FIRESTORM

FIRESTORM

GREG KEYES

BASED ON THE SCREENPLAY
WRITTEN BY MARK BOMBACK AND RICK JAFFA & AMANDA SILVER
BASED ON CHARACTERS CREATED BY RICK JAFFA & AMANDA SILVER

TITAN BOOKS

Dawn of the Planet of the Apes: Firestorm
Print edition ISBN: 9781783292257
E-book edition ISBN: 9781783292264

Published by Titan Books
A division of Titan Publishing Group Ltd
144 Southwark Street, London SE1 0UP

First edition: May 2014
1 2 3 4 5 6 7 8 9 10

A CIP catalogue record for this title is available from the British Library.

Printed and bound in the United States.

Dedicated to Terri Hunnicutt and Warren Roberts

PROLOGUE

Roger Mason was crossing the middle ground between wakeful and asleep when something snapped him to full awareness. He wasn't sure what it was, although he felt as if it had been a sound of some sort.

He glanced around slowly to get his bearings.

Fog drifted through the massive coast redwoods, and it felt in that moment as if he wasn't just a few miles from San Francisco, but in some distant era when this forest had stretched unbroken from what was now Santa Cruz all the way to southern Oregon. Other than his campsite, there was nothing visible of the works of man.

He was slumped against the trunk of one of the ancient titans, facing his tent. He had only closed his eyes for a matter of minutes, or so it seemed.

What had he heard?

Trying to stay still, he listened intently, but whatever it was, it didn't repeat itself. Maybe it had just been the start of a dream, the nonsense music of hallucination.

"Nothing," he sighed. As usual. Maybe it was time to go home. He had been out here for more than a week, alone, without a phone or any other ties to the rest of the world. Normally, he loved these trips. The illicit thrill of outsmarting the rangers, of camping where it wasn't legal. The solitude. The possibility that finally, after all of these years, his dreams would come true. But now, at last, he began to think that not only was it time to go home, but to stay there.

For almost thirty years he had camped in the Muir Woods, among some of the tallest trees on Earth, searching for evidence of the creatures that the Native Americans called 'Sasquatch,' and that others called 'Bigfoot.' Many times in that first couple of decades, he'd felt certain that he had *barely* missed seeing one of the elusive, ape-like creatures, only by the smallest hair. That just one more trip would pay off big.

He knew the arguments voiced by the skeptics—that there couldn't be just one or two Bigfoot. That for a species to survive, it needed a breeding population that numbered in the hundreds, at least, and that such numbers of giant creatures couldn't possibly stay hidden for as long as they had. But the mountain gorilla had managed to remain hidden until the twentieth century, hadn't it? And there were other such examples.

Bigfoot was most likely the descendant of *Gigantopithecus*, an ancient relative of the orangutan that had died off in Asia, but crossed the land bridge into the Americas. Orangutans lived pretty solitary lives, never in large groups. One could walk through a jungle, close to a breeding population of orangutans, and never know it. It stood to reason that *Gigantopithecus* had exhibited similar habits, and Bigfoot would be just as invisible.

Or so he had thought. Lately, though, he had begun to have his doubts. It felt as if he had wasted a lot of his life, and had nothing to show for it.

With a sigh, he pushed himself up and prepared to break camp.

That's when he realized that he couldn't hear anything. *Anything*. No birds singing, no squirrels chattering. The forest was silent as a church on Monday.

Roger felt the hair on his neck prick up a little.

Then, in the stillness, he heard it, the sound he had thought was a dream—something between a hoot and a grunt, a rising tone repeated again and again. Sounding almost—but not quite—human.

"Holy hell," he muttered. Because he knew the sound, or something very like it. He had done his research, prepared himself to be able to recognize the signs. What he had just heard sounded very, very much like the long call of an orangutan.

Or Bigfoot.

"This is it," he said under his breath. "This is really *it*."

He tiptoed over to his sound recorder and turned it on. For a long moment he thought the call wouldn't reoccur. But to his delight, it did—closer and louder than before.

He moved through the trees, treading as silently as possible, and reached the edge of a clearing. There he gingerly reached for his video camera and raised it, trying to keep still. Judging from past experience, he probably only had one shot at this.

These things spooked so easily.

The moments seemed to stretch on forever, the way the days before Christmas had, when he was a kid. Then he saw the trees rustle, and at the edge of a small clearing something moved. He suddenly knew what it was like to be born again, to have an epiphany, to have his life completely validated.

It walked upright, but not with a human gait, and it was entirely covered in dark fur. There could be no mistaking what it was, although perspective made it seem smaller than he had imagined all those years, when thinking of this moment.

He almost forgot to start his camera as the Sasquatch continued on its solitary journey. He zoomed in as close as possible, remaining at a safe distance, trying to get enough detail so that this film couldn't be dismissed as some sort of a fraud—as so many others had in the past. His would be the definitive, the incontrovertible, most famous Bigfoot film of all time.

Glancing up from the eyepiece, he was startled to see another of the creatures appear behind the first.

"A pair..." he murmured, under his breath. His luck was unbelievable. Only rarely had more than one Bigfoot been found together, and never with visual proof.

But then there was another.

And another. Five, twenty...

"Oh, my God," he gasped, still filming. "This is incredible!"

All of a sudden the one in the lead stopped and slowly turned its head toward Roger. In that instant, all he could see in his viewfinder were its eyes—green-flecked, intense, intelligent.

And the Bigfoot saw Roger.

Suddenly he didn't feel safe at all.

Snap!

A twig broke behind him. He whirled around.

The face filled his vision—savage, inhuman, with one milky, blind eye and a livid, glaring one. Its expression was of a malice so pure that it struck Roger like a physical blow. He felt suspended in terror, unable to speak, to move. Incapable, even, of closing his eyes against the terrible visage confronting him.

Then it opened its mouth, and it *shrieked* at him.

Roger didn't remember dropping the camera, or screaming, or running. But when he came back to himself, much later, his hands were empty, his lungs were heaving, and his throat was raw. He glanced behind him and saw nothing but the immense boles of the redwoods, and the fog enshrouding them.

Then he began running again.

With a decidedly grim satisfaction, Koba watched the human flee. He did not care for humans much. He had suffered at their hands and the tools those hands had held. He hoped this was the last one he ever saw.

But he had his doubts.

Once he was satisfied that the man was gone, he turned and looked out through the huge trees to where Caesar was watching him from the clearing.

He feared for a moment that Caesar would be displeased, as he had been when Koba had attacked Will, who had followed them into the trees. But then the ape leader tilted his head in approval, and Koba felt a rare flush of satisfaction. Caesar approved of his actions; therefore Caesar approved of him.

Koba dropped to all fours and ran to join his leader, but a gesture cut him short.

Food, Caesar signed.

Koba paused, chagrined that he had forgotten. Things were happening inside of him, strange things—images, thoughts, connections he had never made before. Sometimes it was distracting. The outdoors itself was distracting, the feel of wind, the smell of leaves, the great wide sky overhead. For so long he had lived in darkness, in pain and misery. And now to be *free...*

That was a sign and a word he had never known, until

Caesar had taught it to him.

Free.

He returned to the human's camp and hunted through the things he found there. After a moment he located a bag of food. Gripping it under one arm, he returned to Caesar, lowering his head as he approached, offering the bag.

Caesar touched Koba's arm, and then his cheek. *Good*, it meant. He took the bag, slung it over his shoulder in a peculiar, human-like way, and scrambled up the nearest of the trees. Koba and the others followed, to where the rest of the troop waited, still in the high canopy.

In a moment they were all on the move again, the soft rustling of the trees the only sound marking their passage.

Because now Caesar required silence. Silence was their survival.

The dark sky had come and gone five times since Koba's liberation and the battle with the humans and their killing tools. They had won that fight, but the humans hadn't stopped chasing them, of course. Their flying cages crossed the skies above, and troops of them roamed the woods, but Caesar was clever. He sent out scouts to find small groups of their pursuers, or loners like the one Koba had just encountered.

They were to be frightened, though not harmed. They would report their meetings, but when hunters came, the apes would be gone to some other place. In this way they had led their pursuers in vast, twisty circles. In this way, they survived, here in this awesome place that was at once so strange and so familiar.

For this place, Caesar had taught Koba another new word, another new sign.

Home.

1

David Flynn woke around four in the morning, as he usually did. It didn't matter what time he went to bed, how much he'd had to drink, whether he had run a marathon or spent all day writing. At four, he woke up. It had started when he was in his early twenties, when he'd moved from Atlanta to the Bay Area. Even after ten years, his body wouldn't let go of the Eastern Time Zone.

He started to sit up, and felt the extra weight in the bed before remembered that Clancy was still there. Her fine, long hair spread out on the pillow. It looked dark in the faint light, but in the day it was the color of hay, with touches of goldenrod where the sun had lightened it. She was only half-covered by her sheet, and he studied her a moment, wanting to trace the contours of her body with the tips of his fingers. He liked the feel of her skin, the shape of her.

But he didn't want to wake her. She usually didn't stay over, but she had some sort of early appointment downtown, and his apartment was a lot closer than hers. He was pretty sure "early" didn't mean four o'clock.

He eased out of bed, went into his small living room,

and glanced at his laptop. He could stand to tighten up the piece on the appropriations cover-up in City Hall, but he was frankly kind of sick of it at the moment. So he switched on the television, cruised through several infomercials and syndicated comedies before one of the news channels caught his eye. They were showing footage of the bizarre events on the Golden Gate Bridge five days ago, when hundreds of apes had escaped from all over the city, fought their way through police blockades, and escaped across the span. It was certainly the strangest event on record in San Francisco, and what made it stranger was the complete blackout of information that had followed it. All of the parklands north of the bridge—the Muir Woods, Mount Tamalpais—everything had been closed, and all but the most essential roads blockaded.

While there were a lot of rumors swirling around about how the apes had escaped in the first place, there was very little of what he as journalist would call *fact*. Mayor House and Chief of Police Burston had assured the public that everything was under control, that the numbers of the apes had been exaggerated, and that the eyewitness reports given by those who had been there were the result of hysteria.

Most of the footage of the event, flickering across the screen, was amateur, taken with cell phones, and it had been a particularly foggy day, anyway, so it was difficult to assess the claims one way or another.

The scene cut to a studio, where a local talk-show host was interviewing a man with a dark, thin face. David recognized him as Clancy's boss, Dr. Roberts, so he turned up the sound a little.

"...primatologist at Berkeley," the host was saying. "People involved in the incident claim very peculiar behavior coming from the animals. They say that the apes acted with organization and purpose, and seemed to have a plan. As someone who studies primates, how would you assess these claims?"

"Well, first of all," Roberts began, "apes *are* intelligent, and capable of learning a wide range of behaviors. They are also social, and do act in concert. Chimpanzees, for instance, will sometimes band together to hunt colobus monkeys for food."

"I thought apes were vegetarian."

"That's a misconception," Roberts pointed out. "Chimps are omnivores—they eat a lot of insects, in particular. Gorillas a little less so. The only species that is almost entirely herbivorous are the orangutans."

"Interesting," the host said. "But we've gotten off subject."

"I think several things are going on here," Roberts said, nodding. "The first is that we humans tend to see everything in our own image. We anthropomorphize. We do it even with dogs and cats—assign human motives and emotions to them. We have an even greater tendency to do that when apes are involved, because they seem more like us. The other factor is that most of these apes were born in captivity, and in many cases trained to act human—for movies, television, circuses. The apes you see on TV are usually young, still cute, and not too dangerous. But when they get older and lose some of their charm—not only in appearance, some get very aggressive—they are often 'retired' to shelters or sold to laboratories for medical testing. So they may well have been superficially mimicking human behavior. The final thing I think that comes into play here is ourselves."

"You mean other than anthropomorphizing?"

"Right. We humans are natural storytellers. It's what we do. There have been some pretty good studies that demonstrate that eyewitness accounts of any kind—especially when strong emotions like fear and surprise are involved—are substantially inaccurate even a few hours after the events. That's because to make sense of what we've seen, we background it with some sort of logical framework. We tell ourselves a story that makes sense in our own minds—then we tell the story to each other. The details that make the most sense to the most people stay in the story, while the rest drop out. It gets bigger."

"So you're saying that what Mayor House says is true..."

David actually jumped out of his seat when a hand fell on his shoulder.

"Sorry," Clancy said. "I didn't mean to scare you."

"Wow," he said. "Yeah. Was the TV too loud?"

"Not really." She nodded at the television. "It was Piers's voice. Thought I was back in his class or something."

"With no clothes on?" He raised an eyebrow.

She glanced down at her state of dishabille and grinned.

"Funny man," she said. "I can put something on, if you want."

"No," he said. "No need to go out of your way." He turned the sound down. "There," he said. "Better?"

"Yep." She nodded. "So why are you up? Bed too crowded?"

"No," he said. "I always wake up around four. I've learned I can either lie there, staring at the ceiling, or get up for an hour or so and piddle. Then I can fall back asleep."

"I can think of a third alternative," she said, stepping around behind him.

"I don't know," he said. "I'm kind of tired, and I know you need your rest."

"Uh-huh," she said, kissing the nape of his neck. It sent tingles through his whole body.

"Now, that's not fair," he said.

"I never said I was fair," Clancy replied, kissing him again, working around toward his ear. She reached around his chest to pull him against her.

"Fine," he said, "let's try this so-called third alternative."

Afterward, she nestled against him, and he felt himself starting to drift.

It felt nice, but there was something possessive about it that worried him. He liked Clancy—she was fun, smart, sexy, and very accommodating in bed. She was also pretty casual. She knew he saw other people, and she didn't seem to care. She never asked anything of him that he wasn't willing to give, and there was never any implication that this was going in any particular direction, or that she had a goal in mind.

At least, it had never felt that way until now.

"I'm going to be gone for a while," she said, drowsily. It was eerie, as if she had read his mind.

"I thought you just had an appointment downtown."

She was silent for a moment.

"Look," she finally said. "I know you're a reporter, but if I tell you something, can we keep it—you know—off the record?"

"Sure," he said, feeling alert now.

"I'm not supposed to tell anyone about this," she said. "I signed a non-disclosure document."

"About what?"

"I've been hired by the city to go up to Muir Woods and check out the apes."

"Check out the apes?"

"Yeah. They're trying to figure out the best way to capture them. Me, I'm just interested to see how they're adapting to an environment so different from what they evolved in."

"Isn't that dangerous?" he asked. "Aren't they violent?"

"Not usually," she said. "Not unless they're pressed, or feel threatened. Whatever happened on the bridge—that's not normal. Hey," she added, "I know my stuff—I'll be okay."

"The Dian Fossey of the Muir Woods," he murmured.

"Dian Fossey was hacked to death by gorilla poachers with machetes," Clancy pointed out. "I think maybe in this case you should think of me as the Jane Goodall of the Muir Woods. Better ending."

"Or maybe just Jane, like in Tarzan," he replied.

"Does that make you the Lord of the Jungle?"

"If I remember right, that would make us cousins," he said.

"*Eew*. Well, you *are* from the South."

"Hmmf," he said.

"I'm excited about this," she told him after a moment.

"I can tell," he said. "I hope you have fun." He yawned then, and closed his eyes.

"Thanks for letting me sleep over," she said. "I know it sort of freaks you out."

"Does not."

"It's okay," she said. "You have nothing to worry about." She squeezed his shoulder.

"Call when you get back," he said. "We'll do something. We'll hang out."

"That sounds good," she said. "Okay, that's enough—let me catch another hour of sleep." Then she rolled over, and within just a few minutes he heard her breathing even out.

A few minutes later, he was dropping off, too.

Talia blinked as sweat stung her eyes, and for a moment all she saw through her blurred vision was the blood.

Sometimes she felt her whole life was about blood. She knew other emergency-room doctors who would have nothing red in their homes—drapes, carpets, tomato sauce, grenadine. At least one trauma surgeon she knew had become vegetarian, because seeing so much raw human meat made the idea of steak or hamburger unthinkable. Once she had considered that to be silly. Now she was starting to sympathize.

"Wipe," she said. Tran dabbed her forehead with a cloth as she went back to examining the chest cavity. The kid was a holy mess—and he *was* a kid, probably no more than fifteen. She wondered why anyone would want to put three bullets in him.

But that wasn't her concern, was it? Her job was to put him back together.

"This is going to be a long one," she said. "See if you can find Dr. Selling. I want him to look at this spleen."

Six hours later, close to shaking with exhaustion, she pushed back from the patient.

"I'll close him up," Selling told her. "You go get some coffee."

She nodded and slipped out of the operating room. She went first to the lavatory to splash water on her face and put her long black hair back up, wondering if it would be better to cut it short. Then she proceeded over to the little room they called the Café Trauma. Someone had actually put a sign up, written on cardboard and picturing a coffee cup above a crossed femur and scalpel. Café Trauma consisted of a sink, a small fridge, a coffee maker, a snack machine, a drinks machine, a card table with four chairs, and a smallish flat-screen TV.

There wasn't any coffee brewed, so she started a pot

herself, then stepped out to see what was incoming. Fortunately, there was nothing as serious a triple gunshot wound, but there was plenty more lined up, and she still had three hours on shift.

She returned to the café and gulped down some of the somewhat disgusting coffee. Randal from Acute Care came in just in time to see her expression.

"Not exactly Starbucks, is it?" he said.

She shook her head, making a face and staring into the cup.

"Every time I drink this swill I swear I'm going to go straight from work to buy a grinder and some decent beans to bring in," she said. "But I always forget. This stuff just makes it all the more tempting to switch to speed or something, which wouldn't be good." Then she turned toward him. "What's up?

"You went to that symposium on respiratory infections last month."

"Mm-hmm," she said. "Sexiest symposium ever. Better than that rectal bleeding thing, even."

"I've got a woman I'd like you to take a look at."

"What are her symptoms?"

"She's sneezing up blood," he said.

"Allergic rhinitis?"

"She says she never has trouble with allergies—I had a look, and didn't see anything," he said. "I've ordered a CT scan, but they're backed up. Plus, she has a temperature of a hundred and four. She's also showing some signs of subcutaneous bleeding."

Talia was about to take another grudging drink, but stopped with the coffee cup halfway to her mouth.

"How old is she?" she asked.

"Thirty-two."

"Let me see her," she said.

* * *

Judging from her fair hair, the woman was probably light-skinned anyway, but at the moment she was positively pallid—except in places where light-greenish patches had developed. Her eyes were dull and moved around sluggishly, so Talia knew immediately that this wasn't just a bleeding polyp in her sinuses. Or if it was, she had some other, unrelated illness, as well.

"Have we bled yet?" Talia asked softly, standing at the room's entrance.

"I was about to," Randal replied.

"Send for labs, priority," she said. "I'll take a look."

She went into the room, glanced at the chart, then at the patient.

"How are you feeling, Celia?" she asked.

"Not so good," the woman managed, weakly.

"Any idea where you got this bug?"

She shook her head.

"I don't usually get sick," she said. "I don't have a GP, so I waited, hoping it would go away."

"I'm going to ask a couple of questions that might sound strange," Talia said.

"Okay."

"Do you work closely with animals?"

"No," Celia replied. Then a thought seemed to strike her. "I have a cat."

"Have you eaten anything out of the ordinary?" Talia asked. "Taken any prescription or non-prescription drugs? Tell the truth—this is important. You won't get in trouble."

"I can't think of anything," the woman said, shaking her head. "I was just in France, but I'm not very adventurous, food-wise."

"France? How recent was that?"

"I just got back to San Francisco a few days ago."

"Did you go anyplace else? Anywhere in Africa or Southeast Asia?"

"No, no place like that."

"Okay," Talia said. "We're going to draw some blood and send it to the lab. Meantime, we'll give you some chicken soup in the arm and something to bring that fever down. How does that sound?"

The woman smiled weakly and nodded.

"Let me look at your eyes for a sec," Talia said, moving in close. She took out a small penlight and shone it on one, then the other, holding the lids open with her free right hand.

"Okay," she said. We're going to be moving you to another room. Have you got anyone in the waiting room?"

Celia shook her head. Talia nodded, picked up her coffee cup, and exited the room.

Outside, she took Randal aside.

"Some subconjunctival bleeding," she murmured. "Could be some kind of hemorrhagic fever."

"I was afraid you were going to say that," Randal said. "Like what? Yellow Fever? Ebola?"

"Whoa, Tex," she said. "I said it *could* be, but it's still not likely. She might just have a bad case of the flu and a nose bleed. But let's be on the safe side. Put her in a clean room. Strict isolation, okay? Just in case. And let's turf it to someone who really knows about this stuff—Collins, maybe, or Park. Okay? And don't spread any Ebola rumors around. I was just thinking out loud."

"Okay," he said.

She had almost finished her coffee when Ravenna stuck her head around the corner.

"Incoming SCUD," she said. "Motor-vehicle accident."

"My lucky night," Talia sighed, and she went to scrub up.

* * *

By the time she had the guy stabilized enough for real surgery, her shift was almost up. Which was good, because she was dead on her feet. She was pulling herself together to go when she ran into Randal.

"Get her settled in?" she asked.

"Yeah," he said. "And you know what? We got another one."

"Another what?"

"Another blood-sneezer. Old African-American lady. I sent her straight to isolation."

"Huh," Talia said, and she frowned. "I don't know. This is starting to sound like a thing. Have you called around?"

"I've kind of had my hands full," he said.

"I'll check it out tomorrow," she said.

She wore her scrubs home, showered, and pulled out a pair of pajamas.

"It's just us, baby," she told the pj's. "We can be together all night."

She fixed herself a Moscow Mule and just sat for a moment, savoring the slight sting of the ginger beer and lime over the kick of the vodka. She checked the messages on her landline. Some of her friends thought she was a bit out of it for having one, but landlines worked in power outages, and they worked when towers or satellites were down. And here in earthquake-land, that seemed like a good thing.

Also, landlines—hers anyway—didn't have texting, so she could safely give the number to people from whom she didn't want to get texts all of the time. Like the people who had left the four messages on her phone. Her father, a guy named Dean she had met last week at a bar called the Choirboy, another guy named Serge who got her number from, of course, her father. And another one from her father.

Tonight, he counted as two people.

Deleting the messages, she sat back and took a sip. Halfway through her drink she remembered to turn on her cell phone. It had been off all day.

She had a text from St. John, a guy with whom she had done her residency. She hadn't heard from him in a while—he worked at another hospital in the Bay Area, also in the ER. Curious, she checked the message.

> Hey Tal—funny disease today. Hemorrhaging, high fever. Couldn't diagnose, turfed to ICU. Two cases. U have any? Let's get a drink sometime.

"Wow," she said to her pj's. "It must be a thing."

2

As the helicopter descended, Malakai began to think he had made a mistake—perhaps a fatal one. He had been ambushed before, in Rwanda and in South Kivu. In Uganda he'd been led into a trap he'd barely escaped. But this was California, and it was possible that his instincts had grown sleepy.

They were kicking in now, though, big time. What he saw below him didn't make sense.

It didn't fit with the public story, either, which meant something was happening that powerful people did not want to be common knowledge. That could very well mean he was entering into a situation he might not as easily walk out of.

He had expected to meet with a few park rangers, some police or National Guard or whoever dealt with these sorts of matters. Instead what he saw was a cluster of prefabricated buildings bearing the symbol of Anvil, a military contractor that he personally knew had been involved in some pretty nasty business around the globe. He knew that because he'd worked for them himself, during the Second Congo War.

Of the four people with him in the helicopter, two of

them had sidearms. He might be able to grab the gun of the nearest, shoot the other, take control of the situation...

Maybe twenty years ago. Maybe even ten.

But not now.

Oh well, he thought. *We'll see, I suppose.*

The chopper landed, and he wasn't murdered immediately upon touchdown, so he figured this wasn't payback of some sort. They wanted something from him, and most likely it was only after they got it—or if he couldn't provide it—that imminent danger kicked in. Nevertheless, he was on the edge of a forest with which he wasn't familiar, surrounded by people he did not know.

Everything about it screamed "covert." Whatever was happening here, only very few people knew about it.

He was escorted into one of the buildings, which had been set up as a spare sort of office. The desk was fairly large, but the only thing on it was a plain manila envelope. Behind it stood a man of middle years. His suit was expensive and tailored. The man escorting Malakai seemed to shrink a little in his presence.

"Mr. Youmans," the man behind the desk said. "My name is Trumann Phillips."

He reached out to shake Malakai's hand. His own hands were soft and smooth, suggesting a man of soft living. But Malakai had dealt with men like this before. The set of his shoulders and the hard glint in his eye suggested some sort of predator. This man was used to getting what he wanted, and probably not squeamish about how he got it. Or from whom.

"Tell me, Mr Youmans," Phillips began, taking a seat and clasping his hands together. "What have you heard of the situation?"

"What the television tells me," Malakai said carefully. "It's all a bit confused—doesn't really make sense. Some apes escaped from a laboratory and freed others from a zoo. They had some sort of a fight with policemen on the Golden Gate Bridge. Most of them were killed there, but a few escaped into the Muir Woods." He spread his hands. "To here, I take it."

Phillips nodded.

"That's the bare bones of it," he said. He unfolded his hands and leaned back in his chair. "You know something about apes, don't you, Mr. Youmans?" he continued.

"A thing or two, I suppose," Malakai replied. "But you must know that already, or I wouldn't be here. I consult for those who study apes in the wild—help track and find them so they can be studied. I work with various rescue groups, as well, and am employed by several zoos."

"Yes," Phillips said. "But back in the day you wore other hats. Safari guide, for instance. Mercenary. And you poached mountain gorillas and chimpanzees."

Malakai shrugged. "If I'd done anything like that, it would have been illegal. So I don't suppose I did it."

Phillips eyebrows dipped a little, and Malakai felt the danger lurking there.

"I'm not concerned with the legality of anything you've done," Phillips said. "I'm concerned with your qualifications. And the results you achieve."

"Mr. Phillips," Malakai said, softly, "You contacted *me*, sir—not the other way around, so I wonder why this talk of qualifications. Yes, I know how to hunt apes. And yes, I know how to capture them. And I daresay—if it is necessary—that I know how to kill them. If those are the qualifications that concern you, I'm your man.

"If not..." He shrugged again, trying to seem confident while wondering what his "if not" might lead to. A flight back to San Francisco? An unmarked grave in the Muir Woods?

Phillips sat silently for a moment, tapping his finger on the table.

"You signed a confidentiality form before coming in here," he said.

"I did," Malakai agreed.

"You understand the penalties involved in breaking that contract?"

"It does not matter," Malakai said. "Asking for my word would have been sufficient to secure my discretion."

Phillips gave him a long, hard look in the eye.

Malakai gave it back unflinchingly. A moment of truth was coming, a wind blowing through.

Phillips finally nodded.

"Fine," he said. "Here's the job. Lead a team into the woods. Find the apes. Capture them."

"How many are there? Which species?"

"Chimps, mostly, including some bonobos. A few orangutans and gorillas."

"They'll be all over the place, then," Malakai said. "The different groups won't stick together. Depending on how many there are, it could take a while."

"We believe not," Phillips said. "We believe they keep together as a group."

Malakai blinked, but didn't say anything. That didn't make any sense at all, but then again, neither did anything he knew about the incident on the bridge. He'd half believed the whole thing had been some sort of weird American publicity stunt, staged for a reality show of some sort.

"How many did you say, sir?" Malakai asked. "How many apes all together?"

"It may be as many as several hundred," Phillips answered.

"That is... a lot," Malakai said. "You want me to capture a few hundred apes?"

"As many as possible," Phillips said. "At least one from each species would be nice." His lips thinned into a smile.

"That's the job," he said. "Now, shall we discuss compensation?"

The compensation was considerable, which didn't make him feel any easier about the situation. Nevertheless, he accepted the job.

A young man with a nametag that identified him as "Flores" escorted him to his quarters.

"You get the special treatment," Flores said. "No barracks for you. You get the suite."

The "suite" was a square prefabricated hut with a sort of entry room, a small bathroom with a sink and toilet, and two bedrooms. It was unoccupied except for his backpack and small suitcase.

"Where is my rifle?" Malakai asked.

"You won't need it," Flores said. "We'll do any shooting that needs to be done. And that reminds me—if you have a phone or anything like that on you, I'll need to hang on to that for as long as you're here."

"May I ask why?"

"I'm just told that this is a very sensitive situation," Flores said. "No communications allowed except through official channels."

Frowning, Malakai produced his phone and handed it to the young man. Flores gave him a quick, apologetic pat down, and then seemed satisfied.

"See you at chow," he said. With that, he left.

A quick look though his things revealed that—as he suspected—they had been searched. His tablet was gone.

He picked the room to the right, moved his things in, and sat on the bed.

Malakai hadn't smoked a cigarette in five years. Now he wished powerfully that he had one.

For some reason, the orangutans always heard the helicopters first, and from their disturbed calls Caesar knew that one or more of the flying machines must be approaching again. He quickly worked his way to the top of the canopy, followed by Rocket, a gray, almost hairless chimpanzee who was one of his seconds.

For a moment he could only stare, caught as always by the wonder and magnificence of the woods. The morning fog was all but gone, and the tops of the great trees bent under a gentle breeze. A blue-colored bird with a black crest was complaining noisily about his presence, and, above, a much larger bird drifting above on expansive wings. He remembered the first time Will had brought him here, how the forest seemed to shape itself around him, take him in, fill something inside of him he hadn't understood was empty.

He shook off the reverie and set himself to the task at hand—keeping his troop alive and safe.

Rocket spotted the helicopter first, and a moment's observation showed the machine coming straight for them.

Find this many, he signed to Rocket, holding up six fingers. *Go, and be quick.* Then he raced back down, leaping from tree to tree, toward the main body of his troop. Most were in the middle canopy, and he searched through them, making low calming noises, until he found one the orangutans, Maurice. Maurice knew the hand language that Caesar had been taught.

Calm them, he told Maurice. *Make them quiet, and lead them in that direction.* He pointed off toward a thicker region of the woods, away from the approaching helicopter.

Then he moved further on down, to those who were too injured to climb or walk well. Most had been hurt in the fight at the bridge, some badly. Most of them did not know the hand signs, although a few of them were learning quickly.

As his feet came to ground, he saw a young female tending to an injured gorilla. She looked up and then bounded toward him. He recognized Cornelia—she wasn't wounded, but had taken it upon herself to care for those who were. She put her head down and held out her hand when she got near, but only just in time, as if she was reluctant to do it at all. She seemed agitated, but that often seemed the case with Cornelia.

Helicopter coming, he told her. *That way. Stay with Maurice.*

She raised her head, a little defiantly.

Moving hurts them more, she signed, gesturing at the injured. *Need rest.*

Caesar shook his head.

If rest, die, he told her. *Go. I lead them away.*

Need rest, Cornelia persisted.

Caesar pant-barked at her, a clear threat. Cornelia's eyes widened, but then she put her head down, backed away, and went to help the wounded to their feet.

Satisfied, Caesar took back to the trees. Moments later Rocket joined him with three orangutans and three other chimpanzees, one of whom was Koba.

Caesar had found Koba at the Gen Sys labs. The bonobo had been given Will's mist, as had the apes from the San Bruno refuge. He was smart, and he was tough, and this far had proven very useful. But he was a little unpredictable.

Together, the eight of them rushed toward the upper canopy, straight toward the sound of the flying machine.

He had prepared them for this, just in case, and the seven who accompanied him knew what they would have to do. But the beating of the blades grew louder, and then the shadow fell against the uppermost boughs. Caesar was suddenly fearful that they were too late.

When he reached the top of the tree he saw his worries realized. The machine was already past their position, headed straight toward his troop.

He cast about desperately until his hand found a dead branch. He snapped it from the tree and hurled it with all of his might. He watched it turn, end-over-end, and hooted with triumph when it struck the rear rotors of the helicopter. He shook the treetop, screaming at the top of his lungs as Rocket and the others joined him and added to the din.

The helicopter banked and came back toward them.

Good, Caesar thought, in relief.

Dallas, a young chimp, screeched and braced to hurl himself at the helicopter.

"No!" Caesar shouted. Dallas hesitated, then aborted his leap.

Something hissed through the air and struck a branch. Caesar recognized it—one of the darts that made apes fall asleep. He flicked his gaze up and saw the shooter perched in the aircraft, taking aim again.

Follow, he commanded.

Dallas was so excited he almost disobeyed, but then he submitted, and they all went, launching themselves from tree to tree, dipping out of sight into the canopy but always reappearing, trying to keep the flying machine occupied and draw it away, always away from the troop, toward the high ground to the north.

* * *

The sun was on the horizon when Caesar called the seven of them down. Hoping they had drawn the hunters far enough, they settled beneath the protecting branches of the trees and the fog that had rolled in from the sea. They waited for the helicopter to leave.

But it didn't leave. It kept circling, and after a time, Caesar heard another join it. And another.

Sam, another chimp, began to whimper.

What? Rocket wanted to know. *What to do?*

Don't know, Caesar replied. *Wait.*

But he didn't like it. Soon it would be dark. Humans couldn't see any better than chimps. Everyone would be blind. Why were they still there? Could the machines see at night? He knew it wasn't impossible.

Caesar glanced over at Rocket, who rewarded him with a look of utter trust, and he felt his gut tighten. Because he knew something Rocket didn't.

Back in the "shelter" where he had been held prisoner, he had known what he wanted to do, and he had worked out how to do it, piece by piece. First he had figured out how to get out of the cages at night, then how to gain dominance over Rocket and the others, then how to escape the facility. He had gone to Will's house and found the mist that made apes smarter. One thing at a time, all put together beforehand.

He had had a *plan.*

Now he was just reacting. He hadn't expected them to follow him out here. This was where apes belonged—people belonged in the city. Things had been wrong before, but now they were as they should be. It seemed to him so obvious that he thought the people would understand, especially since he had been careful to hurt as few of them as possible. He didn't want humans as enemies. He didn't want them as *anything*.

He just wanted apes to be free.

In hindsight, he should have known better. But his plan had ended with them in the woods, safe, and free. He hadn't thought it through any further.

They were free, but they were far from safe. His only hope was to evade the humans long enough that they decided it wasn't worth the trouble.

His thoughts were interrupted when bullets began shredding the leaves above them. He knew from the sound these weren't the kind that knocked apes out—these guns sounded like the ones humans had used on the bridge. Loud. It was unexpected. Since the bridge, the humans had tried to capture them, but never to kill them.

Down, he commanded.

They scrambled to obey and, one by one, the eight apes dropped as quickly as they could without injuring themselves. By the time they reached the rich leaf mold of the forest floor, it was very nearly dark. The ground here was steep and somewhat rolling. Caesar motioned for them to follow, and they began moving away from the helicopters. He felt exposed and out of sorts. When it was dark, apes were supposed to be in a tree, as high as possible.

They moved through the fog. There was a moon, but very little of its light worked its way through the vast, leafy ceiling above.

He heard something and stopped, tapping Rocket on the shoulder. Rocket passed the order around by touching the rest.

Caesar heard the sound again—a thin, faint human voice, like he used to hear coming from the phone when Will was using it. He looked around frantically, trying to find the source.

"Up!" he whispered to the others.

As they started back to the trees, guns barked, this time

the quieter hiss-pop of tranquilizer rifles. A dart thudded into the redwood inches from Caesar's face. He saw them now—men in black clothing, wearing some sort of masks.

I did exactly what they wanted me to do, he understood suddenly. *Stupid.*

They swarmed desperately up into the trees, darts hissing past them. He heard a human cry of fear and then an explosion of real gunfire. An ape screamed in pain, but Caesar's ears were ringing enough he that couldn't distinguish who it was. They were fleeing in absolute darkness now. He flung himself into space, reaching for the next limb, hoping it would be there.

It wasn't.

He fell with a yelp, arms flailing. He caught a branch, and it felt as if his arms were being pulled off, but he swung from it, again reaching into the night, trusting this place he loved, desperately hoping it would save him.

More guns chattered in the darkness. He went desperately higher, knowing the helicopters were still there, hearing the dread beating of the wind they made, but knowing he had to get away from the men with the guns.

They gathered together in the middle canopy in the shelter of a mass of twisted limbs.

Caesar tapped Keling, one of the orangutans. He couldn't see any better than Caesar, but orangs were better at finding their way through the branches, day or night. Keling understood, and allowed Caesar to climb on his back. The others followed his example, the chimps each climbing on to the orangs' backs, and soon they were creeping slowly from tree to tree. There were a few more pop-hisses of gunfire, but it seemed random.

The sound of the helicopters faded as they went, and Caesar reasoned that if the machines weren't following them, the humans probably weren't either. He signaled Keling to take him down. They couldn't stay in the area, not with these humans who could see at night, and although it went against his instincts, they could travel much faster on the ground and lead any humans who might track them even farther afield.

Caesar kept them going uphill until dawn, and then they collected together.

In the light he realized Dallas was missing. Everyone else was tired and sore, but otherwise unscathed.

Wearily, Caesar led them back into the trees, where they changed their direction, hoping to intercept the others from the troop. Hoping as well that the false path they had just made would keep the humans occupied for at least a day or so.

The next morning, after some decent coffee and a bagel, Talia rolled into work feeling pretty good, and reasonably hopeful. Mornings usually weren't too bad, especially in the middle of the week.

This morning, however, the waiting room was almost half full, and the triage nurses were getting a workout. Her first hit was a three-year-old boy whose index finger had been all but severed by having it inserted into the hinge side of a door somebody had slammed. The kid was fairly calm, all things considered, especially after they gave him something for the pain. But his parents were hysterical, especially when the boy was wheeled off to surgery.

When Talia picked up the paperwork for her next patient, she saw right away that he had flu-like symptoms, and was bleeding from the nose.

"Hold him in triage," she said. "I want to check something out."

Randal wasn't around, but she found the room assignment for his patients, and called that floor.

Ravenna was staring at her as she put down the phone. Talia heard someone sneeze in the waiting room, followed almost instantly by a loud expression of disgust.

"What is it?" Ravenna asked.

"There were two women in here last night," she said. "Both had a fever and some kind of sinus thing. One crumped last night, and the other is circling."

"What killed the one?"

"Multiple systems failure, it looks like," Talia replied. "But they haven't done a post mortem yet."

"What is it?"

"I don't know," she said. "But I have a feeling we're about to see a lot of it. How many have come through triage this morning with these symptoms?"

"So far I think we've had six," Ravenna said. "Not all of them are bleeding—some just have the fever."

"Okay," Talia said, letting out a deep sigh of resignation. "This is out of my league. Who is the health coordinator?"

Herrin, the health coordinator, had a voice so smooth it was almost oily, and an attitude that "patronizing" wasn't strong enough to describe.

"Dr. Kosar," he explained over the phone, "We haven't been notified by the CDC or the World Health Organization of an outbreak or even of the *possibility* of an outbreak."

"Of course not," Talia said. "Because it's happening here, in the ER, and not at their facilities."

"Nevertheless, eight cases isn't enough to declare an emergency," Herrin said.

"One of those eight is dead," she replied. "And the

other probably will be before this call is over." She scanned the latest report from the front desk. "And actually, we're up to ten now. We don't know what this is, we don't know how contagious it is—"

"Dr. Kosar," Herrin said, cutting her off. "You're primarily a surgeon, aren't you?"

"I'm an ER doctor," she said, trying to keep the pretty swear words where they belonged, way down in her belly.

"But you mostly deal with and refer trauma, not infectious disease, is that correct?"

"Yes," she said. "That is correct. But I damn well know an infectious disease when I see one, and this one is nasty."

"Then we need someone whose specialty is infectious diseases," Herring said. "I'll look into it—when and if the situation demands it."

"There's a reporting process, right?" Talia persisted, feeling the discussion getting away from her. "Because the CDC can't declare on outbreak unless someone gets the data to them."

"There is indeed a reporting procedure," he assured her, "and it will be followed."

"Great," she said, knowing it was useless. "But we need to set up our isolation procedures now," she added. "While you look into it."

"I'll get back to you, doctor," Herrin said. She heard the line go dead.

"Oh, shit—no he *didn't*!" she exploded.

"What?" Ravenna asked.

Talia looked at the phone and considered calling Herrin back just to swear at him. But she knew she wouldn't get him this time. His secretary wouldn't even put the call through.

"From this moment on," she told Ravenna, "Everyone in this ER is going to wear a face mask, do you understand? Patients included."

"Okay," Ravenna said. "I just hope we've got enough."

"If we don't, go 'borrow' some from upstairs," Talia told her.

Six hours later, the old lady was dead, and so was a young man who had come in that morning. She got a call from Herrin's office. The CDC and the WHO had both declared the outbreak of an unknown viral infection, and the hospital was prepared to implement isolation and quarantine procedures.

Hanging up the phone, Talia swore colorfully in both Czech and English for a few moments, before returning to work.

3

They caught up with the troop when the sun was at the top of the sky. The larger group was moving slowly through a thickly forested valley not too far from where he had left them. As relieved as he was to see them, Caesar had hoped they would have made better progress.

Maurice swung out to greet them, his long arms negotiating the great trees with enviable ease.

Worried, the orangutan signed.

Caesar nodded.

Me too, he said. *Humans have machine eyes to see at night. Did you know this?*

No, Maurice replied.

Think on it now, Caesar said. *Trouble for us.*

Stay on top of largest branches at night, Maurice suggested. *Can't see us there.*

What about gorillas? The gorillas were the worst climbers, and were generally uncomfortable if they were too far off the ground.

Maurice scratched his head.

Think about it more, he said.

Caesar glanced down and saw Cornelia swinging up

toward them. She settled on the bough, again offering her half-hearted submission.

What? Caesar asked.

Hungry, she said. *Apes eat much. Especially gorillas and orangutans.*

True, Maurice put in, and rubbed his belly. Caesar looked more closely at his friend. He seemed drawn around the eyes, more slow-moving than usual.

Cornelia plunged on.

We must find food.

Caesar considered that for a moment. She was right, of course. They had found food at human campsites and in abandoned cabins near the edge of the wood, but that was all gone. Now that he thought about it, his own stomach felt as hard and empty as a shell.

Wild apes, he said. *Apes captured from the wild. They will know what to eat.*

No, Cornelia said. *I was born wild. Woods not like this. Different woods. Different food.*

Frustration exploded through Caesar's weariness. He rose up and bared his teeth. Cornelia slunk back a bit.

What, then? he demanded.

She looked up at him. Her posture was submissive—but her gaze? He saw challenge there. As if she was male.

Wild apes know how to figure out what is food, she said. *Need time.*

Good, he signed. *Figure it out.*

Quickly, he added.

Takes time, she repeated stubbornly. *Also, many apes are wounded. Cannot keep up this pace. Need to settle, nest. Heal.*

No time, Caesar said. *When humans leave, we nest.*

We starve before that, Cornelia insisted.

That was enough. Caesar lunged at her, and she scuttled

back, then began to descend.

True, she signed, defiantly, once she was out of range. He watched her go, fuming. But then he settled against the tree-trunk.

Sleep, he told Rocket. And he closed his eyes.

He slept the rest of the day and the night. When he awoke, he found Maurice there.

Three apes died in the night, the orang told him.

Caesar absorbed that for a moment, and then acknowledged the news.

Maybe Cornelia… Maurice began.

Caesar cut him off with a rough bark. Maurice looked mildly apologetic, but he didn't back down.

I know she's right, Caesar finally said. She was annoying, but she had made good points. She had been thinking.

And he was tired of reacting. It was time to plan.

Find Rocket, he told Maurice. *We three must talk.*

"It's amazing, isn't it?" Clancy said, her eyes preternaturally wide. "So beautiful." She reached up to brush stray strands of straw-colored hair from her face.

Malakai gazed out the window of the Humvee as it bumped along the service road, considering the massive columns of the coast redwoods and wondering what the trees in the understory were. Back home he could have named any plant you showed him. This forest was a cipher to him.

"Have you been here before, Mr. Youmans?" the woman asked, apparently undeterred by his failure to respond to her comments.

"No," he replied.

"The first time I came here, I thought it was like the most amazing cathedral anyone could imagine," she gushed. "It's like the trees are holding up the sky. Dinosaurs knew trees like this, did you know that? Relatives of redwoods used to dominate the globe. Now they exist in only a few places."

Malakai suppressed a sigh.

He had discovered upon waking in the two-bedroom prefab hut that another occupant had joined him there—Clancy Stoppard. She was a primatologist, she studied at UC Berkeley, and she wanted to help rehabilitate apes to the wild. He got all that within thirty seconds of meeting her. She was pretty and upbeat and twenty-seven years old, and he wondered how long it would be before he killed her. If he had known she was to be on his team—worse yet, in his hut—he might not have signed that contract.

He hoped another few moments of silence might send the proper message. There were, after all, five other people in the Humvee she could be bothering.

But such was not the case.

"Where are you from, Mr. Youmans?" she asked.

"I'm from San Francisco," he replied.

"No," she said. "I meant… you know, your accent."

"I was born in the Belgian Congo," he clarified. "What is now called the Democratic Republic of Congo."

"Oh, really? What part of the country?"

It was funny how often people asked that, even when they knew not the slightest geographic detail of his native land. He would tell them, and they would blather something useless.

"North Kivu," he replied. "Near Butembo."

He hadn't thought it possible for her eyes to widen further, but they did.

"That's near the Virunga National Forest," she said. "Where the mountain gorillas live."

"Yes, that's true," he said. "You are quite knowledgeable."

"I hope to go there one day," she said. "Is that where you acquired your knowledge of primates?"

"My uncle took me to see the gorillas when I was just eight," he replied. "And many times after that."

"That must have been *amazing*."

Amazing wasn't the word he would have chosen, but he didn't have much interest in continuing with the conversation. Fortunately, a moment later, the vehicle rolled to a stop.

Malakai opened the door and stepped out onto the rich leaf mold, looking up toward the treetops, trying to put this forest together in his head. Inwardly, he did find the trees rather impressive, but that was sort of the American thing, wasn't it? Everything bigger. The question on his mind was how the apes would perceive this place, how they would bend themselves to it and it to them. What they would forage, where they would drink, sleep, and take refuge.

The other members of the expedition—four men and another woman—piled out of the back and began loading their tranq guns. Two of them, however, had automatic rifles, and they all had sidearms. Malakai found himself longing for one of the weapons himself. He felt naked without a firearm, especially in the woods. And most especially when almost everyone else around him was heavily armed.

"Guns?" Clancy noticed, too. "Those are real guns?" she said, her expression startled. "We won't need guns other than the tranqs."

"The apes were violent on the bridge," Corbin said. He was a blunt-faced man of maybe forty years. Malakai had him figured for an ex-Marine.

"Yeah," Flores, his guide from the day before, said. "And one of 'em tried to take my head off last night."

"Flores," Corbin said, "shut up." He gestured with the muzzle of his AR-15. "This way." He led them about a hundred yards from the road, then pulled out a handheld global positioning device and studied it. He gestured, and they continued a short distance.

He didn't have to tell Malakai when they reached the site. The scuffle of prints, the empty shell casings and shredded vegetation did that. Malakai walked carefully, trying to see everything without disturbing it.

"This is a chimp print," he heard Clancy say. She picked up a spent rifle round. "Somebody was shooting at them."

Well, Malakai allowed, *she isn't a* total *idiot.*

"They came down from the trees here," he said. "Five, maybe six. They weren't all chimps." He stooped to look at a larger print.

"That's an orangutan," Clancy said. She frowned. "They said this happened at night?" she added. "Why would they come down to the ground at night? Chimps and orangutans are diurnal. They stay in trees at night, where they're safe."

"Maybe because they weren't so safe in these trees," Malakai replied, nudging one of the casings with his foot. "That's a big round, .50 caliber, probably from a mounted weapon. Somebody was shooting from the air. It was probably fired from a gun mounted on a helicopter."

Clancy's brows lowered, and she frowned.

"I was told we were trying to recover the apes," she said. "Not kill them."

"They're dangerous," Corbin asserted.

"How dangerous could they be to helicopters?" she demanded.

"They took one down on the bridge," Flores said.

"Flores!" Corbin barked.

That wasn't in the news, Malakai thought, but he didn't show it. He was following the tracks again. He remembered that a policeman had been killed in a chopper accident, but no mention was made of the apes causing the crash.

"The idea," Corbin said, still talking to Clancy, "was to force them to the ground so troops with night-vision gear could capture them."

"Capture them?" she snapped. "With machine guns?"

"The choppers just raked the treetops," Corbin replied, looking exasperated. "They didn't shoot down at them. Which would have meant shooting down at *us*, by the way. We only meant to tranq them."

"You were on this detail?" Malakai asked. "All of you?"

Corbin nodded.

"Here's where the ambush occurred," Malakai said, pointing.

"Chimps can't see at night," Clancy persisted. "They would have been helpless."

"And yet you didn't manage to hit any of them," Malakai noticed. He turned to Corbin. "Am I right?"

"Not to my knowledge," Corbin replied. "And let's keep it down. They could be near."

"They aren't," Malakai said, walking about ten yards. "They went back up into the trees… here."

"So there's no telling where they went?"

Malakai bent to study a dark spot on the leaf mold.

"I wouldn't say that," he replied, and he started moving uphill to the north.

"Is that blood? Clancy asked. "That's blood, isn't it?"

Malakai pretended he didn't hear her.

Following the blood trail wasn't easy. The chimps kept changing direction, although they were generally moving up toward Mount Tamalpais.

The task became even harder when they came to the source of the blood, late in the afternoon. A chimp was curled into a fetal position at the base of a tree. Malakai approached with some caution, but judging by the amount of blood present beneath the ape, he didn't think he had too much to worry about. His suspicions proved true when he nudged the chimp with his foot. He reached and grasped an arm, lifting it, and pulled.

The chimp flopped over on his back.

"He hasn't been dead for more than a few hours," he told Corbin. "Rigor mortis hasn't set in yet."

"Gross," one of the others said.

Malakai heard Clancy sob, and glanced in her direction. Her face had gone white, and tears were running down her face.

"I don't understand," she said. She stepped nearer the body. The chimp's eyes were open and glassy, staring out of the bright world and into the darkness beyond. Clancy looked at Malakai as if there was some question he could answer.

Oh, for God's sake, Malakai thought, and suddenly he was angry. She was upset about a dead ape? How many men, women, and children had he seen like this?

Ridiculous.

"I thought you weren't using real bullets," Clancy said in a shaky voice.

"That must have been the one that jumped me," Flores muttered. "He just came out of nowhere, and I dropped my rifle so I pulled my sidearm. Pure instinct."

Malakai shut out the rest of the exchange. He hunted around the vicinity some more, and then began moving north again.

The sun was well on its way into shadow—and he was on the verge of giving up—when he found a track.

And then another. The apes had come back down from the trees––again, at night. He tried to picture the entire scenario. They had been driven down from the trees by the helicopter, and they ran into a detail wearing night-vision goggles. When fired upon by the ground troops they had gone back up into the trees, but only long enough to outdistance their pursuers. Then—against their natural inclinations—they had come back down.

That was—strange.

Near sundown they crossed a road, and after a bit of fiddling with his GPS, Corbin determined that it was the same road on which they'd left the Humvee, so he sent Flores back to retrieve it.

"We're less than a mile from where we started," he complained.

Malakai shrugged. What could he say to that? They weren't trying to set a land-speed record. They were trying to find some very peculiarly acting apes.

He glanced at Clancy. She hadn't said much since they had found the dead chimp. He could be grateful for that, at least. Her lips were set in a tight line, and she looked miserable.

He took Corbin aside.

"When Flores gets back with the truck," he said, "why don't you have him take the young lady back to base?"

"Hell," Corbin said. "That sun's almost down. Unless they're over this next ridge, we're all going back."

"I'm not," Malakai said. "I'm camping here."

"Why? Do you think they'll come back?" He looked around, as if the thought disturbed him. "We can be back at camp in half an hour, and be back here before the sun rises to pick up the trail."

"I'm camping here," Malakai repeated. "I don't know this place, these woods. I need to become acquainted with them. And I may hear something useful. If there are hundreds of apes out here, they will surely make some noise. An orangutan call can travel a great distance, I've heard."

"We have listening posts all over," Corbin said. "I'm not under orders to sleep out here, and we didn't bring any camping gear."

"I don't require company," Malakai said, "or gear, although a blanket would be nice."

Corbin hesitated.

"I'm not staying with you," he said.

"That's fine," Malakai replied. He stepped away from the man, and searched around a bit, looking for a suitable site.

"I'll be up there," he said finally, pointing to a bit of high ground with a sheltered eastern side. With that, he began to climb.

He was gathering twigs to start a fire when he heard the Humvee arrive below, then leave. A few moments later he heard footsteps and looked down to see Clancy climbing the slope. She was carrying something in a bundle.

"They had some rain ponchos in the back," she said. "We can use them as blankets."

He nodded and continued gathering wood for the fire. Though he was determined not to show it, he was irritated. He had been looking forward to being alone with the night and his thoughts.

When he didn't say anything, Clancy began helping gather wood. When they had cleared a space around the little pile, he produced his lighter to start it, she coughed up a humorless chuckle.

"Pretty sure this is illegal," she said.

"No doubt," he replied. He watched as the little flame fed on the smallest twigs and moved out to the larger. Then he sat on a bare spot, and stared into the fire.

Clancy sat directly across from him, but she wasn't looking at him.

"You think I'm an idiot," she said, after a moment.

He sighed.

"I think you're naïve," he said.

"I am that, obviously," she said. "But I'd rather..." Suddenly she stopped.

"Rather what?" he asked, regretting it the instant he spoke. He wanted her to *stop* talking, not continue.

She watched the fire for a moment.

"I knew the chimp was dead when I saw its eyes," she said, finally.

"Sure," Malakai replied. "It's easy to see when the life is gone."

"It just seems to me," she said, pausing, "your eyes are just like his."

He poked a stick into the fire and watched the sparks weave upward.

"That's quite poetic," he told her.

"How did you get to be like that?" she asked. "What happened to you?"

"I was born," he said.

"I know there's been a lot of war where you come from—"

"Look, miss," he said. "I'm here to do a particular job. I intend to do that, and nothing more. I am not an ethnographic subject for you to study. If you stayed here so that you could interview me, then you've made an error."

"I just thought—"

"Think something else," he said.

The fire was going pretty well now. He started arranging

the poncho. Out of the corner of his eye, he saw Clancy spread hers and lie down. He lay on his back, staring up at the night. The clouds that had covered the heavens for much of the day were gone, and the stars were staring back at him. He remembered lying like this on Mount Virunga, with his uncle—so very long ago, it seemed. The constellations were different here, and Mount Tamalpais was hardly a mountain at all, so the feeling of familiarity was… surprising.

"I didn't," Clancy said, her brittle voice breaking the stillness. "Didn't come up here to interview you. I stayed to keep an eye on you. You know something the others don't, and you haven't said anything about it."

"What's that?"

"Apes don't act like this. Chimps—and most certainly orangutans—they just don't."

"Well," he said, "you noticed that, did you? So why didn't *you* say anything?"

"I don't know."

"Yes, you do," he said quietly, making a decision. "You know these people we're working for—they can't be trusted."

"I get that, believe it or not. The whole thing is too hush-hush." She looked uncomfortable. "I'm not sure I want to know what they're really up to."

"Yes, you do," he told her. "You say you saw me back there, saw something missing in my eyes. But I also saw you. If you did not want to know, you would have already quit. You would be on your way home right now, to your boyfriend, no doubt."

That actually drew a half-hearted laugh from her.

"You really think you have me pegged, don't you?" she said.

"Am I wrong?"

She was silent for a long time, long enough that he thought she might be asleep.

"No," she whispered.

Some things couldn't be avoided, and the weekly dinner with her father was one of them. It wasn't that Talia didn't love him, but she knew what he was working up to, and she didn't really want to deal with it at the moment.

But she was here, in a steakhouse where she couldn't afford the entrees, feeling underdressed and very young. She might be almost thirty, but her father had a way of making Talia feel twelve.

"How's your fish?" he asked, eying her seared Alaskan char with some suspicion.

"It's delicious," she said. "How's your steak?" she countered, eyeing the massive Porterhouse.

"It'll do," he replied. He glanced back at her plate. "Your mother would order the fish, too," he said. "I never understood that."

"It's good," she said. "And it's healthy. You're the heart surgeon. You know this."

"My heart is fine," he said. "My heart is perfect. I'll probably outlive my grandchildren. If I ever have any."

"Okay, we're not starting on this," she cautioned.

"What happened to that fellow, the reporter?" he asked. "I see his articles all of the time."

"That's… that's ancient history, Pop," she said. "And none of your business anyway."

"You're my daughter," he said. "Everything about you is my business."

"Well, we're going to have to disagree there," she said, studying what was left of her fish.

There were a few moments of uncomfortable silence.

"We've been getting some strange cases in the ER," she finally said, trying to break the ice, to remind him that she was a doctor, a woman with a profession. "It presents like a hemorrhagic fever of some kind, but it turns out it's a retrovirus."

"You're a surgeon," he grunted. "Why are you dealing with viruses?"

"God, you sound just like... Uh!" She paused and gathered herself. "I'm an ER doctor. I deal with lots of things. I splint broken fingers. I deal with drug overdoses and alcohol poisoning, with the flu, miscarriages, gunshot wounds—you name it, I've probably dealt with it on some level."

"You trained a surgeon," he pressed. "I didn't pay for eight years of college for you to work yourself to death in an emergency room."

"I'm paying you back—"

"Very slowly, Natalia," he said. "But that's not the point."

"No, it *is* the point, Pop."

He sighed.

"Look," he said, "I've discussed it with the partners. We're all agreed that you'd make a fine addition to our practice. It is a good practice, and I like the sound of Kosar, Kosar, Drayton, and Hamilton."

"I love you, Dad," she said, looking him straight in the eye. "But no. It's not what I want to do. I'm doing what I want to do, for now at least." Then she shrugged. "In the future, who knows? But at the moment this is me."

He sighed again, then went back to work on his steak.

"The retrovirus," he said at length. "Is it dangerous?"

"Yes," she said. "Yes it is. In fact, it's a nightmare. It appears to be airborne. The incubation period is incredibly rapid. Fever, bleeding from mucus membranes, especially in the sinuses, followed by rapid multiple-organ dysfunction. The time between onset of symptoms and death is a matter of days."

"What's the mortality rate?"

"Ten people have died of it in San Francisco that I know of and about a hundred have been diagnosed with it here. There are cases reported in other cities. So far no one has recovered."

"No one?" He leaned back in his chair. "Really, Natalia. This sounds dangerous to me. Maybe you should take some time off."

"By tomorrow, there are some predictions we could see a jump in mortality—a hundred or more. The more healthcare providers have to deal with that, the fewer there will be to deal with things I deal with. If I take off, I'll leave them even more short-handed. I'm not prepared to do that."

He shook his head.

"I'm very careful," she said, heading him off. "Everything washed, everything sterilized."

"Yes," he said. "Even when you were a little girl, always washing the spoon and forks twice—once with soap, again with rubbing alcohol."

"Drove Mom crazy," she remembered.

"Yes, it did," he agreed. Then he turned back to his steak.

"I don't like this business," he said. "This virus, or you in an emergency room, for that matter. And it really hurts me that you won't join the old man in his practice."

"I don't want to hurt you, Pop."

"I'm not done," he said. "All these things, I have some trouble understanding. But know this—I *am* proud of you, Natalia."

She stared at him, feeling a slow smile grow on her face, even as her eyes threatened to tear up. He couldn't look at her, of course. He was cutting his steak with deliberate strokes, as if he were opening up someone's chest.

"Thanks, Pop," she said. "That's nice to hear."

"Now that's out of the way," he said, "if you should change your mind..."

"Just eat, Pop," she said.

4

Dreyfus cleared his throat, took a sip of water, and ran a hand over his shock of slightly shaggy, brown hair. Then he faced the reporters who had gathered in the lobby outside of his office. The steady murmur of conversation died down as they waited for him to speak.

"It's good to see you all here today," he said. "I appreciate you turning out. I'll keep this brief, because there's no big reveal coming, I think. Many of you speculated openly that when I stepped down as chief of police last year, my intention was to run for mayor. Today, I'm just here to confirm that.

"The financial assets and affairs of this city, frankly, have been badly mismanaged, and it's going to take a steady hand and a lot of hard work to get us back to where we need to be. I've served San Francisco proudly for all of my adult life. As chief of police, I made our force leaner and more responsive, more effective than it has ever been. I can do the same for this city and this county. If the citizens of this community see fit to give me the opportunity, I *will* do so."

He smiled. "That's it," he said. "Brief, as I promised.

But I'm more than happy to answer any questions you might have."

Hands shot up.

"Rick," he said.

"You're aware of the so-called 'Monkeygate' affair, Chief Dreyfus?"

"It's just 'Mr. Dreyfus' at the moment, Rick. But sure, it's hard not to be aware of it, given the media—if you'll forgive me—*circus* surrounding the events that occurred."

That drew a few chuckles.

"In a statement three days ago," the reporter continued, "Mayor House cited the incident on the Golden Gate Bridge as a failure of your 'leaner' police force, and claimed that the late Chief Hamil of the San Bruno Police Department was a casualty of your policies."

"We're all sorry for the loss of Chief Hamil," Dreyfus said. "My heart goes out to his family. But he died out of his jurisdiction, in a helicopter accident. What he was even doing in San Francisco is entirely unclear. I don't see how that had anything to do with the relative strength of the police force I put together. And Rick, you were being polite—Mayor House said I 'crippled' the SFPD. But if that's true, why did crime drop in every year of my administration? How was it that we put away three major crime lords?

"And as far as the present state of the force goes, it's been more than a year since I left the post. Chief Burston is a fine golfer, I know, and he frequently golfs with the mayor. As far as I can tell, however, that's his only qualification for the post. It seems to me that Mayor House is poisoning the well. He's trying to make you believe that our force is inadequate in order to justify his use of outside contractors to address the so-called 'monkey problem' instead of using local law enforcement.

"I respectfully disagree with him."

The gathering exploded when he said that, members of the press crowding closer to his podium.

"Sonja," he said, nodding in the direction of another reporter.

"What contractors would those be?" she asked. "And what is your evidence to support this claim?"

"Well, I may not be chief of police anymore," he said, "but I'm not totally out of the loop. The name of the contractor is Anvil. My staff has prepared a brief for each of you on this matter, which you will be given as you leave. I think you'll find more questions are raised about this incident every day. Why contractors, and why has the mayor's office been so quiet about it? There was ineptitude, that's true, but I won't let the brave men and women who protect our streets be the whipping boys in this matter."

"Mr. Matthews." He pointed at another reporter. Matthews was a distinctly young man with reddish hair and a serious expression.

"Sir," he said, "what—if anything—can you tell us about the virus?"

"Well it's hard to tell yet," Dreyfus replied, choosing his words carefully. "There's so much we don't know about it."

"The CDC estimates that thousands are infected in San Francisco alone," Matthews persisted.

"I didn't say it wasn't a serious matter," Dreyfus said. "But it would be irresponsible of me at this point to say or do anything other than what the CDC recommends. Avoid social contact when possible, wash and bathe frequently, and above all let's not have a panic. Misinformation and fear have killed more people in situations like this than disease itself."

Before Matthews could continue, he motioned to yet another reporter. But she carried on the topic.

"The mayor has suggested the possibility of quarantines,"

she said. "Do you think this a good idea?"

"So far only a handful of people have died," Dreyfus replied. "As tragic as any loss is, I must again caution any politician—or the media, and that means you folks—against provoking hysteria. In my view, by calling for military-style quarantines, the mayor runs the danger of doing exactly that."

"But, sir," Matthews shouted, "everyone who gets this thing dies. We may be looking at thousands dead in the next few days."

"Son, I know you're concerned about this," Dreyfus said. "We all are. But unlike some, I'm not comfortable commenting on a matter this fraught with peril while speaking from a position of limited facts. There are experts in these matters. I am not one of them. Neither is Mayor House. I've really exhausted all I have to say on this for the time being, so please—I'm sure there are other things that interest you. There, Assam?"

"Yes," Assam replied. "Regarding your position on the SPLOST last year, I wonder if you would maintain that stance if elected, and employ such a tax."

Dreyfus nodded, happy to be off on another topic.

"Hey, Daniel," Dreyfus said. "Glad you could drop by."

Daniel Ngyun was in his late thirties, but retained a lot of boyish charm. He was physically trim, wore suits with colorful shirts and ties, and had a pleasant voice. He was also one of the youngest presidents ever elected to the San Francisco Board of Supervisors.

Dreyfus rose to shake his hand, then pointed him toward a seat.

"Well," Ngyun said, "I thought you dropped the bomb about Anvil very nicely."

"I'm really in your debt for that bit of information, Daniel," Dreyfus said. "You could have let the press have that yourself. Some say you were considering a run."

"I might have, if I thought I had a chance to beat you in the primary." Ngyun smiled. "But we both know I don't. All we might manage to do is sabotage one another, enabling House to stay in. Anyway, this is my first term as president of the board, and I kind of like the job. In a few years you may be looking over your shoulder at me, but for now, I hope you beat the bastard. Life will be easier for me without him."

"Just out of curiosity, do you know *why* he's using these Anvil guys?"

"I wish I did," Ngyun said. "It makes me nervous. Everybody on that side of the building is barking at flies, and I'm being kept out of the loop as much as possible."

"Well," Dreyfus said, "if I win, that won't be the case, I can promise you that."

"I look forward to it," Ngyun said. "And by the way, if I was in your shoes, I would back off on the whole Hamil thing. You and I both know he was a dufus, but he was a chief of police—albeit not ours—and he died trying to defend San Francisco. Sort of."

"I thought his chopper crashed just after takeoff."

"Yeah," Ngyun said. "That's the story they put out. But I've heard something different."

Dreyfus leaned forward, one eyebrow rising.

"Oh, yes? Tell me more."

"A couple of witnesses early on claimed the chopper was at the bridge, and that it was brought down by a gorilla."

"What witnesses?" Dreyfus asked.

"Well, that's the thing—no one is claiming it, not anymore. We can't turn up a single reliable witness."

"That makes no sense," Dreyfus said. "It would make him look more like a hero, not less. House could probably use that to his own advantage."

"Yeah," Ngyun agreed. "At this point it's just a rumor." He stood and held out a hand. "Good seeing you," he said. "But I've got to go—I've got another meeting."

Dreyfus stood up and walked around his desk to shake hands.

"Thanks again."

"You're welcome. And good luck."

"This virus is the biggest unknown in the race," Adam Patel said. It was an hour later, and they were having gin and tonics in Dreyfus's office. Patel was his aide, an intensely competent man with clipped black hair and an English West Country accent.

"This could be House's 9/11, his Hurricane Sandy," Patel continued. "If he handles it well, his numbers could jump through the roof. Or it could sink him. Either way, since you don't currently hold public office, you're kind of out that equation. There isn't much you can do to seem mayoral. You can't benefit from it much, but you also won't be burned by it."

"I'm not inclined to think of thousands of people dying as 'benefiting' me," Dreyfus replied, dryly.

"You know what I mean."

"I guess." He paused, then continued. "Is what that kid said true? About the survival rate?"

"Yeah," Patel admitted. "Worldwide, there's about fifty dead, ten here in San Francisco. But so far every single person diagnosed with this thing has died. Young, old, male, female, black, white, Latino, Asian."

"Sure, but the only people who get diagnosed are

the ones who get so sick they seek help, or pass out or whatever, right? So the sample may be skewed. There might be plenty of people it hardly affects at all."

"Maybe," Patel said. "But the crazies on TV—the pundits, the preachers, the conspiracy theorists—they've got this now, and they're going nuts with it."

"Yeah. I'm afraid there will be a panic," Dreyfus said. "If the only thing I can do is what I just did—try to stand in the way of that, publicly—then maybe that's what I should do."

"You did just fine today."

"No, I mean it's time to get me on some of these shows. I want to be out front on this."

"Too risky," Patel said. "I don't advise it." But Dreyfus shook his head.

"There's going to be a panic," he said. "People will remember me as a voice of reason. And if I'm wrong, and this all goes away—people won't remember I had anything to say about it at all.

"Call the shows. Get me booked. Now."

"Okay, boss," Patel relented. "Whatever you say."

"Another thing. I want a private investigation of this whole Monkeygate thing. I want to know why people on the force, guys who used to trust me, are so skittish of talking about this whole thing. Even Troy is sitting on something—I know when that sonofabitch is lying to me. And now this business about Hamil... Something stinks here, and it smells like a cover-up. I want to know what House is hiding, because I promise you, if we find out what it is, we can take him apart. I feel it in my gut."

5

Koba laid the chimp onto the dew-damp leaves and stepped away.

He didn't like things that looked alive but were not. He peered around the clearing instead, watching Caesar and the others. It had taken two of them to carry the dead orangutan. Caesar had borne the other chimp—the one that had died in the night.

He said that putting the bodies here—far across the woods from where the main troop was hiding—would mislead the humans, make them look in the wrong place. It made sense to Koba.

He watched Caesar study the fallen chimp for a moment, then squat and gently close its eyes.

A sort of shock ran through Koba, then. It felt like it started in the back of his skull, and he had a sudden, vivid image of someone doing the same thing—a human hand closing an ape's eyes.

He shook his head, but it didn't help. Sometimes when he slept he saw this, and he felt as if he was falling. But he had never thought about what it might have meant. Yet now the feelings were intensified. He remembered those eyes open, gazing at him.

And more...

Koba is small, and watching his mother make hand language with Mary. They live in a big room with a metal grating on one wall. Everything else is white. Koba is playing with one of his toys, a stuffed one that looks like a kitten. He has played with a real kitten before, and wants a real one, but this is what they gave him.

Mary is asking Koba's mother what she would like to do today. Mother answers that she would like to go outside. Koba is excited about this because he likes going outside. Mary says they can go outside after Koba plays with the buttons a little bit, and maybe does some letters.

So Koba goes over to the buttons. Mary asks Koba to find peanut. He finds the right symbol and presses it. She tells him he has done well. She asks for him to find "blue" and then "red," which he also does. Meanwhile his mother plays their private game with him, making the hand signs for these same things. After he is done, Mary gives him a cookie, and then directs him to the letters.

Koba is less certain about the letters. He knows they stand for things, but it's not like the buttons. Mary puts four letters together. They look familiar in that order, but he can't remember exactly what they mean.

Mary tells him.

"This is K-O-B-A," she says. "It's your name. Koba. Now let's do mine."

She makes M-A-R-Y with the letters. He notices one is the same as in Koba. He isn't sure what this is supposed to mean.

Mary is pleased, though. She gives him another cookie, and then they go outside. Koba feels the wind ruffle his fur and climbs around on the tree. He loves the tree, to swing on it and jump from limb to limb.

After a while he goes down and plays with his mother.

"Tickle me," he signs to her, so she does, and he is happy. He presses himself against her, then runs back over to the tree, feeling his arms stretch out and grow warm. The sun is warm, too.

He finds a thing crawling on the tree. It is about the size of his smallest finger and is covered with black fuzz.

Mary sees him studying the thing and comes over.

"Caterpillar," she says. "Fuzzy caterpillar."

Koba plays with the caterpillar. He tries to sign to it, but it doesn't answer. He puts it back on the tree and watches curiously as it crawls away. Then he returns to playing.

After a while Mary tells them it is time to go back inside. Koba doesn't want to go. He wants to play more outside. Mary calls Kuo to bring the leash. Kuo comes and tries to put the leash on Koba, but Koba jumps back.

"Naughty Koba," Kuo says, laughing, and tries to put the leash on again. Koba jumps back again. He likes this game. He and Kuo play this game all the time.

"Hey, Koba, what's that over there?" Kuo says, pointing. Koba knows what will happen—this is how the game always ends. He pretends to look, and the leash goes over his head. He submits and goes with Kuo.

Inside, Kuo gives him a hug and tells Koba he will miss him. Koba wonders why, because Kuo is usually there at night.

But tonight a new person comes. His name is Roger.

The next day, lots of people come to see Koba's mother talk to Mary with her hands, and then watch Koba press the buttons. They laugh when he is asked to find "peanut" and he presses it several times because he likes peanuts. He likes it when they laugh.

Then something strange happens. They put something else in the room with Mother and him. It is big and fuzzy and black.

Mother does the hand talk, but it just looks at her. Koba tries to talk to it to, but it doesn't even look at his hands. It just walks away.

"Do you know what that is, Koba?" Mary asks. "Can you tell us what that is?"

Koba looks uncertainly at the thing, and then at his buttons. Finally he starts pressing them. Furry. Snake. Bug.

Mary laughs.

"Are you trying to call her a fuzzy black caterpillar?"

Koba presses the button that means "yes."

Everyone laughs.

"He doesn't know it's a chimp?" someone asked.

"No, because Wanda—that's her name—can't sign," Mary says. "Washoe, one of the first language apes, called the first chimps he ever met 'big black bugs' because they couldn't do sign. Chantak, an orangutan, called non-signing orangs 'red hairy dogs.' Koba thinks of himself as a person, and people talk. If something can't talk, it's not a person, so Koba thinks it must be something else."

Koba wonders what Mary is talking about. He doesn't know what the word 'chimp' means.

He points at the new thing.

Big black caterpillar, he signs.

Big black caterpillar, his mother signs back in agreement.

That night Koba has trouble sleeping. The big caterpillar is still in their room, and it scares him. But his mother tickles him and tells him he is beautiful, like a banana or a red flower or a kitten, and he finally goes to sleep.

The next day Mary lets them go outside again. Everything is a little bit wet, which Koba likes. It makes everything smell different. It never smells this way inside, even when they wash the cages. He thinks maybe it is the sky he is smelling, which today is big and blue. He tries to reach out and touch it, but it is higher than the top of the cage.

The big black caterpillar just goes to the top of the tree and sits there.

When Mary says to come in, Koba doesn't want to. He wants Kuo to play the game with him. But instead of Kuo, Roger comes out. He tries to put the leash on Koba, but Koba jumps back. He tries again, but Koba jumps back again. Then Roger starts yelling words Koba doesn't know, and it scares Koba. He wonders what he has done wrong, why Roger is yelling at him, why he doesn't end the game. He finally gets so frightened he submits, and Roger puts the leash on him. Then he yanks it so hard it hurts Koba's neck. Koba is so startled he yanks back, then, and in a flash of anger, jumps at Roger.

He doesn't intend to hit him—and he doesn't—but Roger stumbles back and falls down. He yells some more.

Mary takes the leash.

"You don't have to be so rough," she tells Roger.

"He's just a dumb animal," Roger tells her.

Koba wonders what a dumb animal is.

That night, Roger yells more words Koba doesn't know. He has a sack in one hand, and a bottle in the other. He is drinking something that smells bad from the bottle. He hits the cage with his fist, and the big black caterpillar starts screaming.

Roger gets the leash. He comes into the cage with the leash and the bag, and walks over to him. The bag is long and looks heavy, like there's something in it.

"You're so smart," Robert tells him, "then learn this lesson. See this? Leash. When I show you this, you let me put it on."

Koba stares at the leash, not sure what he is supposed to do. He is scared—the big caterpillar is still screaming, and it disturbs him.

When Roger moves forward, he cowers back.

"Oh, no you don't!" Roger says, and he swings the bag at him. When it hits Koba, it knocks all of the wind out of him, and he can't breathe. Lights seem to flash in his eyes.

Koba good, Koba good, he signs desperately, but Roger swings the bag again. Koba can smell what's in it now—oranges.

This time Roger misses Koba, because Mother jumps at him. She bites his hand.

Roger screams, and then he hits Mother with the bag. He hits her again, and again, until she backs into the corner, pulling Koba with her. He hides behind her.

Roger finally backs out of the room and closes the door.

"Stupid animals," he says. He takes a drink from his bottle and then goes somewhere else.

Koba nuzzles up to his mother. He grooms her fur. She puts her arms around him.

Tickle, he signs.

So she tickles him until he falls asleep.

When he wakes up, Mother is very stiff. He can't make her arms move. Her eyes are open, but she doesn't seem to see him. She is cold.

Mother see Koba, he signs, but she doesn't answer.

He tries to make her fingers sign, but they are hard and won't move.

Later, Mary comes in and tries to sign to Mother. Then she comes in the cage and touches her. She starts making strange noises, and water comes out of her face. Koba nestles up with Mother again, scared, but not sure of what. Mary puts her hand on Mother's face and when she moves it again, Mother's eyes are closed.

She is asleep.

Mary takes him outside, but Mother won't go. He plays, at first worried about Mother, but then he becomes occupied witch watching the clouds, which are moving slowly but making interesting shapes. Some of them look like some of his buttons.

When Mary calls him in, he doesn't want to play his game—he wants to see Mother. She should be acting right again by now.

But when he goes in, Mother is not there. Just the big caterpillar.

Mother, he signs to Mary. *Koba want Mother.*

"She's gone, baby," Mary says. "I'm sorry."

The next day, Koba doesn't want to play the game with the buttons. When he goes outside, he looks for Mother, but she isn't out there. He wonders where she is.

A few days pass like this. Each day, Mary tries less and less to make him play with the buttons or talk with his hands. Finally, one day she picks him up. He likes it, because without Mother, there is no one to touch him.

"You're getting so big," Mary tells him. Then she makes a windy sound.

"Koba," she says, "I know you won't understand all of this, but our program funding has been cut. It's complicated, but you won't be living here anymore. I won't get to see you anymore."

Mother, Koba signs.

Mary shakes her head.

"You're going to a nice place with nice people," she says. "You'll be okay."

And the next day a man comes and put a leash on him. He puts him in a little cage in a thing that moves, and they go to another place. It takes a long time, and Koba cannot even stand up in the cage. He gets sick from moving. He gets scared and bored and unhappy.

Koba blinked, and stared at the dead apes, at the eyes Caesar had just closed, and then he understood. His mother had been dead. Roger had killed her, somehow, with his bag of oranges.

Something nudged him, and Koba started. It was Caesar.

Koba, he said. *Go back to Maurice. Be on guard there.*

For a moment, Koba felt a flash of anger. Guard the wounded? He wanted to be with Caesar. He wanted to hunt, to fool the humans, to fight them again if need be.

And he wanted to protect Caesar.

But he also wanted to please Caesar, and that meant doing what he said. So he gave submission and reluctantly went up the nearest tree. But he paused and looked back as Caesar and his band went off in the other direction.

Caesar had divided the troop into three smaller bands. One was with Maurice. It was the largest and included the wounded, the infants, and wild apes who knew how to find food. They were staying mostly in one place. The second group was with Rocket—they were to draw humans away from Maurice and his band, to hunt small animals, and to find human food where they could.

The third group was led by Caesar himself, and would do much the same as Rocket's bunch. When Caesar had asked Koba to help carry the bodies, he had hoped he would remain a part of Caesar's band.

But it seemed Caesar didn't really trust him. No one ever had, he realized. Until now, that had not bothered him. But he *wanted* Caesar to trust him, and he wasn't even sure why. It would mean something, he thought—but he couldn't think what it would mean exactly.

When she got to work, Talia still had a little bit of a glow from her father's grudging pseudo-approval. But the reality of the situation soon overwhelmed that.

The CDC had been quietly trying to prepare the public for what could be a serious epidemic, rolling out ads on how to best avoid the disease, and what to do and where to go if symptoms manifested. Local and national news caught on a little before things were ready, and this was the result...

The waiting room was packed, and there was a line out the door. A lot of them were wearing masks, some improvised. Everyone thought they had symptoms, although triage was turning most of them away because they were perfectly healthy.

She dove right in, and it was more than an hour before she took a break from setting a broken arm to grab a cup of coffee. The little flat-screen television in the café was on, and she stood and watched for a minute. Dreyfus, the former police chief, was announcing his candidacy for mayor. She wasn't sure she liked him enough to vote for him, but when he was asked about the retrovirus and he started cautioning against panic, she nodded.

It was the right message. She hoped people heeded it.

She checked her text messages and saw that David Flynn had left one. She hadn't heard from him in a while, and wasn't sure how she felt about it now. When she read the message, though, she realized he was writing a piece on the virus, and wondering if she had any insights to share. So she just nodded knowingly, and put the phone away.

Talia was about to look at what was next when she heard screaming coming from one of the triage rooms. She bolted out the door and down the hall.

When she got there, she found a man in his mid-thirties, brandishing a knife at Ravenna. The nurse was visibly shaken, but she didn't look hurt.

"Okay," Talia said, holding out her hands, palms forward, and trying to sound calm. "What's going on here? What's the matter?"

"What's going on," the man shouted, "is this stupid bitch says there's nothing wrong with me. But I know I've got it. I *know* I do. And I want the vaccination or whatever. The cure."

She heard a scuffle of feet behind her and saw that Biggs, the security guard, was there, with his pistol drawn.

"Wait!" she shouted. "Just hang on. I'll see you, Mr.—?"

"Max," the guy said. "I'm Max."

"Okay, Max, I'm Dr. Kosar. Come with me."

The man looked uncertain.

"Come on," she said, and she gestured gently with her fingers.

He lowered the knife. Talia stepped over as Ravenna edged away. She studied Max for a bit.

"Yes," she said. "The nurse made a mistake. Come with me."

He looked wary, but followed her, knife still in hand.

"Randy," she said, as soon as they were out of earshot

of the waiting room. "Prepare an IV for Max here, and make sure the MH and sodium levels are adjusted."

She turned back to Max.

"We're just going to give you some fluids, get you hydrated. We call it buffing, here in the ER." She glanced pointedly at the knife. "You won't need that anymore."

"I think I'll hold onto it," Max said.

"Fine," she replied.

"You're pretty for a doctor," he said.

"Thank you," she said. "Okay, here's the IV. Ever had one of these before?"

"I guess," he said. "When I was a kid."

"So I have to find a vein and put a needle in it. Are you okay with that? You're not going to stab me if I prick you? It's going to sting a little."

"No," he said. "I can handle it."

"All right, then let's get it done."

It seemed like a long time before she found the vein and got the catheter in. She felt as if her heart was trying to push itself out of her body. Max's pupils were dilated and she was pretty sure he was on something—meth, probably. She wouldn't have time to move if he used the knife.

But then it was in, and Randall hooked up the bag.

"All right," she said. "That's all we need to do for now. Why don't you just lie down, get comfortable?"

"I think I'll stay sitting," he said. "And I want someone to stay with me. So that guy with the gun don't come in here."

"I'll stay for a few minutes," she said. "But I have other patients I need to see."

"I'm sorry I was rough on that other girl," he said. "But she kept saying I don't have any of the symptoms, but I do. This friend of mine, Jay-Cee, he got it. He said he got it from a monkey or something. And he and I… you know, we smoked a little weed together. So I know I've got it."

"Well, you were right and she was wrong," Talia said. "When we have this many, it's hard to be right all the time."

"Yeah. I guess."

The knife fell out of his hand as the methohexital took effect, and she caught him as he fell face-forward toward the floor.

"Tell security they can have this asshole now," she said.

6

Malakai woke in the gray before dawn. The fog lay thick across the land, and he was as wet as if he had been in a brief rain. He remembered hearing somewhere that fog came on cat's feet—perhaps it was in a poem. But to him it felt more like it had come in like a giant slug.

He stood and fingered the damp bark of a tree. The water had actually beaded there, as if the tree were a glass of ice water on a warm, humid day. It rarely rained in the Bay Area in summer, but the condensation from the fog provided water for the giant trees and other forest life.

He was reminded powerfully of another forest, another mist—the cloud forest in the Virunga Mountains. He had awoken there, too, cold and damp. He and his uncle had spent the previous day trekking up from the tropical lowlands to a place so strange that his eight-year-old mind could hardly imagine it. He remembered how struck he had been with the beauty of it, and how he said so. Babbling in wonder.

Like Clancy, for God's sake.

But he had been eight. Clancy didn't have that excuse.

His uncle had cut a trail with his machete, and Malakai reflected that at that time, he had never seen a machete used for anything other than cutting vegetation. It was like being caught up in a magical tale, carving a tunnel through the green forest that might have been growing on a cloud. To him, it had felt as if *anything* might happen. For long moments, he had almost forgotten the tight emptiness in his belly, and the look of his mother and sister when he last had seen them—drawn, emaciated.

His uncle would point to this and that and call each thing a sign. To Malakai, they mostly just looked like bent leaves and scuffs on the ground. But there was one place even he could spot, an area where branches and leaves had been crushed in a roughly circular area. Some of them looked almost as if they had been woven together.

"A gorilla nest," his uncle told him then. "And not very old."

They continued on for a bit, and then his uncle suddenly stopped. Malakai thought something was the matter. But then his uncle pointed across a little valley, and there they were.

He had tried to imagine them from his uncle's stories, but this was a case where the story did not match reality.

His heart pounded as they moved closer, coming to within ten yards. He could still feel that, the hammering in his chest, the cold of the mist on his skin, the smell of the broken vegetation, the thinness of the air in his young lungs.

And the gorillas.

They watched his uncle and him arrive, peering with almost human regard. The largest, a silverback, crouched a yard or so off of the ground, on a bent tree. Malakai thought they would be attacked, but the gorillas seemed only curious. A small one—a toddler—came over and brushed his uncle's legs before running back to his mother.

He remembered a story he had once heard, about a god who had three sons—Whiteman, Blackman, and Gorilla. Blackman and Gorilla sinned against their father, and so the god took his favored son Whiteman to the west, along with all of his wealth, which Whiteman inherited. Gorilla and his kin went to live in the forests. Blackman remained where he was born, but was impoverished, yearning for the wealth inherited by Whiteman.

His mother didn't like the story because it wasn't Christian. But for the young Malakai it had created a certain longing. His father, after all, had been a white man, and he had gone west, to America, where all men were rich, and left him to starve with his mother and her people. He dreamed that one day his father would return, and lavish gifts upon him, although his mother said it would never happen.

Yet Malakai was the descendent of both brothers. Shouldn't some of the wealth fall to him?

Maybe one day.

And at last he was seeing the descendants of the third brother. How amazingly like men they were. According to the story, these were his cousins.

He wondered if a white man or a black man could make a son with a gorilla mother.

Malakai almost grinned, remembering that childish thought. Looking back, he knew that the story of the three brothers was just another deplorable remnant of European colonialism. Gone was his youthful naïveté.

He turned back to camp to get his things and found Clancy was awake, scribbling in a little book of some sort in the dim gray light of dawn. Like him, she had probably been stripped of her phone, computer, and such.

"Good morning," she said.

"It is," he said, surprising himself.

"Do you like sleeping outdoors?" she asked.

"I once swore I would never do it again," he told her. "When I came to America, I raised my fist and promised myself that from now on I would sleep in soft beds and on clean sheets."

"Sort of like Scarlett O'Hara," Clancy said.

"The rich woman who was so sad to lose her black slaves?"

"I guess that was inappropriate," she said, coloring a little. "I just had that image of her raising her hand, and swearing she would never go hungry again."

Malakai shrugged. "I swore that, too," he said. "And yet here I am, sleeping on the ground, and hungry."

"And agreeing that it's a good morning," she added.

"All right," he said. "Try not to become irritating."

He gathered up his things as she continued writing, and then set off. Clancy looked up, and called after him.

"Where are you going?" she asked.

"Where do you imagine?" he replied. "I'm tracking the apes."

"You're not going to wait for Corbin?"

"No, I think not," he said.

"Fine," she said, stowing her notebook and standing up. "I'm coming with you."

He shrugged and waited for her to prepare. Then they went down the embankment, and he found the trail again.

"Did you hear anything last night?" he asked. He kept his voice pitched low.

"I thought I did," she replied. "An orang, maybe. It might have been nothing."

"No," he replied. "I heard it, too."

They walked in silence for a bit.

"I don't know very much about orangutans," he admitted.

"My experience has been mostly with African apes."

Clancy was frowning, and it seemed in danger of becoming her permanent expression. The happy, babbling girl of yesterday seemed gone—perhaps forever.

One can only hope, he mused.

"There's an old zookeeper's joke," she said.

"Oh, yes?"

"One night while locking up, the zookeeper accidentally drops his keys in front of the gorilla cage. Next morning, the keys are still there, so he picks them up. Another time he drops his keys in front of the chimps. They all start screaming. He looks down, sees that he has dropped his keys, and picks them up. The next night, he drops his keys in front of the orangutan cage. The next morning the keys are gone, the orangutan is gone, and so is every other animal in the zoo."

"Not exactly a joke, is it?" He smiled. "So they're smart."

"It's more that they're deliberate," she said. "They take their time. They don't freak out the way chimps do. They are really good problem-solvers."

"Do you suppose it was an orangutan that organized the—I don't know—prison break?"

"Orangs are sort of solitary," she said. "They don't live in social groups the way chimps and gorillas do. But sure, maybe. I mean, none of this makes any sense to me. Sure, some apes could escape from a zoo or shelter or whatever. But everything they did after that—and the way they're behaving now—it's completely out of the box. I almost feel like there have to be people involved in leading them."

"People in ape suits?"

She actually smiled at that.

"I don't know about that. But apes can be trained to do things way outside of their natural behavior. What I would like to know is what they were being taught in that shelter."

"Well, that's a hypothesis," Malakai said.

"You're making fun of me," she said,accusingly.

"No," he replied. "I was thinking along those lines myself. And I'm also wondering what our contractor friends have to do with all of this."

"They're a little scary, aren't they?" Clancy said.

He nodded.

"You're scarier," she said.

"And yet here you are," he replied.

"Yeah," she said. "Here I am."

They had been on the trail about fifteen minutes when Malakai's walkie-talkie started squawking, demanding his attention. By that time they were well up the southwest slope of Mount Tamalpais. The trail continued along the ground, and in some cases the chimps had left the trees entirely to traverse grassy meadows.

He took out the walkie-talkie and answered it.

"Youmans," he said.

"What the hell do you think you're doing?" Corbin demanded, his voice thin and metallic on the small speaker.

"Hunting for apes," Malakai said.

"Well, get back down here," the mercenary demanded. "We've got three more bodies."

"Your men shot them?"

"No. These had old wounds. Probably got them in the fight on the bridge, and just now died of them."

"Are they near the others?"

"No, down the other way. Almost to the beach."

Malakai considered that for a moment.

"I'm going to follow this trail out," he said. "Then I will be back down."

He shut off the transceiver, and stuck it back in his pocket.

"Three apes died of old wounds, all in one place," he mused.

"Chimps have been known to drag dead bodies around," Clancy said. "If they had several dead, they might have put them together."

"Or they might have moved them miles, to make us look in the wrong place."

"That's—"

"Un-ape-like," he said. "Yes, I know." He slowed to a stop. They had been crossing a field, but now they came back to a tree line—and there the tracks ended. The last ones were quite fresh.

"They traveled on the ground while it was dark," he said. "Then they took to the trees."

"Chimps stay in trees at night," she replied, giving him a strange look. "They would be terrified of traveling on foot in the dark."

"Yes, you've already noted that. But if they *had* to travel, it would be best way. You can't swing from branches you can't see. And as well, they left us this nice trail—and I guarantee you that if we keep going in this direction, we won't see a single ape."

"So you think they're deliberately misleading us?"

"I do," he replied.

"This gets weirder all the time," Clancy said.

Caesar wondered briefly if it had been a mistake to send Koba back to Maurice's group. The one-eyed chimp was good in a fight, and it would be good to have him there to protect the wounded. The thing was, Caesar hoped to avoid a fight, and Koba was somewhat impulsive. He had attacked Will, after all.

Caesar wondered about Will. He missed him, sometimes so much that it hurt him inside. But his place was here, with the apes he had liberated.

With the apes he had changed.

Up ahead, Furaha let out a series of small hoots. Furaha had been born wild and captured as an adult. He knew some sign, and had breathed Will's mist. He was fast, and now he showed it, setting off through the trees with Rafael, another wild-born. Caesar watched with great interest as they separated, then converged, then dropped in a scramble to the forest floor.

A moment later Furaha reappeared, holding something under his arm. When he arrived, he presented it proudly to Caesar.

Food, he said.

Caesar took the limp body. It looked something like a cat, with dark patches around its eyes.

Used to hunt monkeys, Furaha said. *No monkeys here.*

Good. Caesar said. *How do we eat it*?

Furaha made a gleeful little sound, and started to tear the thing up.

Caesar was so hungry he ate more than he had intended before letting the others finish it. It tasted strange, and he was reminded of the time he bit a human's finger. The taste of blood.

We hunt more, he said to Furaha. *You show us*.

They returned to the larger troop as the sun started down the sky. They were laden with a variety of game. His band had all fed as they hunted, so they laid these carcasses out to share. The other apes came signaling their deference to him, crouching and holding their hands out—although some were so hungry it was clearly a strain. None would come near the meat Caesar placed in front of himself, though. He motioned to Maurice.

Come, he motioned. *Yours.*

Maurice stared at him for a moment. He looked very weak.

Not food for me, he signed.

I give it to you. You need it.

Not food for me, Maurice repeated. *Orangs don't eat meat. Eat fruit.*

Chimps eat fruit, Caesar said. *Chimps eat meat.*

Orangs eat fruit, Maurice said.

Caesar thought about that for a minute, then motioned his band over.

We hunt again, he said. *Hunt different food.*

As they walked back over their own tracks, Malakai mulled the situation over. His first instinct was to just walk away. He could pick any direction and find civilization in a few hours—less, if he chose the right compass point. But regardless of his misgivings, he was starting to become intrigued with the situation.

Who actually employed Anvil? The City of San Francisco, it would appear. But why would the city use contractors, when they had a police force, National Guard, and other trained professionals to engage in this situation?

He had been certain from the beginning that someone was hiding something—that this was about more than a bunch of apes loose in the wilderness north of town. Was Clancy right? Was some sort of terrorist organization using trained apes for some unknown purpose? Or perhaps the US government? Whatever the case, the apes were clearly evidence that needed to be eliminated.

Oddly, he had begun to wonder why.

In carrying out his mission to find the apes, following the trails they had left was clearly the wrong way to go. But there were other ways. Figure out what they needed, for instance, and find the sources of those things.

Water came first—all animals needed water. But water wasn't really a problem, as waking up half-soaked had proven. There were plenty of streams, large and small, so staking out a waterhole wasn't going to accomplish anything. Food, though—food would be hard to come by. Chimps could probably forage the easiest. Tree bark, mushrooms, some leaves should be edible. They also ate insects, and when chimps got hungry enough they hunted monkeys and other small mammals.

Gorillas preferred fruit, but could get by on tree bark, leaves and bamboo for a while.

"What do orangutans eat?" Malakai asked.

Clancy glanced at him.

"I'm not sure I want to be involved with this anymore," she replied. "These guys play too rough. It might be their job to capture these apes, but they don't seem to mind killing a few in the process."

"It's hard to capture an ape without killing a few," he said.

"You sound like you know that from experience."

He didn't reply to that.

"Listen," he said instead. "I can call Corbin. I'm sure he can find out what orangutans eat—probably by looking online for half a minute. But if I call, he's going to wonder why the mission primatologist wouldn't answer even a basic question." He paused to let that sink in. "The way I see it, the only person involved in all of this, who has the welfare of the apes at heart, is you. So now you plan to remove yourself from the situation? I don't believe it."

Clancy walked a few paces ahead, then slowed again.

"You have a sneaky mouth," she said. Then she sighed. "They eat mostly fruit. Tropical fruit, like durian."

"I've had durian before," he said. "It stinks."

"Not to orangs."

"What else?"

"Not much else. Honey, if they can get it. A few kinds of bark and leaves. But what they really need is fruit."

"So where are they getting it?" he asked.

"Maybe they aren't," Clancy replied. "Maybe they're starving. Or if I'm right, and there's a person or a group of people behind this, they're probably crating food in for them. I don't think Anvil has enough manpower to secure the borders of this entire area, do you?"

"No," he said, "I do not."

Up ahead of them, the Humvee appeared on an access road they had crossed that morning. Malakai had suspected that their walkie-talkies doubled as tracking devices—now he was sure of it.

Corbin watched them come. His expression was, to say the least, unfriendly. When they reached the vehicle, he cut the mercenary off before he could get started.

"This trail goes nowhere," Malakai said. "I'm just as sure that the one with your new corpses is no better."

"This is ridiculous," Corbin muttered. "They're just stupid monkeys."

"Monkeys aren't stupid," Clancy said. "And apes are even less so."

"Are you saying you can't find them?" Corbin asked.

"No," Malakai said, "I didn't say that. I just need a different tool."

"And what might that be?" Corbin asked.

"A computer, I should think," Malakai replied. "But first I will have a bath and something to eat."

7

"Fights broke out in several supermarkets today. This scene from Pacific Heights, captured via mobile phone, seems typical. The altercation began over distilled water, which has been vanishing from store shelves as allegations surface that the virus is present in city water. Canned goods are also growing scarce, which has also become a source of friction as many in the city have begun 'bunkering'—staying at home and limiting contact with the outside world, hoping to wait out the deadly infection sweeping through the city and, apparently, the world.

"This all follows the announcement that up to a thousand people in the Bay Area alone have died as a result of the virus, and tens or even hundreds of thousands may be infected. About the same number have died worldwide, which suggests that San Francisco is ground zero for the disease.

"Mayor House has called out the National Guard and begun efforts to isolate and quarantine the affected portions of the population. Emergency groups are arriving to relieve local medical facilities, which are already overwhelmed."

"Well, you called it," Patel said, as the Channel Seven anchor moved on to cover the effects of roughly half the work force not showing up, either because they were sick or trying to avoid being sick.

"A few fights over bottled water?" Dreyfus snorted. "This is nothing. Tomorrow there could be ten thousand dead, and the next day ten times that. We're going to see full-blown riots soon. He's going to have to declare martial law."

"This is a hell of a thing," Patel murmured. "Hey, speak of the devil."

The screen showed Mayor House dodging questions outside of City Hall. He was wearing some sort of filter over his mouth and nose.

"Son of a bitch," Dreyfus said.

"Can't say as I blame him," Patel said. "The stores are sold out of those, too."

"Yeah," Dreyfus said. "But it gives me an idea."

"I don't like the sound of that."

"Have my car brought up."

"Where are you going?"

"To a hospital."

As he approached St. Francis Memorial Hospital, Dreyfus saw that the police were manning traffic barriers about a block away. When his car approached the roadblock, Dreyfus rolled his window down. The officer recognized him.

"We've got sort of a situation here, sir," he said. "I'm not supposed to let you through."

"Who is in charge here, son?" he asked.

"Captain Paterno, sir."

"Could you give Charlie a call and see if he'll let me in?"

"Yes, sir." He stepped away to his car. After a moment he returned.

"Go on through, sir," he said, gesturing. "You'll find the captain two blocks over." He paused. "You'll have to leave your car here."

"That's fine," Dreyfus said. He pulled the car to the curb.

The "situation" turned out to be a mob of people clustered around the emergency entrance. Police had cleared a space back from the entry, and the people nearest the front were pleading with them. Some were screaming

He found Captain Paterno leaning against his car. He was almost a decade younger than Dreyfus, but they had worked together briefly before Dreyfus made detective. The cop looked as if he might have picked up a pound or two, but he was still relatively lean.

"Hey, Charlie," Dreyfus said.

"Chief," Paterno said, holding out a hand, and then he looked sheepish. "Sorry," he said, "force of habit." He paused. "Wish you *were* still the chief, though."

"That's very kind of you to say," Dreyfus said, clasping Paterno's hand. He nodded at the mob. "How long has this been going on?"

"No more than an hour," Paterno said. "It was one of those flash crowds, or something. Like everyone suddenly had the same idea."

"They're all sick?"

"Some of them are just demanding antibiotics. You know, we've had about two dozen drugstore robberies this morning. They skipped over the usual painkillers and such, and went straight to the antibiotics."

"Yeah, of course," Dreyfus said. "They're probably worth more than cocaine right now." Out of the corner of his eye he saw that some of the press had noticed him, and a camera crew was headed his way.

"Hold the fort, Charlie," he said. "This could get ugly real fast. I'm not the chief anymore, but if you want my advice, you'll need more men here."

"I've asked for more," Paterno said. "But a lot of officers called in sick, and the rest of us are stretched pretty thin."

"Well, you're doing a hell of a job," he said, getting it out just in time for Channel Five to record it.

"Hi, Frances," he said to the reporter. She was a slight, birdlike woman, but looking very competent in her dark blue suit.

"Mr. Dreyfus," she said. "I wonder if we can talk to you?"

"Well, you're talking, and I'm listening," he replied.

"You're no longer the chief of police. What brings you down here today?"

She held the microphone toward him.

"I'm not the chief, but I still care about this city," he said. "I wanted to see what was going on. Can't really do that from my office, despite your fine reporting."

"Aren't you worried about contracting the virus? You aren't even wearing a respirator."

"Well, aren't you, Ms. Chang? Worried, I mean?"

"Well, this is my job," she replied.

"I'd like to think it's mine a well," he said. "I've tossed my hat into the political ring. The least I can do is inform myself of what our troubles really are."

"Do you—"

She stopped as gunfire exploded, somewhere—first one shot, then a volley of them. Dreyfus ducked reflexively, his eyes picking through the crowd. He couldn't see who was shooting, because the mob suddenly surged forward, engulfing the police near the door.

"Oh, shit," the reporter said. Then to her cameraman, "You didn't get that, did you?"

Paterno drew his pistol.

"Best get out of here, sir," he said.

Dreyfus saw why. Most of the mob was crushing itself into the hospital entrance, but a significant faction had turned toward Paterno and the other officers on the perimeter. Judging from that, he guessed that it must have been the police who started shooting, or that the crowd thought they had.

"Murderers!" one of them shouted.

Dreyfus didn't really think about what he did next. He stepped in front of the officers.

"*Stop it*," he shouted. "Stop it right there!"

But it didn't look like they would. They didn't seem to have a leader, as such, so he picked out the biggest man he saw—a fierce-looking fellow with copious tattoos and a brick-square face—and locked him with his gaze.

"Don't do this," Dreyfus said.

Taken aback by the direct address, the man did stop, and so did many of the others, more or less. Some continued to inch nearer. They were a motley collection—some were in suits, others in jeans or shorts and tie-dyed T-shirts. Most were on the younger side, but none of them seemed like people who would ordinarily charge at police.

Except there was a certain look in their eyes, a look he had come to know all too well in his years on the force.

"They started shooting," the big man said. He thrust a finger at Paterno. "*The cops* started it."

"I don't know what happened," Dreyfus said. "I didn't see it. But this isn't how to sort it out. I can tell you for a fact that these men behind me have done nothing but try to ensure your safety."

"There is no sorting this out," a young woman screamed. "We're all gonna die. They have the cure in there, and they won't let us have it."

"I haven't heard anything about a cure," Dreyfus said, trying to keep his voice controlled and reasonable.

"Where did you hear that?"

"It's *known*, man," someone else said. "It's on Twitter!"

About twenty cell phones shot up to corroborate his assertion.

"I just want antibiotics," the big fellow said. "I don't know anything about any cure."

"Let's just all calm down," Dreyfus said. "You're good people. I can see that. You don't want to hurt anybody."

The madness was starting to fade in some of their eyes. More than a few glanced back at the mob that was still trying to funnel into the emergency entrance. There were no more gunshots, but there were plenty of screams.

"Look," Dreyfus said, pointing. "They're trampling over each other. What's that going to get them? Is that how we behave in this city?"

A few started to look slightly ashamed, as if waking up hung over, and recalling all the stupid things they had done the night before.

"I'm just scared," a young woman with braids said. "I'm so freaking scared."

"So am I," Dreyfus told her. "We all are. These men behind me are. But we don't just turn on each other like this. We find solutions. I know that help is on the way. Medical help. I'll see to it. I'll see to it. It's going to be okay."

And he saw belief kindle where the madness had been. If they asked him how he would see to it, he didn't have an answer for them. And at the moment, he didn't hold any position of authority, and couldn't reasonably deliver on his promise.

But they weren't going to question him, because they *wanted* to believe. They had seen him on television many times as the chief, and most of them probably knew he was running for mayor, so in their minds he was somebody whose word could be trusted.

Besides, he believed it himself. Come hell or high water, he would do something.

"There's an easier way to do that," Clancy said, from over Malakai's shoulder.

One of the contractors, a young woman named Sela, watched them with a bored expression. Corbin was pacing.

"How so?" Malakai said, staring at the list of businesses on the screen.

She leaned over and took control of the mouse.

"Well, there's a map, see? I put a point on it here, where we are, then hit 'search nearby.' Exactly what are you searching for?"

"Supermarkets. Convenience stores. Any sort of market."

"Okay," she said, typing as quickly as she could, despite the awkward angle. She typed in "supermarket" and a series of icons popped up.

"The closest ones are in Mill Valley," she said. "It's not that far from the edge of the woods, but the apes would have to cross a lot of urban area. And go through whatever perimeter these guys have set up."

"You think they're going grocery shopping?" Corbin said.

"They need fruit," Clancy said. "We're just trying to figure out where they can get it."

"A small group of them could easily breach your perimeter," Malakai added. "And they are not strangers to urban settings."

"Okay," Corbin said, "but they don't have the Internet. How will they find these places?"

Malakai regarded the man for a moment, wondering just how long he could survive without computers, satellites, cell phones, and all the rest. Not long, he suspected.

"By looking for them," Malakai said finally.

Corbin's brow furrowed.

"Sure," he said. "By *looking* for them. Why didn't I think of that? So now what?"

"We call a few of the nearest stores and see if they've been broken into."

Corbin thought about that for a moment.

"Okay," he said. "Just watch what you say, okay? Communications are restricted." He punched a button. "And it stays on speaker."

Malakai dialed the first number on his list.

After a few rings, a woman picked up. Her voice sounded strained.

"Baxter's Market," she said. "How may I help you?"

"Hello," Malakai replied. "I was wondering if you could tell me if your store has been recently burglarized."

"Is this some kind of security service?" She asked, after a brief pause. She sounded irritated. "Are you in India or someplace? We don't accept solicitations on the store line."

"I'm not in India," Malakai said, "And I am not a telemarketer. I am calling on behalf of the City of San Francisco. We're doing a survey—"

"Well, skip the survey and put more cops on the street," the woman said. "Of course we've been broken into. Bottled water, medicine, beer, canned goods—cleaned us out."

"What about fruit?" Malakai asked.

"Fruit? No, they left the fruit. Fruit goes bad. Do you even know what's going on?" She paused for a moment. "Are you *sure* you're not in India?"

"Thank you for your time," Malakai said, and he hung up.

"What was all of that about?" Clancy asked. "What does she mean by 'what's going on'?"

"Never mind," Corbin said. "Don't pay any attention—she's just a store clerk. Make the next call."

Malakai picked up the phone, then held it for a moment, considering.

"Perhaps one of you should make the calls," he said. "I think my accent is causing trouble."

"I'll do it," Clancy said.

Her first two calls met with similar, if more courteous results. Yes, they had been robbed. No, the fruit wasn't touched.

The next call to Hong Tan Market got different results.

"Yeah, all the fruit and pretty much nothing else," the man said. "They came in at night. They took all the fresh fruit, but they got into the canned stuff, too, and the frozen. All the durian. We're not a big place, but they got it all." His voice turned a little suspicious. "How did you know?" he asked. "This isn't some sort of prank is it? You're not mocking me, are you?"

"It's not a prank, sir," Clancy said. "Did the thieves eat it there? Were there skins or shells scattered around?"

"No, it was just gone. I looked… holy shit! It was the monkeys, wasn't it? The ones who came over the bridge—"

"Hang up," Corbin snapped. "Now."

Clancy looked darts at him, but she turned the phone off and placed it on the table.

"So they're eating," Malakai said. "At least for now."

"Then what do we do, stake out Asian markets?"

Malakai thumped his fingers rhythmically on the table, trying to decide what to say, but it was Clancy who spoke up.

"They're using a fission–fusion strategy," she said.

"What's that?" Corbin demanded.

Clancy looked Corbin straight in the eye.

"I want you to swear to me right now that our mission

is to locate these apes so they can be captured, and humanely," she said.

"Honey," Corbin said, "I promise on my sainted grandmother's grave. That's the mission. We screwed up the other night—and that's exactly why we brought you two in."

"Fine," Clancy said. "Fission-fusion, then. Chimpanzees do it in the wild. When times are good, and they have plenty of food, they gather into larger social groups. When food is scarce, they break up into smaller groups and disperse. I think they're adapting to this new environment. Instead of completely breaking up, they're sending out small groups to forage for their larger community."

"How do you know they aren't just playing 'each ape for himself'?" Corbin said.

"Because they didn't eat any of the fruit where they found it," Clancy replied. "None. They took it all with them."

"Okay," he sighed, pushing back his hair. "So what does this mean?"

Clancy leaned back in her chair.

"So if you stake out the grocery stores," she said, "you might catch a small group of them, but that's all. And given how well they've been doing at dodging you, I wouldn't even count on that."

"So we follow them back to the big group," Corbin said.

"Yes," Clancy said. "Well, sort of. It would still be too hard to figure out which stores to watch."

"You think we should bring the fruit to them," Malakai said.

Clancy touched her nose with her forefinger.

"Exactly," she said. "Send someone into town to buy fruit—anything, but be sure to include some durian, if they can find it, and as stinky as possible. Most likely you'll find it in Thai, Vietnamese, or Malaysian markets, at least in quantity. We can lay a trail of it to a central cache."

"Won't they know it's a trap?"

"They might. But they need the fruit. Cut off their supply—increase your presence on the Mill Valley side of the woods, so they can't forage in that direction."

Corbin nodded and reluctantly grinned.

"You guys may finally be starting to earn your keep."

"Just remember your promise," Clancy said.

"Noted and logged," Corbin replied. He clapped his hands and rubbed them together. "Well, if you're done in here, let's lock up and turn in," he said.

"I'd like to stay for a while, do a little research," Clancy said. "I might be able to refine the plan a little."

"This is a sensitive area," Corbin said. "You're not allowed in here unsupervised. And I'm tired of supervising for today."

Clancy shrugged.

"Whatever," she said. "I guess I am sleepy at that."

Malakai had his doubts about that, so when he heard the faint creak of the door to Clancy's room, he felt a little smile touch his face. He waited a few more moments and then rose himself. He watched her cross the dark compound to the command center and slip into the prefab building.

He hesitated a moment, looking around. He didn't see anyone. No alarms went off, yet he decided not to follow her. If he did, she would probably scream or something. Instead, he waited.

It took longer than he had expected. It reminded him of standing on duty in a camp in Uganda, what seemed like a very long time ago. But that night the quiet had been broken by mortar shells, and then rifle fire. Nothing similar would happen here. Thinking about it, however, he had a vivid image of chimps armed with assault weapons and gorillas with rocket launchers, swarming into the compound, bent on exterminating the humans who were so determined to hound them. He shook his head at the impossibility of it.

And yet…

He stiffened as a sentry walked past, oblivious to him standing in the shadows. He checked his watch.

Thirty minutes later, the man walked by again.

When at last he saw Clancy re-emerging from the building, another twenty-nine minutes had passed, according to the radium dial of his watch. As she crossed the compound, he noticed the sentry about to turn the corner. Once he did that, he would spot her for certain.

"Hey there!" he shouted, stepping from the shadow and moving toward the watchman. The man froze, lifting his gun. Malakai put his hands up and took a few steps to the side.

"Hey, now," he said, his voice lower. "There is no need for that."

"What are you doing out?"

Malakai walked away from where Clancy had been. The sentry turned to follow him with the weapon. Out of the corner of his eye, he saw her freeze, then tiptoe past and into their hut.

"Just looking for a smoke," he said. "I thought you might have one."

"I don't smoke," the man said, lowering his weapon. "You shouldn't either. It's bad for you, and secondhand smoke kills."

"Ah, I've been thinking about quitting, anyhow," Malakai said. "Perhaps you've inspired me." He turned and went back inside, trying to ignore the itch he got whenever someone with a gun was behind him.

Clancy was sitting in a chair next to the small table in the common room when he entered.

"Thanks," she whispered, as he approached.

"Can we talk?" he asked.

She nodded. He pulled the other chair up to the little table.

"How did you know?" she asked.

"You had a look in your eye," he said. "I've seen it before. I've had it in my own eye, for that matter. How did you get in? They didn't lock it?"

"They did," she said. "I jammed chewing gum in the hole in the strike plate while they were watching you fail at the computer." She shrugged and looked up. "These huts don't have high-tech locks."

"Well, what did you find?" he asked.

She hesitated. "Something," she said at last. "Phillips—our boss, the guy running things here. He works for a multinational that owns, among other things, Anvil."

"Okay," he said. "That I could have guessed."

"They also own a company called Gen Sys. The computer is lousy with Gen Sys files. I can't read any of them because they're encrypted."

He waited, figuring she would finish her point, but she didn't. Then she saw the puzzlement in his eyes.

"Gen Sys was the second place the apes liberated," she said. "They were the company using apes for testing drugs."

"Ah," he said. "I see."

"I'm not sure I do," she said, "but it's out there now."

"What do you mean?"

"It wasn't easy, but I managed to send a friend of mine an email. I'm pretty sure it won't be detected unless they go through the whole system looking for it. Anyway, he's a reporter. I asked him to check it out quietly and get back to me."

Malakai absorbed that for a moment.

"How will he 'get back to you'?"

"I guess I'll have to break back in there," she said.

He nodded, realizing how badly he had underestimated this person. He had mistaken wonder and idealism for stupidity.

Of course, she might very well have just killed them both.

It took him a long time to get to sleep.

8

Caesar now knew his way into town.

The first night he had climbed high in the trees, searching for the nearest lights that marked human settlements. He saw them off toward where the moon and sun came from. When the moon rose, he and a small group went by its pale light, slowly and quietly, the orangs feeling the way first.

When they reached the fringes of the town and its streetlights, things went more easily. They kept to trees and shadows, which was not so difficult as there were plenty of both. Caesar had known what he was looking for—he had been with Will when he went to where humans found their food, although he usually had been made to wait in the car. But the places were easy to recognize, with lots of big windows and pictures of food. Will had called them "stores."

A little hunting had found such a place. They discovered a way in through a shaft in the roof, and found bags they filled with fruit, honey, nuts—anything that looked edible. Keling remembered that fruit sometimes came in metal or plastic cans, and Caesar found plenty that had been made cold and hard, but which he knew would eventually warm up.

They had slipped back into the forest, groaning from

the weight, but it was worth it to see Maurice and the other orangutans finally eat something, to know they would not starve—at least, not yet.

The next night the shaft was closed with a piece of wood, so they had needed to break a window. And the next they had found men with guns guarding the store, so they had been forced to locate a different source of food. They found another place, though, and while small, it had very good fruit, including a very stinky one that set Maurice to doing a strange, stately dance of happiness before devouring it.

Tonight they tried a third store—one Rocket had scouted the night before. But when they approached it, they found the windows already broken. There were people inside. At first Caesar thought they were waiting for him—that it was a trap. But then he saw that they were taking things out of the store and loading them into their cars. Humans were stealing from humans.

Why? he wondered.

It didn't matter—this was no place for them now. They would have to find another store.

He was about to leave when cars with flashing lights arrived, and policemen climbed out. The trees around Caesar rustled as his band reacted, remembering the killers on the bridge that had been dressed like this.

"Quiet!" he whispered.

The people in the store tried to get away from the police, but a few fought them. The policemen hit them with sticks. One pulled his gun.

Caesar knew it was time to leave, while the humans were occupied with hurting each other.

He felt in his bones that something had changed. Something was different. He had never seen humans turn on each other in this way, and it sent weird chills through him. It might be that this was their last night foraging in this area. But if not here, then where? They couldn't go back across the bridge. It was too dangerous. Were there towns toward sundown? And if so, were humans turning on each other there, as well?

A part of him hoped so. If they fought themselves, they might forget about him and his apes.

When they reached the last road before the woods, Caesar saw trucks, and more of the men who had been chasing them.

They know, he realized. *They're trying to catch us coming back.*

It took them all night to go around, and they returned empty-handed. It was not a good night.

Maurice approached him, and Caesar waved to him.

Sorry, he signed. *No fruit tonight.*

It never was the long solution, the orangutan said.

Is there a long solution? Caesar asked.

The wild apes have found some things we can eat.

Not enough, Caesar said.

They will find more, Maurice assured him. He tilted his head. *Fruit grows somewhere,* he said. *We will find it.*

I saw humans fight each other over food, Caesar said. *What can it mean?*

That there is not enough food for them, either, Maurice replied.

How can that be? There was always food in the city.

Maurice shrugged.

If there isn't enough food for humans, where will we *get it?* Caesar wondered.

You will find a way, Maurice said, rolling slowly under the branch. *Because you are Caesar.*

* * *

The man's name is Tommy and he lives in a place with many rooms. In one of these rooms there are two cages, and he puts Koba in one of them. The cage is taller than the one that moved, but it is so narrow that he can't sit or get down on all fours—he has to stand, which hurts after a while. He clings to the cage wall to relieve the cramping, but he can't do that for long either. His mother is not there, and there are no toys in it at all. His only toy is his stuffed kitten, and he clings to it. It still smells like Mother.

There is another cage next to his, with something in it.

"Milo," Tommy says, "Meet your protégé, Koba."

Milo looks at Koba, then points at the stuffed animal.

Kitten, he signs.

Kitten, Koba signs back, relieved that Milo is not another big black caterpillar.

Milo doesn't say a lot, though. When Koba gets some food, Milo wants some. When Koba asks Milo to tickle him, he doesn't. Still, it is nice to have someone near.

The next day, Tommy starts teaching him.

Tommy shows Koba a stick. It looks funny, and has a sort of coil on one end of it. He touches Koba with it, and Koba screams as horrible pain shoots through his arm and makes his whole body shake.

"This is called a prod," Tommy tells him. "When I ask you to do something and you don't do it right, I will hurt you with it like I just did."

He sits down in front of Koba.

"Koba," he says. "I want you to smile."

He makes a sign by putting one finger from each hand under his lips and then pulls them upward in a curve toward his ears. At the same time he pulls his lips back from his teeth and draws the corners of his mouth up. It is the expression Koba's mother made when she was terrified of something, and Koba makes it, too, when he is scared.

Tommy wants him to do that?

Tommy hits him with the pain stick. Koba jerks back in terror.

"There," Tommy says. "You smiled. Good Koba. Do it again. Smile."

He makes the sign again.

Shaking, Koba raises his hands up and puts his fingers under his jaw and then curves them up.

"That's the sign," Tommy says. "Now do it with your mouth."

Then he shocks Koba again. Koba thinks his body will curl into a ball of pain and stay that way. It hurts like nothing he has ever felt.

"There," Tommy said. "You smiled, you little sonofabitch. Now, see if you can do it without me shocking the crap out of you. Smile." And he makes the sign again.

Then he reaches for his stick.

Koba flinches back, anticipating the pain.

"There you go," Tommy said. "You're starting to catch on."

He makes the sign again and raises the stick. Koba watches, confused.

"I said smile," Tommy roars, jabbing Koba again.

Tommy waits a minute while Koba shivers and pants and calms down. He takes out a little white stick, and another thing that makes hot flower-air. He touches the hot flower-air to the white stick, then sucks on it. Smoke comes out of his mouth. It does not smell good.

Tommy sets the smoke-stick down. He makes the "smile" sign and then reaches for his shocking stick. Koba knows Tommy is going to hit him again. Koba pulls his lips back from his teeth and makes them curve up toward his ears. It isn't hard, he's so scared.

Tommy puts the stick back down.

"Good boy," he says. "You learn fast."

He does the sign for "smile," but does not reach for the stick.

Koba dithers, uncertain what to do.

Tommy hits him with the stick.

This time, when Tommy does the sign for "smile" Koba pulls his face into a rictus of terror.

"Good boy," Tommy says, and gives him a cookie.

The next lesson is about "talking." Koba learns to hoot-pant whenever Tommy signs for him to. After that they move on to dancing. For this lesson, Koba is shocked many, many times.

Milo is already good at all of these things. He walks upright most of the time, at least when Tommy is around, and he can do lots of other tricks, too.

One day, instead of teaching Koba, Tommy takes both of them someplace in a car. It is a place that looks a little like a room inside of Tommy's house, except that it only has three walls and no ceiling and it is inside a much bigger room. There are other rooms like this attached to it. The lights are very hot, and bright, and Koba is told to stay still. Then a woman comes into the room and says something.

Her name is Alice. Tommy tells Koba to smile, and he does. Then he makes another sign, but Koba doesn't remember what that sign means, so Tommy hits him with the stick. Then he shows Koba clapping, which is what Koba was supposed to do.

Then they start again. The woman says the same thing, and then Koba "smiles" and claps.

They do this several more times. Koba knows he is doing the right thing, because Tommy does not hurt him. The woman seems to be getting something wrong. But Tommy does not shock her.

Koba is never sure about what they are supposed to be doing, but he learns to like it, except for the part where Tommy hurts him. They put him in pants and shirt, or sometimes a skirt. He is trained to do things, often the same things, over and over. Once he is supposed to stack up a bunch of objects so he can try to climb and get some bananas from on top of a big square object. As he reaches for the bananas, however, the pile wobbles and he falls. It hurts, but he has to do it over and over again, until he gets it right.

If he gets it right, he gets something sweet to eat. If he doesn't, Tommy hurts him with the stick.

Milo does a lot of tricks, a lot more than Koba. And he almost never gets hit or shocked with the stick.

One day Koba notices a little thing like a mirror. He sees some very small people in it. The people look like the normal-sized people, who he also can see, and there is one who looks like Milo. They're doing the same things that the normal-sized people are doing. He wonders if the little people are learning what to do from the big ones.

One night, Tommy lets them out of their cages, but he doesn't teach them anything. Instead he watches one of the squares with little people inside, and drinks something. Koba doesn't like the smell of the drink—it smells like the stuff Roger was drinking before he hit Koba and his mother with the oranges in the bag.

Koba looks for Milo and Alice in the screen, but these are different people.

Milo nudges him.

Come, he signs.

He leads Koba to the room where they learn things. He goes over to a big black hoop hanging from a rope and starts to swing on it. Koba jumps on and begins to swing, too. It feels good to let his muscles stretch outside of the cage. For the first time since leaving where his mother was he feels a little happy. There are other things to play on and climb on. There is a ball that Milo teaches him to roll, and they play a game with it.

Koba sees a leash and hands it to Milo. He motions for Milo to put it on him. At first Milo does not understand. He puts the leash down. But then Koba tries again. Milo tentatively comes forward with the leash. Koba hoots and jumps back. Milo tries again, and once more Koba hops back, hooting laughter.

Then Milo starts laughing, too, and the chase begins. They run all around the room. Milo eventually catches Koba, and they tussle on the floor. Only once, when Koba playfully grabs at Milo's ear, does Milo get angry. He scowls and pushes Koba away. But then Koba tickles him, and they start playing again.

After a while, they grow tired, and Milo leads Koba around the house. Tommy is where he was, but now he is asleep, a can of the stuff he was drinking still in his hand. Milo makes the sign for "quiet."

In one room there is a big white box, like the one he was supposed to get the bananas off of, at the place where he and Milo do their tricks. This one is smaller though, and has food in it. So do some other boxes—each one a different size. Milo finds them sweet things to eat. They play some more and then curl up next to each other to sleep. It feels good to sleep lying down, and not standing up in the cage.

Koba wakes with Milo plucking at him. He sees light coming through the windows. Something is making a ringing noise, and Tommy is stirring on the long chair.

Milo pulls him frantically toward the cages.

Tommy, he signs. *Stick, stick—come in cage. Quick!*

Koba remembers that it was Tommy that let them out

of the cages, but he does what Milo says. The cage doors click shut.

A moment later, Tommy appears, the stick in his hand. He looks at them.

"Huh," he says, and then scratches his head. He walks off.

It is the next night, and Tommy lets them out again. This time he watches them play. Koba does the trick they have been practicing; he pretends to be crying, and then Milo comes and gives him a hug. Koba is hoping for a cookie, but instead Tommy offers him the stuff he is drinking. It still smells bad to Koba, and he does not want to drink it, but Tommy shows him the stick and tells him to drink it.

It burns in his nose and throat, and he wants to spit it out, but Tommy has the stick. And so he swallows it.

After it stops burning, it sits in his stomach, turning warm. It feels a little like being groomed, and he remembers his mother. He remembers outside, and the wind, and soon he feels a little warm wind in his head. Milo drinks some too, and then they play together some more. Things are funny that shouldn't be, like when Koba misses his handhold and cracks his head on the floor.

Milo laughs, and so does Koba, although it hurts.

Like the night before, they find Tommy asleep in front of the tiny moving people, and like before Milo finds them some things to eat and they curl up together.

But this time they wake up with Tommy hitting them and yelling at them. He chases them to their cages and makes them get in. Koba stands there, cramped and miserable. Something is wrong with his head. It hurts, and his stomach feels wrong. He can see that Milo doesn't feel well, either.

* * *

It is the next morning, and they are at the place where the little people copy the big ones. Milo is trying to do his trick, but he keeps falling. Tommy hits him again and again, but he doesn't get it right. Tommy leaves to put one of the smoking sticks in his mouth. Most of the other people wander off. Milo is sulking.

A boy Koba has only seen today goes over to Milo and pokes him with his finger.

"Come on," he says. "Do something." Milo just backs up a little.

The boy pokes him again.

"Come on, you stupid monkey, do a trick."

Koba can see that Milo is getting agitated. The boy is challenging him, threatening him. But the boy is not Tommy. The boy does not have the stick.

"You're such a dumb monkey," the boy says. "I bet you eat your own shit, don't you." He pushes Milo on the head. Milo looks confused, and then he is suddenly angry. He screams and lunges forward, biting the boy on the nose. It isn't much of a bite—most of the nose is still there—but it bleeds a lot. The boy starts screaming, and Milo goes behind a chair and puts his hands over his head.

All the people come back, including Tommy.

Tommy hits Milo many times with the stick. Then he puts them in their cages on the truck and they go home. When they get home, Tommy takes Koba from the truck and puts him in his cage in the house, but he leaves Milo in the truck. Then Tommy leaves Koba again, and he is alone.

Koba doesn't like being alone. Being in the cage was bad, but at least Milo had been close. Koba grips the cage and shakes it. He jumps and bangs his head on the top, where the food comes down. He begins to think that Milo and Tommy will never come back.

Milo and Tommy do come back, and Tommy puts Milo in his cage. Milo is asleep. His face looks strange, swollen. Koba tries to wake him up, but Milo doesn't hear him, and after a while Tommy comes in with the stick.

"Shut up," he says. "Or you're next."

Koba does not know what Tommy means.

After a long time, Milo does wake up. He looks around and sees Koba. Milo tries to hoot-pant, or at least that's what Koba thinks he's doing, but it comes out muffled because Milo is not opening his mouth. Milo starts to panic. He shakes the cage, and claws at his face. He pulls his lips up and does the "smile," and when he does, Koba can see something shiny toward the back of Milo's jaw.

After a long time, Milo tires out. He looks desperately at Koba.

Mouth not open, he signs.

Koba doesn't understand. What has happened to Milo's mouth?

It is the next day, and Tommy is making them practice their tricks. Milo seems to feel better, but he still can't open his mouth. Tommy feeds him through a straw. Tommy looks at Koba.

"This is what happens," he said. "This is what happens when you don't behave. You get your goddamn jaw wired shut. You remember that, you little pissant."

Milo is still able to do most of his tricks. He can even "smile", although he can no longer "talk." Koba does most of the talking now.

Tommy still lets them out sometimes, but Milo isn't the same. He doesn't play long. He doesn't look for food in Tommy's boxes. He goes back to his cage. He doesn't sign very much, and even with Milo there, Koba feels lonely.

* * *

Koba felt dizzy as the memories pushed through him, and he realized that while he hadn't been asleep, he hadn't really been aware of what was happening around him, either.

He saw one of the big caterpillars looking at him. They had found the big caterpillars at the zoo. He had wondered why Caesar freed them, along with the apes. They couldn't sign, and they were stupid. *Go away, caterpillar,* he signed. But of course it just stared at him. Disturbed, he climbed away from it, hoping he didn't start seeing things again.

A bit later he found Caesar, and felt excited when Caesar approached him. He quickly supplicated.

Koba, Caesar said. *My band is smaller now. I need fast, strong apes with me.*

I'm with you Caesar.

It's dangerous. Some have died.

Humans have done much bad to me, Koba responded. *Happy to fight them.*

We don't fight them, Caesar said. *We trick, we avoid. We save apes.*

He waved at the hundreds in the troop.

Koba understands, Koba said, slightly disappointed. But Caesar was the leader. Caesar was smart. He knew what was best for them all.

David woke at four, as usual. He heard sirens in the distance, and looked out his bedroom window. All he saw was San Francisco, in darkness. It wasn't all that unusual to hear sirens now and then, but in the last few days and nights the number and frequency of them had multiplied. Things were definitely getting more than a little crazy. He had covered a triple homicide in Chinatown the night before, which had turned out to be a sort of robbery gone wrong. The rumor had gotten out that monkey penis could cure the virus, and so Chinese apothecaries were being ransacked.

Three groups had shown up at the same place and had a shoot-out.

Over monkey penis.

He went to the living room and flipped on the TV, where they were rehashing the riot that former Chief of Police Dreyfus had managed to quell. Then they started showing clips of him from various local talk shows. He was always urging calm, and he came off as smart, deliberate, and in control. Mayor House, by contrast, seemed to be steadily losing it. The polls were starting to look very good for Dreyfus.

He turned off the TV and picked up his tablet to check his messages.

Unsurprisingly, there was an email from Clancy. He had tried to call her the day before, to make sure she was okay, but then he realized she probably didn't have reception up there.

What was surprising was the content of the mail. He read it, then read it again, wondering if it was some sort of prank, but it seemed pretty serious—and while Clancy was playful, she wasn't actually the practical joker sort.

Okay, he thought, *let's have a look at this.*

There were really two parts to what she had sent. One was a brief essay describing the relationship between Gen Sys and Anvil, and her suspicion that the cover-up Gen Sys had begun was still going on under Anvil. The other was a list of the names of the encrypted files she had come across. Ol86G, AgniP3, Chl223, RV113, Teetot, AH1/2F.

None of them meant anything to him, nor did an Internet search turn up anything that looked as if it might be a lead.

A quick search established the basic facts of the matter, however. Anvil and Gen Sys were indeed owned by the same parent company. After searching "Gen Sys + Apes," he found an article that was eight years old. It was about a shareholder's meeting in which the results of a drug trial were to be released, apparently with much fanfare. The drug, ALZ112, was supposed to be a cure for Alzheimer's, and they had tested it on a chimpanzee. The chimp in question had shown considerable cognitive improvement, and was to be introduced to the public as proof that the drug was effective at helping the brain build new cells and repair itself.

Bizarrely, the chimp had gone berserk, broken into the meeting room, and been put down by a security guard. The drug was deemed too dangerous for further trials, and apparently that was that.

He leaned back.

That was that. Except that Gen Sys had been trashed by apes in the lead-up to the whole Monkeygate thing. And now Anvil seemed to be trying to cover something up, as well. And Anvil was in the employ of the City of San Francisco.

From his investigation of hijinks in appropriations at City Hall, he was already convinced that there was a lot more money moving around there than there should be if everyone was on the up-and-up. What if the mayor was being bribed to cover something up? What could be that big?

This was definitely worth checking out. Everyone was focused on the plague. This story could be very big—and it could be all his.

Talia wasn't sure how long she had been on her feet, but they were numb. She had lost count of the hits, and had been admitting people all day. They just kept coming, one train wreck after another.

Her prediction to her father had proven all too true—almost all of the staff were dealing with the retrovirus, leaving her and a handful of others to deal with gun- and knife-wounds, vehicular casualties, and the like. What she was coming to realize was that that sort of morbidity wasn't remaining at the rate she was used to—it was rising. Most particularly she was seeing an increase in assault victims, people with wounds from broken glass, bats, fists, and feet. As the local death toll from the virus hurdled over a thousand, everything else was ratcheting up, as well.

Some of the assault injuries came from their own waiting room, which was now being used for triage. Those who had tested positive for the disease were escorted to one bus, those who weren't symptomatic went to another. The sick were then driven to isolation camps, while everyone else went to quarantine because they had potentially been exposed.

Security was being provided by National Guardsmen. Talia found it unnerving to look out at the waiting room and see men holding assault rifles, but she knew things would be far worse without them.

"Somebody's been tweeting that we've got the goddamn cure again," Randal said. They were patching up an eighteen-year-old boy who looked as if he'd met the business end of a switchblade. "We're going to get mobbed, like St. Francis did."

"They didn't have National Guard at St. Francis," she pointed out, stitching up an intestine.

"Yeah, but people're just getting more and more desperate," he said. "There was a kid in here yesterday—you missed it. His mom had given him some kind of herbal medicine, thinking it would cure him. I still don't know what it was, but he was convulsing when she brought him in. He was in acute renal failure. Died on the table. And of course the mother broke down, started screaming about how our western medicine was to blame. It was a mess."

"Jeez," she said. She noticed how tired Randal looked, and figured she probably looked worse. "That's too bad. He would have died anyway, but this way she blames herself."

"No, she blames us," he said. "Weren't you listening?"

She shrugged. "You really can't expect a mother to be rational two minutes after her son has died. They usually find someone to blame."

"How about the quack who sold her the medicine?"

"That would be way too logical," she said. "Okay, thanks—I think I've got this one now."

"Right," Randal said. "I'll go see what's next."

As he was getting up, he suddenly sneezed. Talia looked up and saw that his mask was spattered red.

"Oh, God, Randal," she said.

9

For a moment, Dreyfus thought Maddy was going to slap him.

He could see it in the set of her shoulders, the thin line of her lip. After twenty years of marriage he knew her that well. She was trying to decide.

Instead, she wrapped her arms around him, and hugged him so hard it almost hurt.

"You frigging idiot," she murmured.

"Look," he said, "I had no intention of getting into a situation. I just went down there to make an appearance, and things happened."

She pushed him back and crossed her arms.

"You never do intend to get into situations," she said. "Yet somehow you always do. God, I thought all of this was over. Twenty years, every day wondering if I was going to have to go identify your body, wondering how I would tell the kids. You finally leave the job—and now this! This is an addiction. You need help."

"I'm not a cop anymore," he said. "That doesn't mean I don't live in the world. I'm trying to make a difference, here."

"You weren't even wearing a mask," she said. "You

might have caught it. This thing." She waved her arms helplessly, as if the virus was even now all around them.

"If I did, I didn't bring it home," he said. "I scrubbed down carefully at the office. Head to toe, and changed clothes. As for the respirator—I'm the 'don't panic' guy, remember? The mayor looks terrified. He wears one of the damn things. I have to be the other guy."

She looked like she was going to continue, but instead she nodded.

"I know you do," she said. "I know you do."

"Hey, Dad, you're home."

Dreyfus looked beyond his wife to see John, his youngest.

"Hey, fellah," he said. "How's my boy?"

"I'm okay, Dad," he said. At twelve, John was already nearly as tall as Dreyfus. He had his mother's cheekbones and his father's blue eyes, but there was a sparkle there that was all his own, that came from no place but John.

"That was some crazy stuff you did on TV," John said.

"You saw that, hmm? I hope you weren't worried. I was never in any real danger, you know."

"It kind of seemed like you were."

"What, is the whole family going to lecture me now?"

"I doubt it," Maddy said. "Edward is upstairs studying with Ellie Song. As long as he's doing that, he's oblivious."

"Yeah," John said, "he's been trying to get her to 'study' with him for months." He made air quotes with his fingers.

"I hope they're studying with the door open," Dreyfus said.

"It's open, dear," Maddy said. "Only by a few inches, but open."

"What do you think, John, should I go up and check on the situation?"

"I think he would pee his pants if you did," John said. "So—yeah."

Dreyfus mussed his son's hair.

"How about you and I shoot a few hoops, instead?"

"Really?"

"Well, you're out of school, and I'm taking the afternoon off. It's been a while since it was just me and you."

"Yeah, okay," John said. "Just let me change clothes."

That night, Maddy reached over for him, and they made love. It was the first time in a while. Life, work, two children—they weren't kids having sex in the back seat of his car nowadays. Sometimes Maddy seemed more distracted than anything.

But not tonight. Tonight there was an intensity, almost a desperation. His body had no secrets from her anymore, and he loved the familiar feel of her, the sound she made when he touched her just so. He remembered the first time, how exciting her body had been to him, how it had been like uncovering a treasure. Now, years later, he still felt the same way.

When it was over they lay a long time without talking, tracing each other with their fingers.

"I love you," he said, finally. "Thank you so much for staying with me all of these years."

"I wouldn't know what else to do." She sighed. "And I love you, too. Idiot."

"Thanks," he said.

She snuggled onto his chest.

"You looked good," she murmured.

"Hmm?"

"On TV," she said. "You looked really good. Brave."

"Handsome," he added.

"Well, so-so," she said. "But you looked strong. Like a mayor."

"Mayor? Hell, why not a president?"

"Or maybe just an old cop with delusions of grandeur," she said. "Now go to sleep."

"You're going to love this," Patel told him when he came into the office the next day.

"Well, if you have love," Dreyfus said, "give it to me."

"We still haven't gotten to the bottom of why House is using outside contractors, but apparently one of his aides loosens up a lot after a few drinks with a pretty girl."

"I don't want to know who this pretty girl is, do I?"

Patel shrugged. "I don't know her. Someone Karen hired. Won't be an issue."

"Okay. So what did he get loose about?"

"For one thing, there are a lot more apes up there in the woods than we've been led to believe. It's not ten or twenty. It's hundreds."

"Hundreds?" Dreyfus frowned. "Really?"

"But that's not even close to being the best part." Patel paused for dramatic effect. "They can't find them."

"They can't find hundreds of apes? Well, it's not so odd that they would want to keep it quiet, then. If hundreds of killer apes were on the loose and I couldn't find them, I wouldn't want anyone to know about it, either."

"Yup," Patel said triumphantly. "I figure we hold a press conference at the entrance to the park. He accused you of weakening the police force, but here you can demonstrate the total incompetence of his contractors. More than a week, and not a single ape captured or killed."

"Hold it," Dreyfus said, staring at the newsfeed.

The death toll in San Francisco was now over ten thousand.

"Why is House worried about monkeys in the woods, when this is going on?"

He stared at the screen. "What does he know that we don't?"

"We can use this," Patel said.

"Uh-uh," Dreyfus said. "There's another shoe, and I want to hear it drop before I get mixed-up in this. No press conference."

He looked at Patel's disappointed expression.

"Leak it instead," he said.

Caesar felt uneasy as he led his group to their rendezvous with Rocket.

The chimpanzee had been leading the humans off over the mountain again, trying to make it appear as if the troop was farther and farther away from the city. It seemed to be working—although they still guarded the forest edge, no human hunters or their flying machines had been seen in the last day or so.

He spotted Rocket up ahead, at the clearing where they had agreed to rendezvous. He swung over to meet with him. The other chimp seemed excited.

Went far, Rocket told him. *Over mountain, much farther.*

And?

More forest. Trees smaller. Human roads, but no machines.

Caesar tried not to show his disappointment. He had hoped the deep stands of redwood continued on, so they could move farther, deeper—away from their enemies altogether. Still, if there was more forest in that direction, and fewer humans, it might be worth moving the troop, even if the trees weren't as large.

The longer they stayed in the same general location,

the sooner they would be found. They still had wounded, but most had either died or grown stronger. More kinds of food had been discovered—mushrooms, nettle, bark, berries, insects, and salamanders in the rich black dirt that moldered on the large limbs of the trees. Small animals to hunt. Even honey had been discovered in one tree.

But they were eating it all, and fast. Soon enough they would have to move.

Yet he knew deep inside that it was in the tall, tall trees that they belonged.

In the direction of the sunrise there were more people. In the direction the sun went down there was open country and water, and a road that cars still traveled on. Beyond the mountain might be their only choice.

Rocket still seemed excited.

What? Caesar asked.

We found something, Rocket said. *I'll show you.*

Caesar gave his assent, and two bands started off together. They went back toward the mountain, to a human trail. There, in the middle of it, were colorful piles of mangos, bananas, durian, mangosteens, avocados, grapes, peaches, and a variety of other foods.

Caesar froze on the branch.

Stop, he hissed.

They did, but most of the chimps were having trouble containing themselves. All of the fruit they had managed to procure had gone to feed the orangs and gorillas, who needed it most. But fruit was good, and it had been a long time since they had eaten any.

Nevertheless, something wasn't right. Fruit didn't just appear like this. Someone had put it here. So they would find it.

He studied the scene a little more carefully and noticed a littering of skins and rinds.

Did you go down there? He asked Rocket.

Rocket looked a little embarrassed, and nodded.

So they hadn't been able to resist after all. But they hadn't been killed, or even shot at. And, in fact, he didn't think there were any humans anywhere near. So what were the humans after?

Then he understood. They were hoping he would take the food and bring it back to the troop. They would follow him.

But what made the humans think they could follow them through the trees any better now than earlier?

Suddenly Koba was there beside him.

Caesar let Koba go, he signed and held out his hand.

Caesar hesitated only a moment, then swiped it.

Koba made another half-circle around where the fruit lay. He seemed to be looking for something in the trees. After a moment he pointed. There was something attached to the tree above the fruit. It was stripped green and brown, but looked like a machine. Koba picked up a heavy branch, climbed up behind the thing, and hit it. It made a metallic crunching sound.

The bonobo hit it several more times before he seemed satisfied. Then he gestured for them to all come.

Shows us little, Koba explained.

Caesar remembered, then. Will had had a thing that made moving pictures of him. It looked different from the thing Koba broke, but it made sense. There had been things like this in the sanctuary and at Gen Sys, too, all designed to spy on the apes. The humans could watch them without being here.

But even if they could see them take the fruit, how would they know where they took it?

Good, Koba, he said. *Smart.*

Koba seemed pleased by the praise, but it also seemed as if he was trying to hide it.

The others started coming down as Caesar once again approached the fruit.

Wait, he commanded. *Watch.*

Then he began picking through the fruit, not sure what he was looking for. Something strange, something out of place. He sorted through some papayas, then a bunch of bananas—and there, fixed to the stem inside the bunch was a white rectangle about the size and shape of the thing Will used to unlock his car from a distance.

A little machine.

A few more minutes of searching and he found another, stuck into a slit in a durian.

Come, he signed. He pulled the thing from the bananas. *Find things like this. Take off of fruit and put here.* He laid his down.

It was a lot of fruit. They sorted it by moving it, checking each piece carefully as they did so. They found eight of the white rectangles. Then Caesar had them check it again. Reluctantly, the others obeyed.

Some of the fruit had been placed in net bags. Caesar took one of them and tied the rectangles inside. Then he turned to his band.

Take all you can carry back to the troop. Koba, go with my band. Get every ape that can move fast enough, and tell them to come get the rest. Rocket, stay here and set watch, high and low.

What about you? Rocket signed.

Caesar grinned and held up the bag.

10

"If the rest of you matches your eyes," David said to the receptionist, "you must be pretty hot."

He knew it was cheesy but, although it was hard to tell behind the filter mask she was wearing, he thought he got a smile from that. At worst she probably thought he was a harmless dufus—which was better than having her know the truth.

A lot was going on at Gen Sys, and most of it seemed to have to do with repairs. The apes had smashed out a lot of windows, and everything else seemed in a general state of disarray. Maybe for that reason, it hadn't been that hard to get in the front door. Getting past the lobby, though—that might be a trick.

"What can I do for you, sir?" she asked, her voice muffled.

"Well, it's not official business," he said. "But an old buddy of mine works here. I haven't seen him in years, and I was hoping I could surprise him, take him to lunch."

She hesitated for moment.

"What's his name?" she finally asked.

"Will Rodman."

She blinked. "I'm sorry, sir, Dr. Rodman doesn't work here anymore. He resigned his position the week before last."

"Ah, shoot, really?" he said. "Did he get another job?"

"I don't know, sir," she replied. "But he did quit just before..." She broke off.

Just before Monkeygate, David finished, silently.

"Anyway, he's not here," she said, her eyes cutting down.

"That's really disappointing," he said. "I really wanted to surprise him. There was this time in college... Oh, hey! I don't want to bore you. It's not your concern. You've been nice. Thanks."

The girl looked around, leaned forward conspiratorially, and beckoned him in. He bent toward her.

"I liked Will," she said. "He was nice, not like some of the people who work here."

Her fingers went to work on her computer keyboard.

"I have his home address here," she said. "Maybe you could ambush him there."

"I knew you were an angel," he said. "It's all in the eyes. What's that address?"

When he reached the address in Pacific Heights, he found the house with quarantine tape around it. The next house was quarantined, as well. And, for that matter, so were most on the street. All of the homes were upscale, Victorians and the like, and in the distance he could see the bridge. The silence in the neighborhood was eerie. There should have been children playing, dogs barking, cars cruising by, but instead there was just the quiet of a graveyard.

He felt a chill, wondering if everywhere would be like this soon. He wasn't sure what the latest body count was, but it wasn't looking good.

After some hesitation, he approached the house and

knocked, but there was no answer. He went around back, and got no answer there either, but he found the door unlocked. Figuring the police were too busy with looting and riots, he decided he could risk a little unlawful entry and stepped inside.

"Hello?" he called. "Anyone home?"

He didn't really expect an answer, nor did he get one, but it set him at ease enough to search around a bit.

It was a nice suburban place with a sunny kitchen and embroidered hand towels in the bathrooms. It seemed in no way unusual until he found the picture on an old upright piano. It featured a man in his thirties with curly brown hair. And he was hugging a chimp, with obvious mutual affection.

"Okay, Dr. Rodman," he said. "You're definitely the man I've been looking for." And he began the search in earnest.

The attic was a weird combination of children's room and monkey playhouse, making it clear that for this family, the chimp had been the child. He kept looking, hoping to find a notepad, computer, some recordings, anything that could tell him more about what Rodman had been working on in the past months, or even years. After a while, it dawned on him. There was no such device in the house. Nothing—no desktop, laptop or tablet. No phones, no file players, nothing on which anything could be stored.

Rodman had either taken it all with him, or it had been removed.

He was on the verge of giving up, reduced to combing through the chimp's room for the second time, when—in the corner, under a pile of drawings that could easily have been made by a human child—he found a landline handset. The battery had lost its charge, of course, but he hadn't seen any landlines at all. There had been plenty of plugs for them, but no phones, which wasn't really all that unusual, since a lot of people were moving solely to portable devices.

He took a last look around, then slipped the handset in his pocket and left.

Back home, he stuck the phone in his charger, hoping it would fit. It seemed to, but he couldn't really tell if it was working. Then he sat down at his keyboard, and started trying to come at the story from another angle.

He went back over some of the Monkeygate stuff, trying to steer away from speculation and stick with what was actually known. Trying to find connections.

To begin with, Will Rodman had been trying to find a cure for Alzheimer's disease. It was more than a job to him, since his father had suffered from the condition. It was his work that Gen Sys had heralded as a cure until the primary test subject, a chimp, had gone bat-crazy in a room full of investors. In theory Rodman's work had been shut down, but what if it had continued? What if some new iteration of his "cure" had driven not just one ape mad, but a whole lot them? Yet the first apes to escape had been kept in the San Bruno Primate Shelter, not Gen Sys. One of the employees had been killed during the escape, apparently when an ape turned a hose on him while he was brandishing a high-voltage prod. There were eyewitnesses who said the security tapes showed the incident clearly, and that the apes had a leader, a chimpanzee who stood and acted more like a man than an ape. Somewhere in the fuss, however, the security tapes seemed to have disappeared.

Like a lot of things—and people—involved in Monkeygate.

After they had escaped San Bruno, the apes seemed to have split into two groups. One went to Gen Sys and busted it up, freeing all of the apes located there. The other bunch engineered the breakout at the zoo. Then they all had stampeded through town, converging at the Golden Gate Bridge.

How would the apes at the shelter have known where Gen Sys was?

Which brought him back to Rodman, who clearly had owned a chimp of his own. One of the test subjects maybe. He checked through the *Sentinel*'s police reports, looking for anything to do with apes, monkeys, or chimps—cross-references that also mentioned Rodman. And after a bit of digging, he found what he was looking for.

Rodman's chimp had bitten one of his neighbors, charges had been pressed, and the animal had been removed to the San Bruno shelter. So there was the first connection to Gen Sys—an ape owned by a lead scientist there was in San Bruno, where Monkeygate presumably began. The second was that the escaped apes had gone back to Gen Sys. The third was that Steven Jacobs—the man in charge of the Gen Sys labs—had died in a helicopter accident, along with the San Bruno police chief.

Now the fourth connection—according to Clancy—was that the parent company of Gen Sys was using a military contractor it also owned to clean up what was left of the apes. Clearly they were still trying to protect themselves from something. Something other than a bunch of escaped primates.

He looked over Clancy's list of file names again. At first glance, he still didn't see anything, but he checked again, just to be sure. Reading them aloud.

When he came to RV113 he stopped. Was that familiar?

It was somehow. He did an Internet search on it, but what came up was something by a composer named Vivaldi, which probably wasn't what he was looking for. So he went back though his typed notes. A search through them didn't turn up anything, but then he remembered a letter-number combination, and so a quick breeze-through found it.

ALZ112.

That was disappointing. The letters were wrong, and the number was off by one. But what if they were part of a sequence?

He had assumed that the ALZ stood for Alzheimer's, since that was what Rodman had been trying to cure. Presumably there had been an ALZ110, and an ALZ111. In theory there would be no ALZ113, because he had stopped the research after his big failure. But—again—what if he hadn't? What if he had carried on?

Yet why change the ALZ to RV? What could RV stand for?

No, he had to be barking up the wrong tree. It was all a series of coincidences—his reporter's brain was trying to find a pattern that wasn't there.

He went and got a beer, cracked it open, and turned on the news. Then he checked the phone, and found that it had taken the charge. He started scrolling through its record of calls. The last recorded call was from several days ago, presumably around the time when the battery called it quits. It was from someone name Linda Andersen.

He turned down the sound on the TV, pulled out his cell phone, and dialed the number. It rang and then went to messages.

"Hi, Linda," he said. "My name is David Flynn, and I'm a reporter from the *San Francisco Sentinel*. I have some questions I'd like to ask if you have the time. Don't worry. They aren't personal."

He hung up. Another long shot. She was probably Rodman's cleaning lady or something.

He turned the sound back up and took a drink of the beer, flipping through the channels in the vague hope of finding something mindless to watch. Instead he ended up being arrested by the weird smile of Jean Vogel, a prominent pundit with strong religious views and apparent aspirations to the US House of Representatives.

"...a deliberate misreading of what I said," she was saying. "People like to take me out of context. But I'm all about context."

"Then when you said that the Federal Government shouldn't be providing aid to such cities as San Francisco and New York," the show's host responded, "are you telling me you didn't mean it?"

"As I *said*, Brett," she said, again smiling her strange, unfriendly smile, "that statement, taken out of context, makes no sense."

"Well, would you care to contextualize it for me then?"

"I would be delighted to, Brett," Vogel replied. "I say that this disease is a local problem, to be solved by the state and local governments. Because if you look locally, where is this disease located? Not in Montana. There are only three cases there. Or Oklahoma—two verified instances. Mississippi, none at all. You can go down the list. These are all places where real Americans love God and fear him, where they do not pass laws allowing the ungodly union of homosexuals. These places are being spared. These places have the mark on their lintel that the angel of death *passes by*."

"Then do I understand you to say that San Francisco and New York have been singled out by God because they recognize marriage equality?" the reporter said. "That this plague is his punishment?"

"Amongst other things, Brett. My point is, they brought this upon themselves. It is *their* problem. There's no reason that the tax dollars of decent, hard-working Americans—citizens with real values—should pay to salvage Sodom and Gomorrah."

"But Ms. Vogel," the host protested, "the disease has spread to many other places. Paris, for instance—"

"Don't even get me started on the French," she said. "It only proves my point."

"But it's well known that diseases like this spread most quickly in densely populated areas with national and international hubs of transportation. The places you mention are mostly rural—"

"Is it?" Vogel countered. "Is that really 'well known'? Or is this just more of the same propaganda from the liberal secular scientists who tell us that we came from monkeys? Look, here's some science, if you dare to hear it. The first warning was AIDS. It was a shot right across our bows, as clear a message as anyone could want. And yet look how it was ignored." She leaned forward. "AIDS was a retrovirus. The current plague is a retrovirus. This is how God works his will.

"I have it on very good authority," she continued, "from a prominent archaeologist, that the plague of the firstborn in ancient Egypt was a retrovirus—"

"That's enough." David sighed, changing the channel again, this time to a cooking show. He drank his beer and listened to some guy talk about brisket.

Then he sat up.

"Oh, shit," he said aloud.

RV113.

Retrovirus 113.

Implying there had been a 112. What exactly had been in ALZ112? He knew viruses were sometimes used in gene therapy...

The phone rang, and he jumped. He picked it up, hoping it was Linda, but the number was unfamiliar.

"Hello?" he answered.

There was a long pause.

"Is this David Flynn?" It was a woman's voice.

"Linda?"

Another pause.

"No," the woman said. "Linda died. Of the virus."

"Oh. I'm so sorry to hear that," he said. "I'm sorry for your loss."

"She was my sister, Mr. Flynn. May I ask what you wanted to speak to her about?"

"I'm trying to find out some information about a man named Will Rodman."

"He was Linda's team leader," she said. "At Gen Sys."

He paused, not quite sure what to ask next, but the woman on the other end of the line spoke first.

"I'm just not sure," she said. "I don't know if I can trust you."

He took a mental deep breath, and plunged right in.

"Is this about ALZ113?" he asked.

He heard her breathing, and prayed she didn't hang up.

"Yes," she said, finally. He waited patiently for her to go on. "I have something I think Linda would have wanted you to have," she finally said.

He felt his pulse speed up a little.

"Is that so?" he said.

"Yes," she replied.

"Well, can we meet somewhere?"

"I don't like to go out," she said. "I'm afraid of the virus. But I'll meet you in Delores Park. I'll give it to you there."

"When?"

"Now, if you can come." She paused, and then continued. "It scares me to have it."

"Okay," he said. "I'm on my way. I'll be there in about twenty minutes."

"It will take me a little longer," she said. "I'll be in a lime-green sweater. I have red hair. I'm, well, thirtyish."

"I'll be there," he said. "I'm tall, with blond hair. I'll be in jeans and a plaid shirt, I'll wear a hat—a Forty-Niners cap."

As he hung up, he felt sort of like someone in a spy novel.

Then it also occurred to him that if this was a spy novel, he might well be walking into some sort of trap.

11

"What happened to the goddamn camera?" Corbin snapped.

"I think we have to assume the chimps got it," Malakai replied. "One or all of them must have known what it was."

"That's ridiculous."

Malakai, Clancy, Corbin and his crew were gathered around the monitors in the command centre.

"Not really," Clancy said. "A lot of these guys have been monitored by cameras all of their lives."

"They didn't notice it when they first found the fruit."

"No," she said. "But this might be a different group."

"It might be the leader, this time," Malakai added.

"Leader?" Corbin grunted.

"Everything they do is organized," Malakai said. "Very well organized. That implies a leader—and, furthermore, a leader with superior intelligence. Or perhaps, in fact, human intelligence."

Corbin looked like he'd eaten something sour.

"There was a guy," he said. "He followed them out here when they first came. We thought at first he might be leading them. But he wasn't."

"How sure are you of that?" Malakai asked.

"Very sure," a new voice said. Malakai looked up to see that Trumann Phillips had entered the room. "He had been the owner of one of the chimps, that's all."

"So you talked to him?"

"He was interviewed, yes."

"That doesn't rule out the possibility that they have a human leader," Malakai said.

"No," Phillips responded, "I suppose it doesn't. So how are things going?"

"Some of them found the fruit a while back—six, seven maybe. They ate some of it and left. They didn't carry any with them, so the tracking chips are still there."

"Maybe they went and got the rest of the, what, herd?" Phillips said.

"Troop," Clancy corrected.

"So maybe the *troop* is gorging on fruit salad even as we speak, every living one of them."

"That could be," Clancy said. "Our theory is that there is one large group of them somewhere, and several smaller bands that are foraging. Based on their behavior in the grocery stores in Mills Valley, we assumed that if they found fruit, they would bring it back to the rest—to the slower ones, the infants, the injured."

"But that doesn't seem to be the case, does it?" Phillips said. Then he turned. "Assemble a strike force, Corbin. Take them to where you dumped the fruit."

"Hang on," Corbin said, peering at the screen. "The markers are moving now. All eight of them."

"Headed where?" Phillips asked.

"Northwest," the mercenary said.

"They've been tracking generally northeast, haven't they? Based on the bodies you've found, the trails, the encounters?"

"We believed they had moved to the north side of Mount Tam," Corbin affirmed.

"This looks more like they're going along the steep ridge trail." Phillips glanced questioningly at Corbin.

"We haven't searched there," he admitted.

"I think the trails over Mount Tam were false," Malakai said. "Deliberate misdirection."

Phillips took a moment to look astonished before exploding.

"Why haven't you said anything?" he demanded. "Why hold it back until now, Mr. Youmans?"

"I voiced my opinion to Mr. Corbin, there."

"Really?" Phillips spun on his employee. "Corbin?"

"It seemed too ridiculous to consider, sir," Corbin replied.

Phillips stared at him icily for a moment.

"From now on you report *everything*, do you understand? We hired these people because they know apes. You do *not* know apes—you *are* an ape. Your job isn't to evaluate their recommendations. It's to report them, and, when in the field, *follow* them."

"Yes, sir," Corbin replied brusquely. His face was bright red.

Phillips turned to Clancy.

"It seems you may be right after all," he said. "Good work."

"How will you capture them, sir?"

Phillips blinked.

"We have an expert team," he said. "They'll come in by air. We have nets, tranq guns, the works. We just needed to know where they were. Now we do, thanks to you and Mr. Youmans here."

Then he turned and left the room.

Corbin, still red-faced, rose to carry out his orders.

"Come on, experts," he said. "You're riding along."

"My expert advice?" Malakai said. "Don't send any helicopters. Not until they stop. Not until we know for sure where the main group is. They can hear the choppers coming from miles away."

The Humvee bumped along the Shoreline Highway, taking steep, hairpin turns. The evening fog was rolling in, but it didn't obscure the view.

There were no giant trees here, but rocky, broken slopes slanting and sometimes plummeting down to where the restless sea battered against rocky cliffs and narrow shingles. Gulls swarmed in the skies like the flying rats they were, and in the distance Malakai made out the singular profiles of pelicans. It had always interested him, what a difference a few miles could make in landscape, especially when the sea and elevation were involved.

This didn't seem at all like the sort of place that apes would feel at home and yet a short traverse from here stood some of the tallest trees in the world.

A red SUV came around the curve, half in their lane. Corbin swore and honked as the vehicle hurtled by.

"I thought all of the roads were closed," Clancy said.

"Can't close this one," Corbin replied. "It's the only way in and out of the communities along the shore. We closed the Panoramic Highway, and there's been plenty of hell raised over that. Hopefully we'll get this whole mess mopped up pretty soon and get out of here."

Corbin glanced at his GPS and suddenly slammed on the brakes, just before a car pullover. There was a brown sign informing them that this was where the Steep Ravine Trail began—or ended. The trail led up a steep hill thick with small trees and shrubs, becoming low scrub as it climbed.

Beyond the hill, only sky was visible from this vantage.

"That's the trail up there," Corbin said, presumably for those who couldn't read.

He popped the door open and stepped out, tranq rifle in hand. He scanned the hill above.

Trying to still his heavy breathing, Caesar watched the car stop, and the man get out. He concentrated on keeping still, on making even his thumping heart less noisy. If the man came over—if he took four steps—the shrub Caesar hid behind wouldn't conceal him anymore.

The other humans weren't paying much attention. They were talking to each other. He could hear them clearly. He watched the man with the gun, and he listened.

"I don't know," Flores said as Corbin took a step toward the trail. "About getting this over with. I mean, we might be safer up here, what with the plague and all."

"Plague?" Clancy asked.

"Some damn virus," Flores went on. "It's killed like a few thousand people in San Fran. Seems like it's pretty nasty. People start bleeding out of their noses, and the next thing you know they're dead."

"When did this begin?" Malakai asked.

"Just a couple of days ago. It just sort of started."

"Sounds like Ebola," Malakai said.

"Yeah, they're comparing it to that. Except it's a lot easier to get than Ebola."

"That's a weird coincidence," Clancy said.

"Weird?" Flores said. "It's more than that—it's scary as shit."

"No," Clancy said. "It's weird that the escape of a bunch

of apes would coincide with the onset of an epidemic, especially an epidemic that resembles Ebola."

"Why?"

"Well, because some scientists think Ebola, like AIDS, got into the human population from animals, and specifically non-human primates."

"You mean we're chasing the plague?" Flores said, his voice getting higher.

"Probably not," Clancy said. "I'm just thinking out loud."

But that would explain a lot, Malakai thought. *A whole lot.*

Like why the stores he had called had all had break-ins. In an epidemic, people panicked. They hoarded food and medicine. And if there was a link between the apes and the epidemic—if the apes were carrying it—it would explain the presence of Anvil, the secrecy, all of it.

"Talk a little louder," Corbin snapped. "Maybe the apes haven't heard you yet."

"I don't know about you," Flores said, "but I don't see anywhere you could hide three hundred apes right there. Maybe one or two."

Corbin frowned and began to walk toward the trailhead, but he hadn't gone more than another step before he glanced down at the locator.

"Crap," he swore. "We missed them, somehow. They're still going. And still headed northwest. They've already crossed our perimeter."

"Headed to Seattle maybe?" a soldier named Kyung joked.

"No," Corbin said. "But there are pockets of redwood forest all along the coast. God, if they get up to Sonoma County, we'll never find them."

"Can they do that?" Malakai asked.

"They would have to cover a lot of open ground, and cross a bunch of roads," Corbin said. He looked back uneasily at the hill hunkering over them. "But we've closed some of those roads, and evacuated some of the homes. If they're moving by night –" he glanced back at his tablet "– they could be headed for the Point Reyes seashore—the ridges are in forest. But surely someone would see them."

Then he climbed back in the car and stepped on the gas, a determined look on his face. The Humvee lurched onward. Malakai kept his eye on the stark line between hill and sky.

Still breathing hard, Caesar watched the man get back in the big car. In a moment, it moved on, following the pick-up truck, the truck into which he had, moments before, tossed the white rectangles as it slowed for the curve near his hiding place.

When it was clear, he hurried back up and over the hill, racing into the sheltering leaves of the forest. But his mind was busy, stirring around all he had just heard. He knew what disease was. Will had been trying to cure a disease, the one that was hurting Charles. It sounded as if many humans were dying of this new disease. And they seemed to think it had something to do with his troop.

He remembered the people fighting at the market. Was it because they were sick? Will's father sometimes acted very strangely because of his illness. He didn't mean to. Caesar remembered the time the man in the house next door had screamed at Charles and grabbed him, pushed and threatened him. That was when Caesar went to protect Charles, and bit the other man, and was sent to the shelter.

Had the man been angry at Charles because he was sick and acting strangely? Or was he afraid? And why did they think the apes brought the disease? There were injured in his troop, but that was different from sick. None of them were sick.

But it meant something. Whether it was good or bad, he did not know.

Delores Park was normally a pretty lively place, but today it was mostly empty. A few brave or deluded parents had brought their kids to the playground. A young couple lay on a blanket, flying a kite shaped like a sailing ship. An old man was walking his dog.

So it wasn't hard to spot the red-headed woman in the green sweater, standing between the playground and Delores Street. As he approached she smiled uncertainly at him. She wore a white filter mask and carried a leather satchel.

"Are you…?" she asked, when he was close enough to hear her through the muffle of her mask.

"David Flynn," he said.

She looked around nervously.

"What are you worried about?" he asked.

She shook her head.

"It's just… You weren't the first person to come looking for Linda," she said. "Someone searched her apartment. They took her computer and some other things. They didn't know she had left it with me."

She handed him the satchel.

"She already knew she was sick, you see. One of the men on her team, he was the first to die."

"The first to die at Gen Sys?"

"No. The first to die of the virus, period."

For a moment all he could do was stand there, stunned.

"You mean in the world?" he said. "How do you know?"

"It's all in there," she replied. "She was going to come

back for it and get it to the press. But she didn't come back. I was afraid, so I held on to it. Then you called." She looked down. "I have to leave," she said.

"I really am sorry for your loss," he said. "You've done a brave thing. The right thing."

"What else should a big sister do?" she said, smiling briefly.

She turned and began to walk, then to run. He watched her go, and realized he didn't even know her name. She had almost reached the street when she stumbled and fell. He started toward her involuntarily, and then checked himself, knowing she would rise long before he could reach her.

Except she didn't get back up.

He started trotting toward her. Had she hit her head on something?

But when he reached her he saw the blood, and how much there was of it, and he knew she hadn't just stumbled.

"Easy," someone said from behind him. "Turn around, slowly."

Mayor House looked—more than anything—tired, as he took the podium. Dreyfus noticed that he wasn't wearing a mask or respirator this time. His campaign was apparently adjusting.

He cleared his throat.

"Good morning," he said. He took a sip of water. "I'm here today to clear up a few misconceptions that have been getting a lot of press lately. There has been so much nonsense thrown around, I'm not sure where to start.

"The so-called 'monkey problem' is well in hand. The idea that hundreds of them survive is purest fantasy. The few that remain will be captured or humanely euthanized in the next twenty-four hours.

"That's all that I have to say about that. That's all there *is* to say about it.

"As to the more relevant and serious matter of the virus," he continued, "we are moving with all due speed to mitigate the situation. Quarantine and isolation treatment areas have been set up by the CDC and the National Guard, in order the give the greatest number of infected persons maximum medical attention, and to keep those who might be infected from spreading the virus until they've been cleared by the CDC.

"I'm sure you're all aware that this problem extends far beyond our city. This morning I've been informed that the governor has invoked martial law and requested federal disaster relief. We're doing everything—and, I repeat, *everything*—we can to fight this plague. As to you, the citizens of this great city, I ask that you work with law enforcement to keep things running as smoothly as possible in this time of crisis. If you're told to report for quarantine, under law, you must do so. You will be there for a few days at worst. Indeed, quarantine is probably the safest place you could be right now. So if you think you've been exposed, please, do what's best for all of us, and obey the law.

"Only by adhering to these time-tested procedures do we have any chance of slowing this thing down."

He looked around, a bit uncertainly, Dreyfus thought. Then he cleared his throat.

"I would like to take a moment for us to all pray together." He looked to one side. "Pastor Dubois, if you would...?"

Dreyfus switched the channel. He didn't have any interest in what Pastor Dubois might or might not have to say.

He landed on one of the cable "news" talk shows, where a red-faced man was holding forth to the host.

Dreyfus thought he recognized the guest as a national talk-radio personality.

"...an engineered situation," the man was saying. "The virus was made in a laboratory by the US government. That's for damned sure. We know they've been working on these biological weapons for years, plus we've got everything Saddam Hussein was working on. Why were there no WMDs? Because we took them all." He leaned forward and used both hands for emphasis.

"I find it interesting—*very* interesting—that not a single member of the President's cabinet or the leadership of his party has contracted this disease."

"I'm sure they're all being very careful," the host said.

"How could they be careful about a disease they didn't know about in advance? The speaker of the house has it. Besides, they don't have to be careful."

"You're saying there's an antidote," the host said.

"Damn straight there is. They *made* it. They wouldn't release it until they made some sort of inoculation or antiviral, or whatever they call it." He mopped his sweaty forehead and went on. "It's also a proven fact that the virus disproportionately affects Caucasians. Once this plague has killed off what few *real* Americans remain, those who endure will find themselves under permanent martial law—in a totalitarian state that Stalin could have only dreamed of."

"So you're saying the people at Argo ranch were justified in shooting the FBI agents?"

"Patriots like Ted Durham and his followers are the only hope we have left. And there are more of them—of us—than you think. Some of us have been preparing for this day for a long time. They tried to use the threat of terrorism to suppress our liberties, but that didn't work. Now they've shown their true colors, shown exactly what depravity they will stoop to. Look at what's happening right here—they call them 'quarantines,' but everybody knows they're death camps.

"Nobody that goes into one of those places comes out. Everyone, everyone that hears the sound of my voice, I call on you to resist. If you have a gun, load it. If you don't, get one. Fight the tyranny!"

"Oh, shit," Dreyfus said.

The Argo ranch thing had happened just yesterday, in western Washington State. A reputed militia group had shot at local law enforcement, killing a sheriff and two deputies. The FBI had been sent in and was also fired upon. Now Guard troops had surrounded the place. A similar incident was unfolding in Idaho, although the scale seemed to be smaller.

"Why are they wasting their time on nut jobs out in the boondocks?" Patel wondered aloud.

"They won't for long," Dreyfus predicted. "They won't have the manpower. There's going to be a lot more of this, people turning on each other—but also banding together."

"And not in a good way," his aide added.

Dreyfus shrugged.

"Those guys have a common enemy. They believe they know who's responsible for their troubles, for everything they think is wrong, and they have a plan for what to do about it. It's better than 'every man for himself'."

"But they're wrong," Patel objected. "It's absurd—the notion that the government did this." Then he stared at his boss. "Are you suggesting we get behind them, or mimic these claims?"

"That's not at all what I'm saying," Dreyfus said. "We need a strategy that unifies everyone, not just people with similar political persuasions. A real common enemy."

"Wouldn't that be the virus?"

"No, a disease doesn't have a face unless you give it one, and everyone is giving it a different face. The fringe right blames the government. The left says it's the multinational corporations to blame. I've heard the claim that it's God's punishment for our hedonistic ways—it started in San Francisco, you see. I've heard that it's Gaia, the Earth Mother, punishing us for pollution, or that it's the virus that killed the dinosaurs, and that it was frozen in polar ice until global warming let it out.

"No, there are too many theories," he said. "We need a common story."

"And what would that be?" Patel asked.

"Damned if I know," Dreyfus said. "Although knowing the truth might be a good start."

Thank you, Maurice signed, before dipping his fingers into the soft flesh of the durian. *I was very hungry.*

You're welcome, Koba acknowledged, feeling a prickle of some emotion he didn't recognize. It felt good, but he wasn't sure he liked it. Or better put, he wasn't sure he could trust it. He had never been given anything that hadn't been taken away.

Except pain.

Maurice ate with a deliberation that was hard to understand, as if each taste of the food was important to him. As if getting it into his belly quickly so that no one else could take it wasn't the main objective.

Maurice noticed Koba watching, and offered him a finger full.

Try.

Koba took the durian doubtfully and placed it into his mouth. It smelled bad. To his surprise, however, the taste was good. A little like a rotten banana.

I see you remembering, Maurice said. *Eyes go funny. You shake.*

This happens to you? Koba wanted to know.

To me, yes. To all of the apes that breathed Caesar's mist.

The mist makes us remember?

Makes us smarter, Maurice said. *Being smarter makes us remember.*

Koba thought about that for a moment. He had known something else was happening to him, without being able to say what it was. Smarter? For him, that word had to do with learning tricks, or using sign. And now that he thought about it, he was using sign differently than he used to. Better.

Not true of big caterpillars, he told Maurice.

Big caterpillars?

From zoo.

Maurice's throat suddenly swelled. Koba wasn't sure what it meant. But it felt dangerous, and he skipped back a bit.

Don't call them that! Maurice said. *They are apes, like you, like me. Not as smart maybe, not know sign maybe, but still apes. Apes together—strong. Like Caesar says.*

Koba gaped, taken aback by the usually gentle ape's show of anger. The big caterpillars were apes?

But of course they were. They just hadn't been taught sign like he had. But they could learn it, as he had. Now that it was pointed out to him, it seemed so obvious, and he felt stupid for not understanding earlier.

Apes together strong, he signed, feeling a sort of heat go through him. He remembered riding on top of a rolling machine as they approached the big bridge, Koba side by side with Caesar, Maurice, and Buck—the gorilla who died saving them all from Jacobs. He remembered that feeling. Together.

Caesar says this? he asked. *Why?*

Because it's true, Maurice replied.

Yes, Koba said. *Caesar is right. I understand now.*

He wasn't sure he did, but the concept left him almost gasping. It wasn't just about respect for Caesar, loyalty to Caesar—it was about respect and loyalty to all apes. Even the ones who couldn't sign.

All of his life he had felt almost as if he had a weight on one side of him that made him walk crooked. That weight was all of the things humans had done to him, and the hatred that came from that. For the first time in his life, he suddenly felt the possibility of a burden on his other side, too—one that would balance him, let him walk straight.

Even the possibility felt good.

What do you remember? he asked Maurice.

I was circus ape, Maurice said. *I did tricks.*

I did tricks, Koba said. *Not for circus. For little pictures.*

Not understand.

Koba tried to explain. After a while, Maurice scratched his head.

We had little screens in our prison, he said. *Had small humans. Sometimes apes. Maybe I saw you.*

Why did they do this? Koba wondered. *Make us do tricks for them, wear clothes?*

Humans think apes funny when they act like stupid humans, Maurice explained.

Why? Koba asked.

It took so long for Maurice to answer that Koba thought that he had refused to do so, or had forgotten the question, perhaps lost in a reverie of his own. But finally the orangutan lifted his hands.

I think maybe they hate themselves, he said.

* * *

After a time, Koba left, and Maurice was once again alone. Beautifully, wonderfully alone. He ate a little more of the durian, feeling warm inside, more content than he had felt in a long time. He listened to the forest, the quiet breath of the wind, to the singing stars of his own thoughts, the *questions* forming there, elegant connections between this and that thing that he had somehow never noticed before.

The feel of bark on his fingers was a luxury he had never imagined. That was an added thing. But he also reveled in absence. The absence of people looking at him, poking at him, yelling at him.

A deep part of him wanted permanent solitude, and at first—just after they left the city—he had thought to strike out on his own. He could explain Caesar's vision to Koba well enough, but part of him resisted the idea of living together with so many apes.

And yet it seemed to him that resisting an instinct was sometimes the only way to move forward. To improve. To understand. And there was so much more he wanted to understand. More than that, he owed Caesar his freedom, and all of this, even these small opportunities to be by himself. Whatever else happened, he owed Caesar his support, his presence, anything he could provide.

So he did not mind when he saw Caesar approaching.

A good trick, he told Caesar.

A trick that nearly got me killed, Caesar replied. *A trick that won't work again.*

There are always new tricks, Maurice told him.

Caesar seemed agitated. He was better than most chimps at keeping still, but the tension in his body betrayed him. Still, Maurice waited for him to speak. It wouldn't do to hurry him.

While I was hiding, I heard the humans talking, Caesar said finally.

Maurice focused his attention on Caesar's account of the disease, and how humans thought apes had something to do with it.

If they think we have this sickness, why come after us, Caesar asked.

Maurice thought somehow there might be a connection to the question Koba had asked him a little while ago—the one about why humans made apes act like foolish humans—but the connection was dim in the constellation of his new thoughts. He would have to work on that later, when he was alone.

Don't know, he replied, instead. *But this might be good.*

How? Caesar wondered.

If enough of them die, maybe they will forget about us. That would be a very good thing.

12

Malakai understood long before they found the tracking devices what had happened, but he also knew Corbin wouldn't believe him, so he let the whole thing play out. He was pretty sure Clancy had figured it all out, too.

They found the tags in the back of a truck parked in front of a restaurant in the small town of Stinson Beach. Corbin swore colorfully for what seemed like a long time.

"They fricking hosed us," he said. "Smoked us like a cheap cigar!"

"Maybe we should try again," Flores said. "Use smaller transmitters. I've seen some smaller than a dime."

"If you did, it was in a movie," Corbin snapped. "The ones we used are the smallest they make."

"That's not even the point, really," Clancy said. "That point is, they figured out what we were up to, and used our plan against us."

"Well then, expert," Corbin said, turning to Malakai, "what next?"

"Drive back to that place you stopped," he responded. "The bottom of that trail."

"Right, that makes sense," the mercenary agreed

grudgingly. "Let's get moving, then!"

They made the drive in silence. When they reached the spot he had suggested, Malakai got out, carefully observing the ground. It didn't take him long to find the tracks.

"Well, do you know where they've gone?" Corbin demanded, hovering over him as he crouched close to the ground.

"Not 'they'," Malakai said, after a moment. "Him."

"What do you mean?" Corbin asked.

"There was only one of them. 'They' didn't figure out what we were trying to do. *He* did. Or *she*, perhaps."

"No need to be politically correct," Clancy said. "Apes have their gender roles pretty well mapped out."

"Yes, but we aren't dealing with apes here," Malakai said.

"The tracks are human?" Corbin said.

"No," Malakai said. "It's the spoor of a chimpanzee. But the mind attached to the foot that made that track is not the mind of an ape. Up until now I've believed that the apes had a human leader, despite your assurances to the contrary. I no longer believe that."

"Couldn't it have been trained to do this?" Corbin asked. "Haven't apes been used in robberies or whatever?"

"Sure they have," Clancy said. "In those movies Flores has been been watching, the ones with the tiny tracking devices." That earned her a nasty look, but she didn't seem to care.

"Imagine the sequence of events," she went on. "He recognized the camera, inferred what it was there for, and then disabled it."

"You said that wasn't a big deal."

"That alone, no. But then he figured out—or at least guessed—what the tracking devices were, and why they were there. He then systematically searched the fruit until he found not one, not a few, but *all* of the devices. Then he used them to draw us away so the rest of his troop could take the fruit. I'll guarantee you there isn't a single piece remaining where you left it. He must have known there was a road over here, with cars on it.

"It's just too much," she concluded.

"What are you saying?"

"Malakai is right. At least one of these apes is smart—really smart. Maybe he's a mutation, the next step in chimpanzee evolution. Or maybe he was deliberately altered in a lab. Chimps are ninety-nine percent genetically the same as us, so maybe someone spliced in the last one percent." She shook her head. "I don't know."

"But this is good news," Malakai said, before Corbin could erupt again.

"How's that?" Corbin asked.

"For one thing, I actually have a better concept now of where they really are," he replied. "And it gives me an idea."

Koba is at the place where they do their tricks and make the little pictures, but they haven't done anything. People seem upset, and some have water leaking from their eyes. He knows now that they call it crying.

He remembers Mary crying because his mother wouldn't move, and it makes him feel anxious. He tries not to fidget, because Tommy will punish him if he does. But Tommy isn't really paying attention to him. He's speaking loudly to a man who is speaking loudly back. Koba feels as if any minute one will challenge the other, and that makes him feel even more distressed. But finally the men stop yelling at each other.

Tommy comes over and takes his leash then, and Milo's.

"It was a stupid show anyway," Tommy says. Then he takes them home.

Tommy drinks a lot of his burning juice and talks on the phone much of the time. He also sleeps a lot, and does not remember to feed Koba and Milo. Koba grows hungry, and anxious again. When he sees Tommy, he "smiles" and "talks." He signs "food." Tommy says something he doesn't understand, and walks away.

One day he finally takes Koba out of his cage and holds out his leash. He leaves Milo in his cage. Milo points to his mouth, then to Koba.

That frightens Koba, and something about the way Tommy is acting scares him, too. So when Tommy comes close with the leash, Koba jumps back.

"Don't you even," Tommy shouts. He pulls out the stick, but Koba is more scared of having his mouth stuck together than he is of the stick. He has been hit by the stick so many times he almost isn't scared of it anymore.

But this time Tommy smacks him on the side of the head, and Koba doesn't even know what is happening. Then he understands that Tommy is hitting him again, and again, and again, and he suddenly knows that Tommy isn't going to stop.

Koba feels something break in him, something hot, like the stuff Tommy made him drink. It wants out of him, and the only way it can get out is through his hands, his feet, and his teeth. He jumps at Tommy, knocks him hard against the cage, and then slams him to the ground and starts hitting him. It feels good.

Tommy covers his head and face with his hands and howls, submitting to him. Koba suddenly feels powerful, in control, and it is a feeling he likes.

His head starts to clear a little. Tommy has submitted. Things will be different now. He steps back from Tommy.

Tommy lifts his head and stares at Koba. He still looks docile, frightened.

Then he screams. He pulls something out of his pocket and slashes at Koba. Koba feels something slice from his eyebrow through his eye and into his cheek. Everything goes black in that eye. With his other eye he sees blood, and it seems to be everywhere. He sees Tommy grab the leash and put it around his throat. Koba is trying to keep the blood from coming out of his face while Tommy ties him to the cage, in such a way that if he doesn't keep his feet under him he starts choking.

Then Tommy starts hitting him with the stick again, and before long Koba doesn't know anything at all.

It is later, and Koba is back in his cage. He hurts so much he can't focus on anything else. The cut across his eye hurts terribly, but now he can see a little bit through it, even if things aren't quite in focus.

Tommy comes by and looks closely at him. He has one of his smoking sticks in his mouth.

Koba tries to look submissive.

Koba good, he signs. *Koba do tricks.*

Tommy laughs then, but it sounds awful.

"You're too goddamn ugly now, anyway," he says. "Now one wants to see you do funny little goddamn monkey things. Maybe if a part in a horror movie comes up, though."

He stares at Koba's face.

"One more little touch, maybe," he says.

Then he sticks the burning end of his smoke stick into

Koba's hurt eye. Koba screams and throws himself back against the cage, but he cannot go far enough to avoid the burning stick.

"I ought to burn out your other eye, too," Tommy mutters. "But then you'd be no goddamn use to me at all." Then he stumbles off. He falls, and makes a hard sound when he hits the floor. Koba barely notices, he's in so much pain.

"God*damn*," Tommy says, pushing himself up. Koba sees blood on his mouth. "Looks like I need another drink. Heh."

He wags his finger at Koba.

"I hope you aren't laughing at me," he says. "If you are, we'll have words later, you and me."

Then he gets up and leaves the room.

Tommy feeds them the next morning. He changes their water. Then Koba doesn't see Tommy for a long time. He and Milo grow hungry, but the thirst is worse. It takes away his strength. His legs won't hold him up, and the cage hurts him where his body pulls against it.

Tommy returns. Koba doesn't know how long it's been. The lights have been off for days.

Tommy is carrying something. It is not the stick. It is smaller, and fits into Tommy's hand in a different way. It has a hole in the end, about the size his little finger might fit into. He points it at him, and Koba knows whatever it is will probably hurt, but he is too sick from lack of food and water to care.

Tommy points it at him for a long time, and then he lowers it.

"Screw it," he finally says. He opens Koba's cage, and then slowly walks away.

Koba looks at the open cage door, unsure what to do.

He wants to go out, find food and water. But he's scared of Tommy.

Suddenly he hears a loud *bang*. Then it is very quiet.

Koba can finally stand it no longer, and he leaves the cage.

He finds Tommy on the couch. He is lying slumped in one corner of it. His eyes are open but he doesn't seem to see Koba. Just like Mother. There is blood everywhere, and the thing is in his hand.

Kobe decides to leave Tommy alone. Even though his eyes are open, he seems to be asleep.

He goes and releases Milo from his cage, and they go to the boxes, desperate for food and water. They find something sweet to drink, and the place where Tommy keeps their food, and they eat and drink as much as they can. Milo vomits, but Koba does not.

Then Koba lies down, and after moment, Milo joins him. After so much time in the cage, it feels so good to stretch out, to move all of his muscles.

He wakes with Milo pulling at him, frantically trying to get him back to his cage, but Koba doesn't want to go. He takes Milo to see Tommy. Tommy is still sitting in exactly the same position Koba last saw him in.

Tommy sleep, he signs to Milo. *Tommy not wake up.*

Milo seems unsure, but when Koba goes to the playroom, Milo waits, then follows. They play for most of the day. Koba thinks that Tommy will vanish, the way his mother did, but Tommy is still there when he looks again.

There are places in the house—square places in the walls, covered with cloth. Sometimes light comes from behind them, and sometimes not. Koba decides to look behind the cloth and see what is there.

What he sees is beautiful. He sees trees, and houses,

and most of all the blue sky and realizes that through this clear, hard stuff is *outside*. This reminds him of the door, the door Tommy takes them through when they get in the truck. It's dark in that place, and it's dark in the truck, but there must be some way out.

He and Milo go into the dark room with the truck. He can see light coming from under one wall, but he can't figure out how to get out.

That's when Milo seems to remember something. He goes to the wall and pushes something. Suddenly there is a loud grinding sound.

Koba jumps at the sound and chitters as the sliver of light gets bigger and bigger until they are looking at outside. He gingerly approaches it. He feels something in him, then gets an idea. What if he and Milo just go into the outside, and keep going? What if there are no more cages, no more tricks, no more beatings or shocks or fire pushed in his eye?

He tries to explain to Milo, but Milo is scared. So they find a safe corner and wait. Soon the outside starts getting dark, and Koba gets a little worried, too. But then he becomes determined.

Next time it is light, he thinks, *I will go outside and stay there, whatever Milo does.*

So he and Milo go back in the house to sleep.

Koba wakes up with a lot people talking. They are everywhere in the house. Some of them are looking at Tommy. Most of them are looking at Milo and Koba.

"Easy there," a man says, as Koba sits up.

"Crap, look at him," someone else says. "Is animal control on the way?"

"They should be here any minute," the first man says.

Koba can see outside.

Koba go outside, he signs.

"Watch it," the second man says. "He's doing something."

Koba looks past the men. He points at outside.

The first man is now holding a thing like Tommy had pointed at him.

Koba go outside, he says again.

"You know," one of the people says, "I think he might be trying to say something. You know, like those monkeys the scientists talk to?"

"This one looks like the chimp on that TV show," Somebody else says, pointing at Milo. "He has that same mark on his face."

"You can't tell one of these things from another," the second man says. "They're all just dumb animals."

"Well, I can sure tell these apart," he says, pointing at Koba's eye. "There's no way I'd forget that."

Koba knows then that the people won't help him. He knows there is only one way he can go outside.

He bounds forward, over the couch where Tommy will never wake up, through the open door. He reaches the grass, feels it beneath his feet as he runs with every ounce of strength in his body.

They run after him. Koba sees a tree and scrambles up it. It is hard—all those days in the cage cause his muscles to cramp, but it still feels good as he climbs up toward the sky. This time he thinks he might touch it, because there is no cage, and he can keep going up, up, higher until no one can even see him.

Something hits him in the side, hard, and it hurts so much he almost loses his hold. He puts his hand there and finds something sticking out of it.

He looks down, and sees lots of people looking at him. Some of them are pointing. He sees Milo, being led on a leash toward a truck.

Then he turns and begins climbing again, but it's more difficult now, and everything is going strange. His hands and feet seem very distant, not connected to him anymore. His heartbeat is like a little fly buzzing in his chest. The sky above seems to be moving around the tree.

The last thing Koba is aware of is falling. He feels as if he is in the sky.

13

David didn't turn, as the voice had directed. He ran like hell. It wasn't a strategy or the result of a conscious decision. It was just what he did.

This time he heard the high-pitched whine of a silenced gun firing sas he sprinted back toward Church Street, with nothing but open ground around him. Then he heard it again. He didn't hear the third shot because he was too busy being hit by it. White heat blazed through his back and the ribs on his right side, and his lungs suddenly felt hot, as if he'd been running all day.

He stumbled, trying to keep his feet under him.

The only part of his brain still working was the part that wanted to live, which meant he had to keep running, no matter what.

Except he couldn't.

"Hey!" he heard someone shout, and realized it was the old man with the dog. He was holding a pistol.

Shit, David thought.

He heard the *thwimp* of the silenced weapon, then the explosion of the decidedly unquiet weapon in the old man's hand—once, twice, three times. David lay there, feeling the blood leaking through his ribs, wondering why he wasn't dead yet.

He finally lifted his head and saw the soles of the old man's feet, close by and pointed at him. When he turned around, he saw a younger man with dark glasses, lying in a similar position.

David sat up cautiously. He saw a few people running away—everyone else had already gone.

He pushed himself unsteadily to his feet. The old man was clearly dead, but he checked for a pulse anyway. The dog, a Pomeranian, whined and licked at his deceased master's face. The other guy—the one who had tried to kill him—had a bloody hole where his nose once had been, and another in the middle of his chest.

David stumbled back to his knees and began to vomit. When he was finally done with that, he shakily took out his cell phone and dialed 911.

The phone told him that the network was overloaded.

He looked around. There wasn't another soul to be seen.

Swearing at the pain in his side, trying to get his thoughts in order, he began searching through the murderer's jacket. He took his wallet and his phone, but didn't find anything else of significance.

Then he left the scene, limping, holding his side. He stopped and looked at the old man again, then at the body of Linda's sister.

God, what have I done? he thought.

He couldn't think of where he should go. All of the hospitals were slammed, and if he went to one, he would probably catch the plague anyway. He had a first-aid kit at home, but going there seemed like a bad idea. Had they followed her or him to the meeting? Was his phone tapped? What if another guy with a gun was waiting for him at his apartment?

How did he have a hole in him? How could someone shoot three people in a city park? This happened to other people, not to him. Other people in other places.

But now it was happening to everyone, wasn't it? He felt a sudden plummet in his gut as he realized how fragile civilization really was. All of this steel and stone and glass around him seemed strong, durable, and dependable. It was built to withstand earthquakes.

But a civilization wasn't made up of its buildings. The pyramids had outlasted the pharaohs and the Colosseum remained long after the Roman Empire. Civilization, in the end, was about rules and norms that people agreed to follow. And that was weaker than tissue. He remembered a satirical article he'd once read, about people who had resorted to cannibalism after being stuck in an elevator for fifteen minutes. He'd thought it was hilarious at the time.

Now it didn't seem funny at all.

He needed an emergency room, but he knew they were all slammed.

Talia, he realized, then. She didn't live far from here.

He buzzed five times before she answered.

"Who the hell is it?" the intercom crackled.

"David," he said. "Talia, it's David Flynn."

He heard the intercom click off, then back on.

"David, I just pulled a seventy-hour shift," she said. "I'm not in the mood—"

"I've been shot, Talia," he sobbed. "I don't know where else to go."

"Shit." A pause. Then the door clicked. "Get in," she said. "Wait for me in the foyer."

She was down a few minutes later, wearing flannel pajamas and slippers. She had a tote bag with her.

"David?" she said, kneeling beside him.

"Thanks, Talia," he murmured as she examined his wound.

"Damn," she said.

"Is it that bad?"

"It could be a lot worse," she replied. "You've made it this far. Let's get you upstairs."

She helped him to the elevator and up to her apartment. She had gotten a new couch since he had last seen it, and moved things around. It looked like she still lived alone, though.

She moved him to the bathroom and pulled his shirt off.

"How did this happen?" she asked, as she examined the wound more closely.

"I met a source in Delores Park," he said. "Somebody shot her, then shot me. Then someone shot him... *Ow!*"

"That's a lot of shooting," she observed.

"Some old guy walking his dog just happened to have a gun, or I'd be dead."

"I think probably everyone who owns a piece is carrying it right now," she told him. "I've seen more gunshot wounds in the last few days than in my entire career." She looked over at him. He'd forgotten what beautiful, dark eyes she had.

"I think it just went through the ribs," she said. "I don't think it nicked your intestines. If they were perforated, that would be bad. Still, there's enough tissue damage that some of it might go necrotic."

"How bad is that?" he asked. "Can you fix it?"

"I can sew it up," she said. "Stop the bleeding. But you need antibiotics, which I don't have here." She caught his gaze and held it. "I don't have any anesthetic, either."

"How about vodka?" he asked.

"You know me that well, anyway," she said. "I'll be right back."

* * *

David woke up, head throbbing, and realized that between the pain and the vodka he had made it all the way through the operation. He was lying on Talia's bed. She had cleaned and sewn him up in the tub, and so she had stripped him down. He was still naked.

She lay about a foot away. She had changed pajamas.

He contemplated the fact that he had never seen Talia in pajamas. Lingerie, yes. T-shirt, yes. Birthday suit, check. Never pajamas. He didn't even know she owned any. And they had seen each other for the better part of a year. It had been good, really good, but then things had gotten busy for both of them, and they hung out less and less. Nowadays he never saw her in the bars and restaurants where they used to go. He guessed that she was either too busy at work, or had hooked up with a different crowd.

Fortunately for him, she hadn't moved to a different apartment.

She stirred, and her eyes flickered open.

"Well," she said, smiling. "You finally stayed the night. How about that."

"I never stayed over?" he said, trying to remember. "That was stupid of me."

"No, that was just you," she said. "How are you feeling?"

"Like I got hammered while someone worked a needle into and out of my skin."

She touched his cheek, and for just an instant he thought it was a gesture of affection.

"You're warm," she said. "I should check your temperature. And you need to hydrate."

She brought him orange juice, and found that his temperature was just over a hundred.

"I go back on shift this afternoon," she said. "But I'll try to get you some antibiotics before that."

She looked so tired. "You should rest," he said.

"I got a few hours of sleep," she said. "It'll do. Hey, I'm young, right?"

"It's bad out there, isn't it?" he asked. She nodded.

"And getting worse," she said. "Half the staff are down with it."

"Don't go back," he said. "Just don't go back."

She gave him another weary little smile.

"Don't think I haven't considered it," she told him. "But too many have already taken a walk. Somebody has to try." She patted his arm. "I'll be back. Hopefully with antibiotics." She rose, went to her closet, and selected a pair of scrubs.

"Talia," he asked. "Why did we stop hanging out?"

She looked down then, frowning a little.

"I liked you," she said. "A lot."

"Yeah," he said. "I liked you, too."

She drew her gaze up to meet his.

"I was tired of liking you," she replied. Then she left the room. A little while later, he heard the front door open and close.

He lay there for a moment, then gingerly levered himself up. He went into the living room, got the satchel, and brought it back to the bed. Inside were an ultralight laptop and several file folders. He switched on the laptop and waited for it to boot up as he flipped through the files.

"Holy shit," he said, after a moment. He found his cell phone, but he didn't have any service, so he picked up Talia's landline and called his editor.

"Sage," he said, when he got hold of her. "Flynn here."

"Where the hell have you been?" she demanded. "I have an assignment for you."

"I've already got a story," he said. "You're going to want to leave some space on page one. And if you've got anybody inside the mayor's office, I'm going to need to get a couple of things vetted."

"You're going to have to give me a taste," she said.

When he was done, there was silence on the line for four, five, six heartbeats.

"You're sure about this?"

"I've got original Gen Sys documents," he said. "Paper and ink. With signatures. I just want to see if we can get corroborating information from House's office."

"I think I can swing that," she said. "Are you at your place?"

"No," he said. "Somebody actually tried to kill me, if you can believe it."

"Are you kidding?"

"No. He shot my source, and he shot me. Then someone shot him—it gets complicated."

"Are you all right?" she asked. "Are you safe?"

"Yeah. You can reach me at this number. Do *not* give it to anyone else."

"Don't you need medical attention?"

"I've got the best I'm likely to get," he said. "Just get that stuff for me."

"I'll get back to you," she said. "Go, write. You've got six hours."

14

One of Rocket's scouts dropped down from the higher branches. Caesar saw that he was agitated.

What?

Humans, the scout said. *That way, coming this way. Many.*

Caesar frowned in frustration. He'd hoped the trick with the white rectangles would have kept them busy for a longer time. But here they were again, the very next day. Would they ever give up?

He was starting to believe they wouldn't.

Show me, Caesar signed. He motioned for the rest of his band to follow.

He chased the chimp through the treetops. The scout's name was Jojo, and when Caesar caught a flash of his face, he saw that the agitation had been replaced by pure joy. Until they freed him, he hand never been outside. At first he had been terrified, but now he had embraced his new existence, his life as it should always have been. A lot of the apes were like this. It was as if they were waking up from a long sleep.

For some, a sleep that had begun at birth.

Eventually Jojo slowed and, down through the trees, Caesar could see the humans. It was hard to count accurately through the leaves, but Jojo was right—there was a lot of them, mostly with guns, moving in the general direction of the troop. Furthermore, they were walking side by side, spread out in a long line. This would make it easier for them to find what they were looking for.

He turned to Jojo.

Return to Rocket, he said. *Tell him I'm leading them to the sunset side of the mountain. Tell Rocket to go to Maurice, have him move the troop up the valley to the sunrise side.*

He glanced back down at the humans, passing beneath him. Then he glanced at Koba, and saw how taut his muscles were, every inch of him a threat.

Koba, he signed. *Stay high in the trees, follow, warn us of flying things.*

Koba stared at him for a moment, then acknowledged.

As Caesar turned back to his band, one of the humans looked up, and their gazes locked.

He had known many human expressions: kindness, love, fear, anger. He had seen meanness in the eyes of Dodge, his "caregiver" back at the shelter.

The gaze of this man was made of something he had never seen, and could hardly understand. But it felt very, very dangerous.

Then other heads turned toward him.

Follow me, he signed. Then he flung himself from limb to limb, down, toward the forest floor. He heard the humans shout as they caught sight of him and his band, and he began the chase. A glance back showed them following.

He felt a prickling on his exposed back, and expected them to start shooting at any moment, but for some reason they did not. That made things a little easier, since the trick was to keep them following, and avoid getting killed.

* * *

When Koba reached the top of the trees, he glanced around, but didn't see anything in the air. He did see the city where the humans dwelt—where he had dwelt, where his mother had died, and he had been tortured.

Why had Caesar put him in the high canopy? The other chimps in the band had better eyesight. After all, he only had one eye. He would be more useful down there, where he could fight.

But it was good up there, so near the sky. He reached for it, but it was still too far away. How far could it be?

Koba shook his gaze from the heavens and refocused on his job. From this vantage point he could see what transpired below, but he was starting to realize something. There weren't as many humans as he had thought chasing Caesar's band. It looked like only eight or nine, at most.

He was trying to figure out what that meant when the unmistakable sound of the flying cages reached his ears. He scanned the sky, and saw the source of the sound. They were in the distance, not moving toward Caesar at all.

They were flying toward the troop.

Suddenly there was a crashing in the tree branches above. Caesar looked up as Koba came hurtling down. He was trying to swing and gesture at the same time. He kept pointing up, so finally Caesar peeled off from the band and followed him. They reached the treetops, and from there he saw the helicopters.

Most not chase you, Koba signed.

And Caesar suddenly understood. This time *he* had been

tricked. The helicopters were moving toward the troop.

Koba, find Rocket. Bring him to the troop, he commanded. Then he turned and raced back the way he had come. As he whipped over the heads of the humans this time, they started firing at him, but within seconds he was beyond their sight, swinging as fast as he could, hoping he wasn't too late.

The ape was gone, rushing off through the trees, but the fierce intelligence of his gaze remained with Malakai. It was like nothing he had ever seen in an ape.

He remembered the first gorilla had had ever seen, when he was with his uncle. There had been something there—an awareness, something on the level of a child, but caged in an outsized body. He had recognized a cousin, but knew it was a distant one.

When his uncle had shot it, the gorilla looked confused. It kept touching the hole and making pitiful noises. He asked his uncle to shoot it again, to make the sounds stop.

"I've already killed it," his uncle said. "He just doesn't know he's dead yet. Bullets are expensive."

He was right, and the gorilla soon died. They butchered it while the rest of its family looked on. None of the apes really seemed to know what had happened.

The thing that had just looked down at him was not like that. The fierce intelligence, the will and purpose, were all there. And they were far from childlike.

That was him, he thought. *The leader.*

"They went for it," Corbin said.

Clancy was just staring at the apes as they quickly receded from view.

"That's the first time I've seen one, since we started this whole thing," she said. "A live one, I mean. I was starting to doubt they really existed." She turned to Malakai. "Did you see…?"

He nodded.

"It's amazing. I wish I could just study this… this… *whatever* is happening. It could change everything we know about apes. About ourselves."

"Whatever," Corbin said dismissively. "Which way?"

"Where's the capture team?" Clancy asked.

"We call them in when we find the herd," he said.

"This way," Malakai said. "Quickly."

He heard the choppers in the distance.

Suddenly a group of chimps went racing off in front of them, screeching at the tops of their lungs. A couple of the men shot at them with their tranq guns, but he didn't think they hit any of their targets.

"Ignore them!" Malakai said. "They're just trying to distract us. Push on."

"The choppers think they have them spotted," Corbin said, holding one hand up to an earpiece. "But they want visual confirmation from the ground."

The apes in the trees buzzed at them again, but this time no one fired.

"There are signs everywhere," Malakai muttered, looking around, seeing the remains of nests, the scuffed areas. "They were here, not long ago. A lot of them."

"They're on the move again."

"Yes," Malakai said, "but this time there are too many for them to hide their movements."

The helicopters were already there when Caesar arrived, yet they weren't doing anything, as far as he could see.

Maurice had the troop in motion, but some still were not moving very quickly. Caesar was raging at himself for letting his own tricks be used against him, and terrified that more apes would be killed. What's more, it was abundantly clear that the men on foot would find the troop this time, and soon.

With a shiver, he realized that he didn't have a choice. He had misled the humans as much as he could. After the battle on the bridge, he hadn't wanted to fight again. He just wanted to be left alone. But that wasn't going to be possible.

Overhead, the helicopters turned and began to fly away. Caesar watched them, wondering why. But without the helicopters...

It could be a trick.

He didn't have a choice.

He started moving through the troop, picking out the strongest and fastest.

Malakai noticed that he no longer heard the sound of the helicopters. He couldn't decide if that was a good or a bad thing.

Corbin had noticed it, too, and was on his two-way, arguing with somebody.

That's when, looking up, Malakai caught the motion in the trees, a glimpse of rust. Then another, this one black, surely a chimp.

"They're here," he said, his voice low. The treetops were rustling violently now as the branches above them filled with apes. He saw the orangutans first, moving almost like giant spiders above them. Then more chimps were there, frenetic, bouncing from tree to tree, screeching.

Tens of apes, maybe more than a hundred of them. Realizing what was missing, he shifted his gaze to look through the boles of the trees, searching for the ground troops. And there they were, the gorillas—not acting as gorillas should, but prowling, moving from the cover of one tree to the next.

"Do not shoot," Malakai said, softly.

"Oh, shit," Flores gasped, suddenly understanding the situation.

"They're just apes," Corbin snarled. "Keep it together."

"Where's the friggin' air support?" Kyung demanded.

"It's been recalled," Corbin said. "I can't get a straight answer as to why."

"They're recalling us, too, right?" Flores said.

"They said for us to proceed at my discretion."

"If you tranq one of them, you'll have to fight them all," Malakai said.

"I've called everyone else in. They'll be here in ten minutes."

Malakai continued searching through the trees, watching the numbers grow.

"That could be a very long ten minutes."

"Yeah," Flores said. "And another, what, fifteen guys? Maybe if more of us had real guns, instead of Sleepy Joes..."

He looked significantly at Corbin, the only one carrying a real assault rifle.

Overhead, one of the orangs made a long call, and that set off the chimps, who began screeching even louder. Sticks began pelting down. Not big ones, but lots of them.

Malakai watched the nearest gorilla. It was staring at him as if it knew everything he had done in his life. It did not have the dull intelligence he remembered. Like the chimp he had seen earlier, this ape was different.

Clancy saw it, too.

"It's not just one of them that's smart," she said. "It's all of them."

"I say you'd better use your 'discretion' to check our

asses out of here, Corbin." Flores said, his voice edged with panic.

"They're just monkeys, damn it," Corbin snapped.

"Don't," Malakai said.

As he said it, a group of chimps seemed to explode out of the mid-canopy. For an instant, the one leading them looked as shocked as anyone. Then a gunshot detonated, so near it set his ears ringing. One of the chimps screamed and tumbled from the tree, falling almost at Corbin's feet. Before anyone could react, another chimp leapt down, knocking Corbin to the ground and sending his rifle flying.

The newcomer was a nightmarish customer, with one milky eye and a visage filled with sheer malevolence. It was a kind of face Malakai was all too used to seeing, had seen many times on people whose hatred for another tribe or religion transcended all rational bounds. Everyone seemed frozen as the ape slouched toward Corbin. In that moment, it could easily have torn the mercenary's throat out.

But instead the one-eyed chimp backed away, although it seemed reluctant.

The cacophony from the trees suddenly cut off, leaving them with a surreal silence that was almost claustrophobic. Flores started to pull his weapon up, but Malakai slapped it down.

"Are you insane?" he hissed.

The half-blind ape went over to the wounded one and pulled it up. He lifted it onto his shoulder, all the time staring at Corbin and the others. Then he turned his back, as if daring them to shoot him, before swinging unhurriedly into a tree and climbing away, carrying his fallen comrade.

"Let's... get... the hell... out of here!" Flores said.

Malakai picked up Corbin's gun, keeping the barrel carefully pointed to the ground. He reached out a hand to

Corbin, who ignored it and scrambled up under his own power. The apes had remained silent. But suddenly from the midst of them came a single screech.

And the rest seemed to explode—the chimps screaming, the gorillas growling threats, the orangutans hooting with what seemed to be derision. But Malakai hardly noticed them. It was their unity, their singleness of purpose that sent prickles down his spine. One glance at Clancy told him that she felt it, as well.

"Yeah," Corbin said. "We're out."

For a long moment, Malakai wondered if that was even an option anymore. But as they backed away, the apes just watched them retreat.

Caesar watched them leave, his heart hammering.

If Koba had killed the man...

He made his way over to where Rocket lay on a huge branch, the bonobo sitting beside him.

Rocket? he asked. *Where bullet hit you?*

Rocket looked a little embarrassed.

No bullet, he said. *Surprised. Missed branch.* He indicated his leg. *Hurt,* he said. Then his arm. *Hurt.*

Can you travel? Relief welled up in Caesar's chest.

Not fast, Rocket replied.

Caesar glanced back up at the sky. He still couldn't hear any helicopters.

We have to go, find new place, he said. *They come back with more guns, more machines.*

I'll help him, Koba said.

No, Caesar said, *Sam will help him. You lead his band now.*

Koba's eyes went wide.

You made the right choice, Caesar said. *You chose*

Rocket. You chose ape. I am proud.

Koba supplicated.

Apes together, strong, he said.

Apes together, strong, Caesar repeated. *Now go. Find thick forest beyond the mountain, away from humans.*

Koba nodded. He glanced at Rocket's band. They fidgeted, but with a look from Caesar they fell in line.

We go, Koba signed, and he moved to leave. The others followed. Soon they were out of sight. Wearily, Caesar went down to organize the move. They all thought they had just won an important victory, but he felt in his bones that they were in more danger than ever. This was only the start.

Phillips met them when they arrived back at the base. He didn't look happy.

Corbin wasn't happy either.

"What happened to the air support?" he demanded. "The nets, the traps, the guys who were supposed to put them down after we found them?"

"I'm sure you were informed when it was pulled," Phillips said. "Plans were changed. We have to be flexible. I had every expectation that you had enough resources to succeed in your mission. To bring back at least one lousy ape."

"You weren't there," Corbin said. "You didn't see them. If you had let us take in our AR15s we *might* have had a chance. Or if you called in—"

"The goal is live capture," Phillips said, interrupting him.

"They're monsters!"

"They are not," Clancy said. "They're amazing."

"It doesn't matter what they are," Phillips said. "For

the moment, at least, we're shut down."

"Why?" Corbin demanded.

"You don't need to know that," Phillips said. "Just stand down and wait for further orders."

This, Malakai realized, *is where they kill us.*

15

The streets were nearly empty as Talia drove toward the hospital. She felt as if she was in a demilitarized zone. Garbage was collecting on sidewalks and streets. Wrecked and abandoned cars littered the freeway. What people she did see were almost shadows, scurrying in the periphery of her vision.

Just for the hell of it, she decided to try a pharmacy. It would be quicker, and as a doctor she could order the meds right there. But when she pulled into to the nearest one, she saw that the windows had been smashed in, and the lights were off. Suddenly feeling in danger, she wheeled out of the parking lot and hurried on toward the hospital.

She found the National Guard turning cars back more than four blocks out. A soldier waved for her to stop, then walked over.

"I'm a doctor," she told the man, and showed him her ID.

"You can't drive in," he said. "There's a back entrance for doctors. I can walk you there."

She found a place to park the car, and then walked back to the guardsman, wondering what the hell he meant by "a back entrance." Soon enough, however, she understood.

The entire block surrounding the hospital had been cordoned off, and guardsmen were busy putting up chain-link fencing. A huge line of people was being herded through an entrance in the fence into a sort of tent city that had sprung up like magic in the seven hours since she had left. Outside, buses were pulling up, from which people disembarked. A lot of them didn't seem to be doing so willingly, as the guards had to prod them—and in some cases drag them along.

"What's going on?" she asked her escort, more or less rhetorically.

"We're setting up a quarantine here," he said.

He took her to the doctor's entrance, which was guarded by two men with rifles. They were wearing hazmat gear.

Inside the hospital it was chaos, as every available space was being made ready for the sick. Waiting rooms, offices, the lunch room, the chapel—any place vacant. She felt like she was in a war movie, except almost everyone here had the same problem, and it wasn't a human enemy.

It was the retrovirus.

However, those sick with the virus were no longer being routed to the lobby of the emergency room. That was packed with people, and a glance told her that most of them were in critical or near-critical condition. Gunshot wounds, stabbings, head trauma, broken bones—more than ever, she felt like she was in a MASH unit.

The impression was completed when a middle-aged African-American man in army scrubs gestured toward her. She noticed than that there were several other people she didn't know, all of them wearing similar dress.

"You there," he demanded. "Who are you?"

"I'm Dr. Kosar," she said. "I belong here. Who are you?"

"Dr. Kosar," he said, more quietly. "Sorry for the tone.

Thank God you're here. I'm Captain McWilliams. I've been put in the charge of this ER. I have my hands full, as you can see."

"I'm not on shift until ten," she said. "I..." She looked again at the dying all around her. David would be fine for an hour or two. Then she would slip off with a course of antibiotics.

"Yeah," she said. "Never mind. Let me get scrubbed."

The next couple of hours were a nightmare. Triage consisted of deciding who she could treat, and who was beyond help. She had thought herself hardened to this kind of thing, but this was a whole other level.

McWilliams didn't seem fazed. He was a more-than-competent doctor but, more importantly, he knew how to command. She suspected that, as an army surgeon, he had worked in this sort of chaos before.

After a length of time she couldn't even begin to measure, Talia found herself becoming weaker, more tired by the moment. She realized that she hadn't had anything to eat or drink in hours, so she took a break and had an energy bar from one of the machines. It was the last one. She tried to drink some water, but after half a cup found she couldn't get any more down.

Remembering David, she picked up some antibiotics. Their stores were nearly depleted, but there still was some cephalexin and ampicillin. She felt guilty for taking it, but David deserved treatment as much as anyone. She checked her phone and realized that it had been the better part of four hours since she had left him. That wasn't good. If she had missed something—and there was a chance she had, given the tissue-damage in the vicinity of his gunshot wound—then he might be in trouble. She had patched him up in poor lighting, in her bathtub...

But there was nothing to do about it now. So she went to the lavatory and then splashed some water on her face.

In the mirror, she saw a dribble of pink, just beneath her nose. She reached up and touched it with her index finger.

It came away red.

"Well," she said to the image in the mirror.

In the back of her mind, she had known this was coming. She had kept it back the way everyone did when confronted with mortality, by imagining she was the one who couldn't get it, she was the one who wouldn't die.

She closed her eyes. There was still so much to do, she thought. David was counting on her, Captain McWilliams was counting on her, and the desperate people in the next room were counting on her.

She opened her eyes, wet a paper towel and wiped her face again. She stuffed some wadded toilet paper up her nose and as soon as she was outside, she put on a mask.

Then she found Captain McWilliams.

"I have to go," she said. "I'll be back in about two hours, I promise."

He nodded.

"Get a little rest," he said. "You look tired."

"Thanks," she said. She hurriedly grabbed her things and started back through the hospital toward the physician's doorway. She felt dizzy, and wondered if she would be able to drive. But she had to try.

If she was very careful, kept contact with him to a minimum, she could help David without infecting him.

Then she felt an itching in her sinuses, and started to run, hoping to make it outside, but she was still fifty feet from the door when the sneeze tore out of her.

One of the guards looked over. He was wearing a hazmat suit, without the headgear.

"Excuse me," she said, pretending to scratch her forehead, hoping her hand would cover her face.

"Ma'am," the young guardsman said.

She nodded and tried to keep going, but he placed himself in front of her.

"Ma'am," he said, "I'm going to have to ask you to stop there."

"I'm a doctor," she said, tapping her ID.

"Yes, ma'am. But you appear to have viral symptoms. My orders are not to let anyone through this door unless I'm confident they're clean."

"You can't just hold me against my will," she said. "I haven't done anything."

"You are an active carrier, ma'am." He sounded sure of it. "We are now under a state and federal quarantine and isolation order. You may appeal this—"

"Appeal it when?" she said, and she realized she was shouting. She took a deep breath. "Look," she said. "I have a friend who has a gunshot wound. He needs antibiotics, and I'm taking him some. Then I'll be right back. You can check with Captain McWilliams in the ER."

The young man shook his head.

"I'm sorry, ma'am, but it doesn't much matter what he says. Even if he gave me a direct order, I couldn't let you through this door."

As he spoke, two more guards arrived.

"If you'll just wait," he said, "we'll send for someone to evaluate you."

"Please," she said. "He may die without this."

He hesitated, and she felt a moment's hope.

"Ma'am," he said, "I go off shift in an hour. If you give me the meds and the address, I can give them to him. That's the best I can do."

She studied his earnest face, then withdrew the

antibiotics and the syringe from her pocket. "He needs a shot of this one," she said. "These he takes by mouth." She handed them over to them. "I'm trusting you," she said.

"I'll do it," he promised.

"Thank you," she said. "I'm going back to ER now."

"Ma'am—"

"I don't need to be evaluated,' she said. "I'm a doctor. Shoot me if you have to." She almost hoped he would, because she knew what was coming. But she also knew she had a day or more before she lost the ability to function.

McWilliams shook his head when he saw her, and hustled her into the café, where they would have a little privacy.

"Are you okay?" he asked. He sounded genuinely concerned. That little bit of human kindness was all she needed to push her over the edge, and a soft sob crept out of her.

"Does it look like I'm okay?" she replied.

"I was starting to worry about you," he said. "I thought you were showing symptoms. I'm so sorry I was right."

For a moment, she couldn't speak, and the tears began. McWilliams rested a gloved hand on her shoulder.

"You were going to let me slip isolation?" she finally asked, wiping her eyes.

"I knew you would be careful," he said. "I thought you deserved to deal with this thing on your own terms."

"Can you still get me out?"

"No," he said sadly. "Not at this point. Now I can't plausibly claim ignorance. Were you turned back by a guard?"

She nodded.

"Yeah," he said. "I figured that. I couldn't get you out even if I tried. Best go let them find you a bed."

She imagined lying among the dying, waiting for the

end. It wasn't an appealing thought.

"Can I stay and work?" she asked. "I have some time, we both know that. The symptoms just started presenting. And I'll be careful. I'm always careful."

"I've seen enough of your work to know that," he said. "But careful sometimes isn't good enough." He looked back at the waiting room. "On the other hand, most of them don't have a chance in hell without you anyway. Slim is better than none."

"Okay," she said. "I'll go scrub."

When she got back to the waiting room, the only coffee that remained was instant, and as she poured the wretched stuff she realized she would never taste good coffee again. She wished that she had savored the last cup more. She wished she had gotten around to buying a grinder and some beans for the café.

Her reverie was cut short by a loud, dull, *whump* outside. The lights flickered and went out, and everyone began screaming. After a moment, the generators cut in and the lights came back.

Talia heard the staccato chatter of gunfire, and more screams. Through the glass doors of the emergency room, she could see a bright orange-yellow glow.

"What is it?" she asked McWilliams.

"I think we're under attack," he said.

"Attack?" The light seemed to go funny, as it did whenever there was an earthquake. Attack? Who would be attacking a hospital? And why? All of it seemed suddenly completely unreal, like a bad dream. She would wake up from it, and she wouldn't really be sick, and none of this would be happening.

A guardsman burst in and exchanged salutes with McWilliams.

"What's going on corporal?" he demanded.

"They threw firebombs into the quarantine, sir," he said. His eyes seemed glazed by the same disbelief that Talia felt. "And into the back door. And we've sighted snipers with their rifles focused on the entrances. We're not sure how many, but they shot Cain and nearly got Rodrigues."

"Who are 'they'?" McWilliams barked.

"I don't know sir," the corporal replied. "They didn't exactly identify themselves."

McWilliams absorbed that for a millisecond, and then turned to Talia.

"Get anybody in here who knows anything about burns," he told her. "Do it now."

"We have a burns unit," Talia said. "I can see if anyone is there."

She was hurrying down the hall, trying to think who might be available, when she met two men with a gurney. One it lay a man in a hazmat suit that had mostly burned off of him, and he himself had extensive burns—but not so extensive that she couldn't see his face.

It was the young guardsman to whom she had given the• antibiotics.

As she watched him go past, the feeling of unreality faded. The ground was under her again. This was a nightmare, and there was no waking up from it.

"I'm sorry, David," she whispered, and continued on toward the burns unit. She could still hear the faint reports of gunfire outside.

16

David realized he'd just been staring at the page—maybe for a minute, maybe for longer. He took another drink of water and tried to get his focus back. His side throbbed, and pain radiated out from it to touch him everywhere. It felt, in fact, as if he was a hand puppet on a zombie's hand.

He looked at the clock, and tried to do a little math.

Talia had been gone a long time. Four hours?

Most likely she had reached the hospital, and been drafted for an emergency situation. There probably wasn't anything to worry about.

He took his own temperature and saw that it had climbed to a hundred and four, which explained some things—like the morbid zombie-hand analogy. He went to Talia's medicine cabinet and found some aspirin. He took four and then went back to the laptop. Despite the way he was feeling, the story was taking shape.

Sage called an hour later with the corroboration he needed.

"You sound bad," she said.

"A little fever," he explained.

"Just send me what you've got, and get to a doctor," she said.

"Right," he muttered. "So someone else can get my byline."

"You'll get your byline, you flinking idiot. Get to a doctor!"

"I'm at the doctor's right now," he said. "Now let me finish the damn thing."

He hung up before she could say anything else.

Caesar sat alone in the topmost branch of a redwood, staring out at the city. In the west, the sun was melting into the sea, and beyond the bridge, lights began coming on.

It seemed to him that there were fewer lights than there once had been, that the city was darker. Once again he wondered what Will was doing. Was Will sick with the disease? He hoped not. He could picture Will and Caroline in the kitchen, talking about what they had done that day. He longed to be there again, to be a part of that, part of a family. But it had never been entirely real. When they went places, Will took him on a leash, like a pet. Caesar knew what a pet was, and he knew that was the best thing an ape could hope for in the human world.

The worst—well, there were members of his troop who knew all too much about that. Apes who had been raised with nothing like a family, nothing like love, who had experienced only pain, degradation, and isolation.

And many of them… weren't right. They were damaged inside, didn't know exactly how to act, and maybe they never would. And all of this running, the threat of being captured or killed, the hunger—none of it was helping. But if he could find a place where they could be left alone, he knew things would get better. If some apes were broken, their children would not be. They would grow up with apes, as apes, in the trees where they belonged.

If...

He heard a faint rustling, and to his surprise he saw that Cornelia was approaching. Just seeing her made him feel tired, and he wondered what she had come to complain about this time, what things she thought he was doing wrong.

She approached with deference. Not enough, he thought, but more than she had ever shown before.

Caesar watches the city, she signed.

He nodded.

What are you looking for?

When he didn't answer, she moved closer.

It will be dark soon, she observed.

He shrugged, and waited for her to say something worth a reply. For a moment he thought she would just leave, but was astonished when she reached over and began picking twigs out his fur. He flinched at first, but then he let her continue. It felt good, relaxing, like when Will and Caroline had brushed him or stroked him.

She started on his back, working around to his side, slowly, methodically.

You're a mess, she said.

No time to groom, he signed back. *Always running.*

You did well today, she said.

He jerked away, trying to read her expression. Was she mocking him?

But her expression seemed sincere.

I made a mistake today, he said. *Might have lost many.*

Didn't, she pointed out.

Maybe soon, though, he said. *I was too confident. Stupid.*

She pulled at a twig, a little too hard, and it stung.

Not stupid, she said. *Apes are free because of Caesar.*

Apes are together. Worth dying for.

She continued to groom him in silence for a few moments.

Caesar is the smartest, she added. *Still, should listen to others, take help from others. Caesar alone strong. Caesar with apes, stronger. Apes together, strong.*

Caesar recognized what he had said to Maurice, coming back to him again. Koba had said it, too.

Who says this? he asked. *Apes together strong?*

All of them, she said. *Even ones who don't talk.*

He watched the last of the sunset, then touched Cornelia's shoulder, a gesture of thanks. He'd come up here feeling like something in him was broken. Now he felt it was just a bad bruise.

Together they went down to join the troop.

"Hey, Dad."

Dreyfus looked up as Edward entered the kitchen, stifling a yawn. He was a rangy sapling of a fourteen-year-old, with a bushy mess of brown hair.

"Good morning, Edward," he said. "I'm surprised to see you up so early, with school being canceled and all. I thought you might take the opportunity to sleep in."

"I kind of… kind of thought I might see you before you left," Edward said.

Dreyfus had been reaching for the paper, but he left it where it was.

"Is something the matter?" he asked.

"No," Edward said, his gaze wandering randomly around the kitchen. And then, "Maybe, I don't know."

"Have a seat," Dreyfus told his son. "You want some coffee?"

"Gross. No thanks." He went to the fridge and got

some sort of energy drink instead.

"You worried about the virus that's going around?" he asked.

"Sure," Edward replied, studying the back of his drink can. "Everyone is. Aren't you?"

"Sure," he allowed. "But I can't let it stop me from doing what I think is right."

Edward's eyes lit up a little.

"Like running for mayor?" he said. "Like getting in front of that mob the other day?"

"Exactly," Dreyfus said.

"Yeah," Edward said. "So, there's this food drive—to try to collect canned goods for the quarantine shelters. I was thinking I should… help out. Do the right thing, like you."

Dreyfus sipped his coffee carefully.

"I'd rather you not go out, son," he said.

"But you just said—"

"I know." He sighed, and closed his eyes for a moment. "It's just different when you're a father."

"Hey, you set the example," Edward said.

"Tell me more about it, then," Dreyfus said.

"Mr. Song, our history teacher, is organizing it. He—"

"Hold up," Dreyfus said. "Henry Song?"

"Yes, sir."

"The one with the daughter who was over here the other day for a study session?"

"Dad, this isn't about her," Edward protested, looking down at the table. "I just want to be like you."

"Edward…" Dreyfus said, tilting his head.

"Okay, okay," his son blurted out. "It's *totally* about her. Please, Dad—let me. They have filter masks, gloves, fifty kinds of antibacterial hand wash."

"It's a virus," Dreyfus interrupted. "Antibacterial hand

wash won't do anything to prevent it. Not unless you really scrub. And soap is actually better for scrubbing."

Edward put both hands in front of him, as if he was shaking an invisible box. "Look, Dad," he said. "We're either all going to die, or we aren't. If we don't, I could come out the other side of this with some *serious* points." He paused. "And I would be doing good, even if my motives aren't perfectly pure."

Dreyfus regarded his son's earnest face.

"You'll wear the gear," he said. "Every second."

"Yes, yes," Edward said.

"And you'll wipe down and shower as soon as you come home." He looked his son in the eye. "I'm not kidding about this."

"Neither am I."

Dreyfus nodded reluctantly.

"Okay," he said. "Just be smart, okay? Be safe."

It struck him that in a better world, those words would exist in another context, a context more suited to the life of a fourteen-year-old.

Edward left, and Dreyfus picked up the paper. The headline might as well have jumped out and slapped him in the face.

"Oh my God," he muttered.

LOCAL BIOTECH FIRM CREATED SIMIAN FLU

Mayor's Office Involved in Cover-Up

By David Flynn

The 133 retrovirus devastating the region and other cities around the world originated at Gen Sys, a biological engineering firm located in the Bay Area. An inside informant and company records indicate that the virus resulted from a serum intended as a cure for Alzheimer's disease. According to verified documents, it was designed to help the brain to repair itself. It was tested on primates, and seemed to increase the intelligence of the test subjects.

The virus was developed by William Rodman, a scientist once considered to be on the cutting edge of Alzheimer's research. His procedures were called into question when a trial version appeared to cause a chimpanzee test subject to go berserk. More recently Rodman began testing an improved version, and then quit abruptly, lodging formal complaints that the testing was being moved ahead too quickly. Rodman could not be located for comment, but a source at Gen Sys has claimed that faulty trials led to the infection of humans.

Independent sources and records obtained by the San Francisco Sentinel reveal that Gen Sys and the mayor's office colluded to keep the details of this research, and the events that followed, from the public. They have also tried to actively suppress information concerning the escaped apes that wreaked havoc in the city and on the Golden Gate Bridge before fleeing into the Golden Gate National Recreational Area.

Bank records indicate that Mayor House received as much as ten million dollars from Gen Sys and its parent company, Polytechnic Solutions. Police Chief Burston also was named in the documents, but neither he nor Mayor House could be reached for comment. A spokesman for the mayor, who spoke on the condition of anonymity, stated that the claims are "outrageous and utterly without foundation," but sources inside the administration corroborate the relationship between the mayor and the tech firm.

Official reports from City Hall, claiming that the violence on the bridge was exaggerated, have been called into question. Sources indicate that the primates number in the hundreds, and exhibit unnatural intelligence and aggression. Currently they are reported to be roaming Muir Woods, and Anvil, a paramilitary contracting firm also owned by Polytechnic Solutions, has been hired to handle what has been dubbed "Monkeygate." Trumann Phillips, the executive in charge of the Anvil presence, could not be reached for comment.

The current death toll attributed to the Simian Flu stands at more than 100,000 nationwide and that number is expected to grow exponentially. Medical facilities are overwhelmed with those who have been infected, as well as victims of escalating violence throughout the city.

"Well," Dreyfus muttered. "There's the other shoe." He set his coffee down and headed for the office.

"You think being locked up might cost House the election?" Patel asked.

"There's not going to be an election," Dreyfus said. "No matter what happens to the goddamn mayor. And who do you imagine is going to lock him up?"

"Well, we'll find out soon enough," his aide replied. "They've announced a press conference, and if anything's going to happen, most likely it will happen there."

Sure enough, a short time later House appeared before the cameras. He still wasn't wearing a surgical mask, but looked more bedraggled than ever.

I almost feel sorry for the sonofabitch, Dreyfus thought. *Almost.*

After some adjustments to balance the sound, the mayor began to speak.

"I'm here today to address the allegations directed at me

and my administration, and to state definitively that they are entirely false," he said. "This city is deeply in crisis, and will probably remain so for the foreseeable future. For the moment, that is my one and only priority, and all of the resources of this office are focused on maintaining public safety as much as is possible.

"When the danger is over," he continued, "I will happily submit to any sort of outside investigation the citizens may call for. In the meantime, I remain in charge. This city is under martial law, and I am its executive officer.

"Thank you. God bless you all, God bless the City of San Francisco, and God bless America."

The first mob to storm City Hall formed less than an hour later.

The police and National Guard units repelled the first wave with tear gas and rubber bullets. The crowd backed up, but continued to grow. Police were called in from other parts of the city.

Dreyfus watched all of it unfold on the TV, and he came to a decision. He reached for his jacket.

"It would have been nice to have been mayor," he said with a sigh.

17

When he arrived at City Hall, the mob looked as if it was on the verge of charging again. Despite the bullhorn he held, it took him several tries to get their attention, and for a moment he thought they were going to charge *him*. Then someone in front shouted his name, then someone else, and before he knew it, it became a steady beat.

"Dreyfus… Dreyfus… Dreyfus…"

He raised his hand, and they quieted a little.

"Look," he began, through the bullhorn. "I understand that you're angry. I am too. If what we've heard is true—and I think the evidence is compelling—then Gen Sys, Mayor House, and anyone else involved must and will be held accountable. But for the moment, this city is collapsing around our ears. Already basic services don't exist for many citizens, and the predictions are that it's only going to get worse.

"We can't fall apart now," he said. "We need leaders."

"You mean House?" someone shouted. "Screw that. Screw him!"

That was followed by a messy wave of rage that took a few moments to calm.

"No," Dreyfus said. "I do not mean Mayor House. We have law in the city. We have procedure. It's clear that—guilty or innocent—Mayor House does not have a mandate to govern. Under normal conditions, he would be under indictment even as we speak. Instead he's chosen to go the way of the tyrant, protecting himself with his office and the brave men and women who serve that office.

"He should and must step down. In the event a mayor cannot continue in office, he is replaced by the president of the Board of Supervisors—in this case, Daniel Ngyun, a good man, a capable man. That is what we should demand." He paused a moment to let that sink in, then continued. "To the policemen out there, you all know me. I may not be your chief anymore, but you know what I stand for. The mayor is right about one thing—we are deeply in crisis, and we cannot spare a single life on either side of this line. Not when we know our real enemy.

"We should not be fighting each other. We should be fighting this disease, this Simian Flu. We should demand full disclosure, *now*—about how the virus was created and how it might be cured. In holding back this information from the CDC, Gen Sys, Mayor House, and everyone involved has critically delayed the search for a cure. Who knows what might have happened if, rather than trying to cover their collective asses, they had instantly divulged the blueprint for this virus? There might already be a vaccination.

"So I'm talking to the police now. Stop fighting this fight. Your mayor is now Daniel Ngyun. Place yourselves under his control. That's the law. Everyone else, go home. Trashing City Hall isn't going to help anything. Odds are Mayor House isn't even in there."

* * *

Three hours later Dreyfus got a Skype call from Daniel Ngyun. The picture was pixilated, but the sound was clear.

"Way to put me on the spot, chief," he said.

"Oh, come on," Dreyfus replied. "You said it yourself—if you thought you could beat me in the primary, you would have run. Now you get to skip that part. Anyway, it was the only thing to do. So what's up? To what do I owe the honor of this call?"

"Well, we can't even find Mayor House right now," Ngyun said. "I've removed Burston and appointed Tremont as Chief—"

"Good choice," Dreyfus said. "But I was kind of hoping to fill those shoes again."

"Yes, I kind of figured that," Ngyun admitted, nodding. "But no go."

"Still, I need to do something, Daniel. Maybe you can find a place for me on your staff, or… something."

"From what I can tell, you're doing plenty," he said. "Quelling two riots, all of those talk shows, precipitating a more-or-less peaceful transition of authority. You haven't exactly been a couch potato. But I can't make you chief again."

"I understand," Dreyfus said, his heart sinking.

"I don't think you do," Ngyun responded, and there was a strange sound to his voice.

"I'm appointing you mayor," he added.

"You're what?"

"I convened a full meeting of the board. They didn't all show up, but I had a quorum. Congratulations."

"This is completely out of the ordinary," Dreyfus said. "Normally the president of the board—"

"The president of the board has the 113 virus," Ngyun said. "That's why I'm Skyping, instead of coming over there in person. I don't want to spread it around."

That silenced Dreyfus for a moment.

"Oh, shit, Danny, I'm sorry," he finally managed.

"I'm in the early stages," he said. "But we all know how quick this goes. What could I do in a couple of days? I'd rather—well—prepare."

"Maybe…"

Ngyun smiled faintly, and held up a hand.

"Yeah, I keep telling myself that, too. Maybe." He shook his head. "Good luck, Dreyfus," he said. "You're the man this city needs right now. In all of this you've been the steadiest, most reasonable voice, and the people know it. They'll follow you." He sighed. "My wife and kids are still clean. I'm counting on you to bring them through the other end of this."

"You have my word," Dreyfus said, "I'll do everything in my power. I swear it."

"I know you will. Come down this afternoon for a quick swearing-in ceremony, and then get to work." With a *bloop*, the screen went blank.

Dreyfus stared at it long after Ngyun's image had faded. Then he poured himself a Scotch, trying to absorb what had just happened, feeling the weight start to press on his shoulders.

"By God," he murmured to himself. "This is not how I wanted it to happen." He raised the glass. "To you, Daniel. Godspeed." He took a sip.

He'd wanted to be mayor. He'd wanted to be *elected* mayor. But right now, what he wanted didn't matter. This was how things fell out. And he knew the first thing he was going to do.

He took out his phone and punched in a number.

"Tremont," the voice on the other end announced.

"Hey Chief, I just heard," Dreyfus said. "Congratulations."

"Yeah," Tremont said. "About that. I told them I thought you should—"

"Nonsense," Dreyfus said. "You would have been my pick, too. If I'd had my say. Which in about an hour I will."

"Sir?"

"The board is making me mayor," he said.

There was silence on the other end of the line.

"That's good news," Tremont said.

"Look, I'm not sworn in yet, but I think there's something we should get on top of, right now, before it gets away from us. I know you've got a lot on your plate, but this is important."

"Whatever you say, Mr. Mayor."

What's bothering Caesar? Maurice asked, looking out over their new home, however temporary it might be.

Too quiet, he replied.

Too quiet, Maurice echoed.

Caesar watched a juvenile chimp playing with a young orangutan.

They will come again, he said. *But not the same way.*

I agree, Maurice signed.

They have a tricky thinker with them, Caesar said. *Learned our ways and used them against us. I think they were driving us to the helicopters, but helicopters went away.*

Maybe humans fighting each other, too, like in store, Maurice offered. *Maybe it's the disease you heard them talking about. Things may be getting worse for them. Maybe they don't care about us as much.*

They weren't together, Ceasar replied. *Something about their plan changed. I feel it. But if they try again, they won't try the same thing.* He looked at Maurice. *How would you catch apes?*

Maurice shifted slightly on his branch.

Get rid of trees, he said finally.

Caesar looked at the giants around him.

Humans come on ground, Maurice explained. *Helicopters come from the sky. Apes can go over humans on the ground, stay below the tops of the trees where helicopters can see.*

How could they get rid of the trees? Caesar wondered.

Fire, Maurice replied.

Caesar looked around again.

Burn this? he said. He remembered his trips here with Will, and the other humans he had seen. *This place is important even to humans. They wouldn't burn it.*

If Caesar says so, Maurice replied.

How else?

Maurice held up his hands, making two half-circles with them. He brought them together to form a circle.

Come from every direction, Caesar said. *Thought of that. But we could go up. Like you said.*

They could think of that, too, Maurice replied.

We're waiting on them again, Caesar said, his frustration mounting. *Waiting to respond to them.*

Maybe they won't do anything, Maurice signed.

Caesar looked over at the orangutan, and realized that Maurice was saying something that wasn't true, in order to be funny. What did Will call that?

A joke.

Caesar laughed. He didn't mean to—it just came out.

Maybe they all go in the water and swim away, he replied. *Maybe turn into fish and leave us alone.*

Maurice made a croaking sound that was probably supposed to be a laugh. Nearby apes heard them laugh and started laughing, too, just the way they did when they were playing with things.

Maybe apes still not too smart, Maurice said.

No, Caesar said, remembering a dinner party at Will's home. *Humans do this, too. Laugh when they don't hear the joke.*

Maybe humans not so smart, either.

18

"We're prisoners, aren't we?" Clancy asked him.

They were in the hut that served as their quarters, but it was clear that they were locked in even before he checked to make certain.

"Yes." Malakai nodded.

"Why?"

"It's good news," Malakai said. "It means they're still trying to decide what to do with us."

"You mean as opposed to just killing us," she said.

"You've worked that out," he said. "Very good."

"Crap," she said. "I hoped I was kidding. Would they really kill us?"

"You had to have suspected," he replied. "Everything so secret, no contact with anyone allowed. Does anyone even know you're here?"

"Well, David."

"That's the guy you emailed the other night."

"Yeah. But he sort of knew before. I wasn't supposed to tell him, but I did. He and I—we hang out."

"Hang out? What does that mean? You stand around in front of a store, drinking beer?"

"No. More like we have sex now and then."

"So he's your boyfriend."

"No," she said. "We just hang out."

"We're both speaking English, and yet I don't understand you."

"Holy shit," she said. "That was supposed to be a joke."

He shrugged.

"This is when you get funny?" she asked. "When you're about to die?"

"I've been here a lot of times," he said. "At some point, what else do you do?"

She was silent for a moment.

"You're a bad guy, aren't you?"

His first instinct was not to answer her at all, but then he saw she was really serious.

"Bad guy?" he said. "I don't know. "Remember how I told you my uncle took me to see the gorillas when I was eight?

"Yes."

"It was so I could learn how to kill them. And you know why we killed them? Because we were starving. And why were we starving? Because we were from the wrong tribe in the wrong place at the wrong time. So was I doing a bad thing to hunt bushmeat?"

"Gorillas are an endangered species," she said. "And they're as conscious as we are."

"What did that mean to me? My family was endangered."

"So anything you do is justified, if you do it to save yourself?"

"You see," he said, "this is the sort of question that does not occur to you when you are there, and people are assaulting your sister before they kill her with a machete.

And why it doesn't occur to me now that I should have to justify myself to a spoiled, western child. Whatever I've done, it is done. Any soul-searching would be a waste of time. If you kill someone, do you think they give a shit if you feel sorry about it later? Penitence is nothing but a form of self-indulgence. Some things you cannot wash from your hands, and there's no use in trying."

He saw that she had tears in her eyes.

"Oh, what are you doing now?" he snapped.

"I'm sorry," she said.

"About what?"

"I'm just sorry," she said.

Malakai lurched out of the chair, stalked out of the common room and sat on his own bed. He lifted his hands, staring at them, as if they weren't his at all, but some sort of alien appendages that had been grafted there.

He remembered the look in the eye of the ape leader. The purpose.

He heard a knock. It was Clancy, of course.

"Do you drink?" she asked.

She was holding a bottle of Scotch.

"Where did you get that?" he asked.

"I brought it with me," she said. "It wasn't electronic, and it wasn't a gun, so they let me keep it."

Malakai studied the bottle for a moment.

"Yes," he said finally. "I could use a drink."

She produced a pair of paper cups from the lavatory, and poured them each a shot.

"To whatever the hell that was we saw today," she said, raising her cup.

"To staying alive," he added, and they drank.

"You're not going to cry again are you?" he asked her, after a moment.

"You're just so... *damaged*," she said. "To see something like that—"

"Yes, yes," he said.

"How old were you?"

"Twelve," he said. "I was twelve."

She took another shot.

"Can you tell me more... about your family?"

"Oh, you want a bedtime story now?" he said, raising an eyebrow. "Are you sure about that?"

"Yes," she said, after a moment. "I want to know."

This is stupid, he thought. *Why should I even be speaking to her?*

He took another drink. It had been a while since he had whisky. It felt good in his belly.

"Very well," he said. "If you wish."

"I wish."

"I was twelve, as I said," Malakai began. "I was coming out of the hills." He smiled. "No bushmeat, this time. My uncle had acquired a few cows, and I was bringing them down from foraging. We had food to eat, every day. My mother made this thing, you know, that everybody made—*bugari*. It's just a sort of paste made from cassava or cornmeal. You roll up a ball of it and then you poke a hole, so it is like a little shot glass. And then you dip it in the stew. My mother made the best stew. In poor times, there was not much in it—a few ground peanuts, some hot chilies, coconut, maybe some caterpillars..."

He paused for a reaction from Clancy, but what he got wasn't what he was expecting.

"Gorilla," she added. "Chimpanzee."

"Ah," he said. "No. The gorilla meat we usually sold. More often than not my uncle would be asked to obtain some by a local official or rich man who would loan him a gun. Once we got to keep the head, but you don't make stew from that, you—"

"No," she said. "That's enough. How could you eat something so close to a human being?"

"As a matter of fact, my mother would not eat chimp, for that very reason. But others ate it. You forget, I think, that even human meat has been on the menu in many places and times. Indeed, some people I knew just around that time were eaten by Rega warriors."

"Right," she sighed. "I just... Okay, go ahead. Your mom made great stew."

"The best, but it was better if she had some meat, and that day I knew there was going to be chicken in it, and I was already imagining the taste, eager for it." He closed his eyes. "I can still remember the taste.

"You see, we not only had the cattle, my mother and sister had found sewing jobs. There was a lot of excitement in the air, too, that year—our country had become independent just a few years before. There was a lot of turmoil, but to us it seemed far away. We were a small village, of no interest to anyone.

"My buddy Jean-Francis was with me. He was a year older, I think, a smart boy. He was Hutu and my mother was Nyanga, but that wasn't such a big deal back then."

"What about your father?" Clancy asked.

"Ah, my father," Malakai said. "Well, you know, I never knew him. He was an American, you see, an anthropologist. He came to the Congo to study the natives, and I guess he did. He studied my mother, anyway. Then he left."

"I'm sorry."

"It is nothing," he said. "He was never there, so how could I miss him? And my uncle was there, my mother's brother. He raised me as well as any father."

"I didn't mean to interrupt."

He shrugged. "So we're coming back with the cows, and I'm dreaming of chicken stew with *bugari*, and we hear these sounds. At first we think we've missed a festival of some sort, and we hurry to get closer. But when we realize what we're hearing, we slow down.

"We are hearing gunshots, and people screaming. The people in our village. We leave the cows and creep down closer, to where the trees come up to the fence. And then we see, you know? There are men with guns, killing everyone. Everything that moves. I see little Marie, she's five years old. She's just staring at them, no idea what is going on, and then a bullet hits her, and she's gone like a broken light bulb."

"Why?" Clancy asked, her eyes wide. "Why would they do that?"

"At the time I didn't know. There was a rebellion in my part of the country, by a group called Simba. The leaders were communists, but they attracted a lot of tribal leaders and people who didn't like what was going on in our new country. It was, as you say, complicated. It made countries like the United States very nervous. Nervous enough to put their support behind pretty much any leader who was not a communist. The men I saw that day were mercenaries. Most were white men from South Africa and Rhodesia, but some were from Europe and America. They were under orders to take no prisoners, to kill everyone, to set an example so that no other village would give aid to Simba."

"Did your village give them aid?' she asked.

"I don't know," he replied. "Maybe. After it was over, there was no one to ask."

He paused to give her time to ask another one of her endless questions, but she was silent.

"Anyway," he said. "Jean-Francis sees his little brother,

and he can't stop himself, he jumps over the fence and runs toward the men. They do not see him until he's on one of them. But Jean doesn't know much about fighting, and the mercenary does, and he clubs poor Jean to death with the butt of his rifle. Me, I run when I see this, I run until I remember my mother and my sister are down there, and then I start to go back.

"Our house was a little outside the village, so I was hoping they would be okay. They weren't—they… Well I told you already. My mother was already dead, but they weren't finished with my sister yet. When I saw it, I went mad. There were three of them. I was just running at them, screaming, but they knocked me down, and one held me and made me watch. And then they were going to kill me."

"What happened?"

"What happened is my uncle comes out of nowhere with his machete and kills the one who is holding a gun. The other two didn't have a chance. I remember…"

He stopped.

"It's okay," Clancy said. "You don't have to."

He shook his head. "I remember I could smell the *bugari* scorching, and thinking how it would ruin the whole meal," he said. "That's what I remember going through my mind. Anyway, then my uncle grabs me and we run away, up into the hills, where we can hide. We hide in the jungle for more than a week. Hiding like these apes, here, now that I think of it. But we couldn't climb so well." He looked at Clancy. "Could you spare another drink of that?"

"Of course," she said, pouring him another shot.

He took a long swallow, wondering again why he was telling her any of this. But there was something about being here, about the trees, the mist, the men with guns, that was making it swell up in him, that forced him to put it into words.

"What did you do after?"

"We joined Simba," he said.

"You were twelve!"

"Many men are soldiers by that age," he said. "On both sides. Many still are. In my group in particular, there were many boys, and girls, too, some younger than me. We were baptized, and shamans chanted, and the shamans told us we were invulnerable to bullets. They gave us marijuana to get us high. We stayed stoned most of the time, which was probably for the best because they armed us only with traditional weapons: spears, clubs, bow and arrow. Although our leaders usually had guns."

"Oh, my God."

"I don't think God had much to do with any of it," he said. "My first battle—if you want to call it that—was in this little town, not much bigger than the one I was born in. We had rounded up every man, woman, and child that might be 'westernized.' Police, public officials, anyone that was white, of course—anyone who knew how to read or write French. Then we executed them with spears, machetes, clubs, and what have you. We wiped out whole villages, just as they did. I was so stoned I barely remember any of it."

That part was a lie. He remembered the first man he had ever killed. He was a young schoolteacher whose crime was teaching western ideas. He begged for his life, but all Malakai could think of was his mother and his sister and the burnt *bugari*. The marijuana made everything unreal; the machete in his hand felt like a magic stick as it made pieces of the teacher, and as he did it he remembered butchering gorillas. It was very much the same.

Clancy was studying him, eyes still wide.

"You asked if I was a bad man," he said. "Now you know."

"I am so sorry," she whispered.

"It's nothing," he said.

"No," she said. "I mean I'm so sorry I asked. I'm going back to my room now."

But then there was the sudden noise of a door opening at the other end of the building.

"Oh, God," Clancy said. "Is this it?"

"I don't know," he said.

"Hold my hand," she said.

"What?"

"I don't want to die alone," she said.

We all die alone, he thought, but he resisted saying it. Instead he took her hand as they waited.

The man who came in, however, wasn't one of the Anvil mercenaries—it was a San Francisco policeman in SWAT gear with a respirator pulled over his face.

"Oh, thank God," she said.

Malakai had no such reaction. A uniform did not signify safety. Usually, in his experience, it was quite the opposite. He waited for the man to raise his weapon, for the muzzle flash that would be the last thing he saw.

But the officer studied them for a moment.

"If you folks would come with me," he said, "there are some people who want to talk to you."

They were separated. Malakai was taken to a makeshift shower and scrubbed down by two men wearing hazmat suits. Then he was given a clean orange jumpsuit that reminded him of prison garb.

When he saw Clancy again, her face was pink and she was similarly dressed. She looked scared again.

Trumann Phillips's office was a very different place than when last Malakai had been in it. For one thing, Phillips wasn't there. In his place was a man he had seen on television, a former chief of police. Dreyfus was his name, he remembered. It was thought he would run for mayor.

"I'm sorry for the institutional orange," Dreyfus said, when they were brought in. "It's the only thing we had on hand. Your own clothes are being cleaned and sterilized, and we'll have them back to you soon." He folded his hands in front of him.

"I need to make this quick," he said. "There's a lot to do, and not much time to do it in. Could you please tell me your names?"

"My name is Malakai Youmans," Malakai said, nodding.

"I'm Clancy Stoppard," Clancy said. "We met once at a fundraiser for the zoo, Chief Dreyfus."

"It's actually Mayor Dreyfus now," he said. "I'll have one of my aides bring you up to speed. So you two are the experts they brought in to help them find the apes."

"That is correct," Malakai said.

"Good," Dreyfus said. "So, for now, let me briefly explain that Anvil, the company that hired you, is under investigation for a number of illegal activities. Mr. Phillips is under arrest—we caught him trying to leave by helicopter. The rest of the crew here has been detained. That the two of you were being kept under lock and key suggests to me that Mr. Phillips might not have had your best interests in mind, at this point."

"I surmised that, sir," Malakai told him.

"What I need from you two is to know exactly what we're dealing with here. In terms of the apes."

Clancy glanced at Malakai before beginning, as if she wanted his approval... or complicity. He nodded again, and she turned to face the mayor.

"They're smart," she said. "They're organized."

"How many would you estimate?"

"Two hundred," Malakai said. "Minimum. It could be more."

"Have you had direct contact with them?" Dreyfus asked.

Taking turns, Clancy and Malakai gave a brief description of their encounter. Dreyfus took all of it in without expression.

"Now I want to ask you both this," he said. "Are they dangerous?"

"I think they just want to be left alone," Clancy said. "Even when we provoked them, even when one of them was shot, they never tried to hurt us." Malakai heard the pleading in her voice as she went on. "They probably won't survive the winter. Apes are native to the tropics. I don't think there's enough here for them to eat."

"They've raided groceries already, right?" the mayor said. "Maybe when winter comes, as you say, they'll become more aggressive. More desperate."

"They deserve a chance."

"Mr. Youmans?"

He felt Clancy's gaze burning at him.

"I agree with her," he said. "They probably will die in the winter. If they come into town to loot, shoot them then. Otherwise, I would not waste more man-hours on this."

Dreyfus stared at them incredulously.

"You guys have really been completely out of the loop, haven't you?" he said. "You have no idea what things are like back there, back in the city."

"We heard something about an outbreak of some kind," Clancy said. "But we haven't been allowed to have television or the Internet or anything."

"Well, suffice to say, a few hundred apes coming into town to raid for food might be a lot more trouble than you think by the time winter gets here."

"But think of the scientific value," Clancy said. "What's happening here is amazing. Apes of different species, forming some sort of social group. What we could learn from this—"

"I'll consider everything you've said," Dreyfus said, cutting her off. But he didn't say anything more. The conversation was clearly over.

"Are we free to go?" Malakai asked.

"Since you were in close contact with the apes, you'll need to be held here in quarantine for a few days. You've been isolated out here—so far no one has shown up positive. If you didn't catch it from the apes, you're probably clean. If you don't show any signs of the disease, then you can do as you please. Although once you understand the situation, I highly doubt you'll want to go out."

"We've missed a lot, it appears," Malakai said.

Clancy was watching the news with a look of utter shock on her young face.

"Welcome to 'C' Hut," Corbin said, popping open a beer and flopping into a chair.

It was the first time they had been in "C" hut, the building that had served as an entertainment center for the mercenaries. It contained two pool tables, some videogame consoles, and a large television. There was also a fridge that appeared to contain mostly beer.

The bulk of the mercenaries seemed to be here, including Corbin and his team. Like Clancy and Malakai, they were all now dressed in prison orange. The big difference was that the people now patrolling the compound were San Francisco PD, and the police were the only ones armed.

"What's happening?" Clancy said, staring at the television, her voice trembling.

Corbin picked up a remote and turned up the volume.

"...rioters looting pharmacies, leaving ten dead and fifteen wounded. But our top story tonight comes from Alameda Point, where the site of the former Naval Air Station has been set up as a quarantine and treatment facility, one of many throughout the Bay Area.

"At around two in the morning, large sections of the tent city were set ablaze by masked individuals armed with improvised bombs filled with homemade napalm. So far the casualty count is uncertain, but is thought to be upwards of five hundred dead and hundreds more with severe burns. The crowded condition of the camp worsened a situation that would have been devastating under any circumstances.

"Police haven't announced any suspects, but graffiti outside of the compound features the juxtaposed Greek letters Alpha and Omega. These same symbols were found two days ago near the site of a mass shooting at a clinic in Chinatown. A similar and perhaps related napalm attack was carried out about an hour ago at a quarantine facility maintained at a local hospital. The name and location of that facility is being withheld as police fight to get control of the situation."

"How can people behave like this?" Clancy said.

"Welcome to my world," Malakai said.

"I heard you were in some of that business in Rwanda," Corbin said. "You must have seen some pretty nasty things there."

"I suppose," Malakai said, regretting he had said anything.

"I think if they're scared and angry enough, people will

do almost anything," Corbin said.

"But this... This is San Fra—" Clancy began, and then she stopped abruptly.

"San Francisco," Malakai continued for her. "San Francisco, in the USA, as opposed to some third-world hellhole where people eat gorillas."

Corbin and the rest laughed.

Her face, pink from the industrial scrubbing, darkened.

"I wasn't going to say that," she said. "Some pretty awful things have happened in this country—slavery, genocide, riots, mass murders. It's just... I was there a week ago, and everything was normal. How did it go from that to this so quickly?"

"Because in that less than a week, a total of more than 250,000 people have dropped dead of a plague that kills everyone that gets it," Flores said. "And now they're calling it the 'Simian Flu' because those monkeys out there are the ones that gave it to us."

Clancy frowned.

"We were briefed after talking to the mayor," she said. "My impression is that the virus was developed by Gen Sys."

"Yeah. And spread by monkeys."

"From what I've been told, the prime vector was probably a man that worked at the lab, not an ape."

"Why is it called the Simian Flu, then?" Flores shot back.

"Just..." she sighed. "I've watched more of this than I can take. Is there a computer or a tablet or something around here I can use?"

"Right over there," Corbin said.

Malakai continued watching, however. It wasn't just San Francisco that was collapsing. Paris had descended into a similar purgatory. Mumbai had a death toll at almost half a million. Most major cities around the world had some share in the pandemic. Airlines were grounded over much of the globe, train and bus lines were shut down. Food was vanishing from grocery shelves and warehouses, and wasn't being replaced due to the transportation stoppage. Healthcare systems were so swamped with victims of the Simian Flu that the death toll for every other malady had skyrocketed.

And it wasn't just the human race suffering. All over the country—the world—people were breaking into zoos, killing apes, monkeys, tarsiers, sloths—anything that looked faintly simian, apparently because the actual facts that gave rise to the term "Simian Flu" hadn't traveled with the term.

He glanced over at Corbin, now on his third beer. If the apes really were carriers, then Corbin was the most likely of them to have been infected, although all of them had been near ape corpses. He had touched one.

Well, they would know in a day or two.

Across the room, Clancy abruptly started sobbing, and a moment later she ran from the room.

They had been watching American cable television, so there was next to nothing concerning the continent of Africa, much less his homeland, but later that night he went online to learn that fresh fighting had broken out in North and South Kivu, again shattering the region along tribal and ethnic divisions. He wondered how long it would be before the death toll from starvation, trauma, neglect, and lack of general healthcare would surpass that of the disease itself.

The 133 retrovirus was a hard, cold killer, but the human race was giving it a run for its money.

19

Dreyfus sat in the mayor's chair for the first time, and reflected that nothing was ever what you expected.

He had believed he would one day sit here. He had worked for it. But the chair seemed somehow too big at the moment, and the warm hardwood walls too close. He thought of all of those who had been here before him, one of whom had lost his life in this very office. He wondered how he would be remembered, or even *if* he would be remembered.

"Okay," he told Patel. "Bring him in."

Patel opened the door, and a moment later Trumann Phillips walked in. Dreyfus did not offer him a seat. He preferred to leave him standing.

"Let's cut through all the bullshit," Dreyfus said. "Why did House bring you in?"

Phillips didn't blink.

"I would prefer to answer that question with an attorney present," he replied.

"Are you goddamn *kidding* me?" Dreyfus exploded. "Where do you think you are? The worst thing I could do to you right now is put you on the street. There's a mob out there screaming for your blood. And if they don't kill you, your goddamn Simian Flu will."

"As you must know," Phillips said, "I had no hand in the actual creation of the virus. I don't even work for Gen Sys."

"No, you work for Polytechnic Solutions, which owns Gen Sys. You're their cleanup man." He leaned forward and studied a report on his desk. "Yes, I've done some research on you. You have a sterling record for 'fixing' things. Kuantan, Malaysia, 1997, you 'fixed' a toxic chemical dump that was poisoning the drinking water of thousands of people. Except ten years later the dump was still there, and the people had mysteriously moved elsewhere, or just—hey!—vanished.

"Or that thing in Bangladesh. The alleged malfeasance in Iraq by Anvil, all of the witnesses unfortunately slain in a roadside bomb attack. You were involved in all of that, and I'm sure you know I could go on."

"And as you must know," Phillips said, "I've never been indicted for anything. Because I'm not guilty of anything."

"No, you're just the kind of guy who gets away with things. Until now. Now that we know what to look for, we've got connections between you and House going back twenty years, when he was an assistant DA. You've been fattening him up for a long time, and it finally came time for you to slaughter the pig. You convinced him to let you handle the situation. To keep everything quiet."

"I—" Phillips began, but Dreyfus held up a hand to stop him.

"Just answer the question," he said. "Why were you brought in?"

Phillips hesitated for a moment.

"You know why," he said.

"I want to hear it from you."

"We needed to contain the situation," Philips finally

said. "Our first priority was to keep secret the fact that Gen Sys created the virus. At that point we had no way of knowing how bad it was going to turn out to be. The hope was that by the time anyone found out, if they ever found out, we would have worked out a cure. And for that we needed apes infected with the virus."

"Why?"

"Because it doesn't kill them. We need to know why."

"Why not infect another captive ape?"

"It's not that simple," Phillips said. "In humans, the virus mutates. Apes can't get it from us. And we don't have access to any of the original serum."

"So you've really been trying to catch apes."

"And keep the particulars... insulated. My people haven't been allowed contact with anyone outside. At least not until you put them at their liberty."

"You found them, I understand. Why didn't you follow through?"

"Everyone was paying too much attention to us. There were protesters outside our perimeter. We shut down, hoping things would go quiet."

"Can you still do it?"

The change that came over Phillips's face at that moment was subtle, but Dreyfus saw it. The man was just realizing that this conversation wasn't about what he had thought it was.

"I'm sure we can," he said. "With a little help."

Dreyfus thought about that for a moment.

"What else would you need to make this work?"

"Enough men to actually encircle the beasts—that would be nice," Phillips said. He was beginning to radiate confidence.

"That's going to be tough, given that every able body on the force, in the Guard, and in the reserves is already on task somewhere." Dreyfus sat back. "Still, if I sell it right, I think I can get the governor to commit more National Guard. But I need to know you won't screw it up this time. That you'll get it done."

"I'll get it done," Phillips replied. "But I want something in return."

"I'll bet you do," Dreyfus said. He leaned forward again. "I want you to understand something. I don't like you, Phillips. I would love to see you burn. But if there is a chance to stop this disease, we're going to take it, and you're what I have. You and your team already know the situation. If you get this right, I might just be able to rewrite history enough to keep you from being torn limb from limb by an angry mob."

Phillips lips twisted into a faint, sardonic smile.

"That's the best deal I've heard today."

"It's the best deal you're going to get," Dreyfus said. "The next best deal—you wouldn't like that very much."

"Well, then. Shall we shake on it?"

"I'd rather not," Dreyfus said. "I feel dirty enough just talking to you."

Phillips didn't look pleased—he clearly wasn't accustomed to being spoken to in this manner.

"There are some details of the plan—" he began.

"I know all that I want to know," Dreyfus interposed. "Get some of those things alive. I don't care how you do it. And just to make it clear, I don't want anything from Anvil, or Gen Sys, or anyone else involved in this. Just do your job and quietly go away. I have enough to deal with."

Koba stared up at the moon. He worried about it sometimes, worried that it might fall on him, fall on all of them. Fall on Caesar. He couldn't see what kept it up.

Until Caesar led him into the woods, he had never seen the moon.

Koba wakes and he is not in the sky. He is on something cold.

He is in a cage again, but it is not Tommy's cage. This cage does not force him to stand up, but the floor is hard, and gritty, and cold. The cage is also not very big. He looks around for Milo, but doesn't see him anywhere. There is something in the next cage. He signs at it, but it looks at him blankly, and he realizes it is a big caterpillar.

The light in the place comes from long tubes, high overhead. Sometimes they go off for a long time.

Someone comes to feed him. She reminds him of Mary, so he signs to her. She doesn't seem to notice, so he does his "smile," his "talk," his "funny walk."

She chuckles a little.

"Aren't you funny," she says. "I wonder what happened to your eye."

He tries to tell her by sign, but she just moves on and feeds the caterpillar.

Koba remembers outside and tries to get out of his cage, but finds no way out. Over the next cycle of light and dark he realizes that there are many, many cages, and that they all contain big caterpillars. He is the only one who isn't, he realizes. Some sort of mistake has been made. The next time someone comes to feed him, he tries to explain this, but they won't talk to him. He knows they can talk, because they do the sound talk to each other. Why won't they talk to him?

He hopes that soon they will realize their mistake and that he should be someplace doing tricks, even if his eye is ugly now.

On the other hand, no one has hit him with a stick since he arrived.

The next time someone comes, he tries again. It is two men. They still won't talk to him, but they point to a little bed they have brought with them and open his cage. They put a leash on him. He tries to show them that he already knows the trick of lying in bed, not curled up but lying out straight.

"Good boy," one of the men says.

Then they put things on his hands and feet and across his chest, so he can't move. At first Koba thinks of it as part of the trick, and he tries to "smile" and "look silly." When he does that, they stick something in his mouth, so he can't close it, and they push it in so far that he can't open it any further either. He thinks of Milo with his mouth wired shut, and he starts to panic. He tries to ask them to stop, but he can't use his hands.

They think he is a big caterpillar, and they are going to do to him whatever it is they do to big caterpillars.

They take Koba to a very bright room and they give him a shot. He knows what shots are. Mary used to give them, and said they would keep him from getting sick. They don't want him to get sick, so he feels a little better.

Except that he does get sick. First his stomach hurts, and then he starts to vomit. The thing in his mouth won't let anything out, so he is breathing his own vomit, and he can't get any air.

The next thing he knows he is back in his cage, on the hard floor, still sick. He keeps shaking. The thing they put in his mouth is gone, so his teeth chatter together.

He is like this for several cycles of the lights. Then they come to get him once more. He tries to sign to them again, but he is too weak. He sees that the little bed is ready for him, but he is scared and backs up into the corner of the cage.

"He went quiet last time," one of them says.

"Yeah," the other says. "He's catching on fast."

He pulls out a thing like Tommy pointed at him, like the other man in the house pointed at him. There is a strange, explosive sound.

Something hits him in the chest and knocks him back against the wall. He looks down and sees another thing sticking out of him, like the one that hit him in the tree.

Koba good, he signs desperately. But it's too late. He is starting to feel dizzy and sick and sleepy.

Koba is back in his cage, feeling a horrible pain in his side, like something has been stuck all the way through him. His head hurts, and he starts vomiting again.

He misses Milo and he wants someone to sign with him. He even misses Tommy. He is used to the stick. He could guess when Tommy was going to use the stick, and why. Here, pain just happens.

For a long time nothing happens at all. People come and feed him. They ignore him when he tries to talk to them, and he begins to wonder if he is signing right. Maybe he doesn't really know how to sign, and it is just the colors that come into his head at night that make him think he can.

Maybe Koba really is just a big caterpillar.

There is nothing to do in the cage, and he never leaves it except when they hurt him. He has no toys, so he begins plucking out his hair and arranging it on the floor. He thinks maybe he can make some buttons to talk with. He arranges his plucked hair in the symbols he remembers, but the hair doesn't stay arranged. It moves, it gets disturbed. It is annoying, and so sometimes he screams at it.

He begins signing to himself, signing onto the floor, sometimes for a whole light cycle. His fingers and knuckles bleed from signing against the floor.

There is a long period he cannot remember. Then one day someone comes to his cage. Two people. Koba does not look at them.

"Koba," one says. He knows the sound. It seems familiar.

"This is a waste of time," another voice says.

"Koba," the man repeats.

Koba gradually turns his head. The man is doing something with his hands. At first he doesn't recognize the motion, it has been so long. But then he understands, and a tiny part of him remembers.

Koba.

He rolls to his feet.

Do you know sign? the man is asking. It feels like his mother's arms going around him.

Koba know sign, he answers.

"I told you!" the man exclaims to the other man.

I am not big caterpillar, Koba signs.

The man looks puzzled.

What is big caterpillar? he asks.

Koba gestures at the thing in the cage beside him, then to all of the other cages.

The man laughs.

"What is it?" the other man asks.

"He thinks the other chimps are caterpillars," he says.

"Or maybe he's signing gibberish," the second man tells him.

"No," the first man says. "It's classic. We definitely have

a language ape on our hands."

"That's wonderful if it is true," the second man says. "But God, he's an ugly fellow."

Koba isn't sure what to do. He knows they are talking about him. So he does a "smile." He "dances."

"See?" the first man says. "I checked his records. He was on the TV show, *Monkey of the House*."

"I'm afraid I never heard of it," the second man says. "I've got better things to do than watch television."

"It was canceled after the first season," the first man says.

Koba, the man signs. *Can you do your numbers?*

Eager to please him, Koba starts counting. He gets to three and realizes he doesn't remember the next number. He becomes agitated. What if the man becomes angry with him, and stops signing? He cannot bear the thought. He beats against the cage frantically.

It's okay, the man signs. *Maybe you forgot.* The man makes soothing sounds. Koba feels the panic retreating. And then he remembers. He smiles. He tries to dance.

Four, he signs, and keeps going until the man stops him at twenty-five.

Know sign, Koba said. *Not big caterpillar.*

"He's remembering fast," the first man says.

"Good," the second man replies. "We can use him then. Get him ready."

"Koba," the first man says. "My name is Amol. This is Mr. Jacobs. Would you like to work with us for a little while?" Koba isn't sure of what he is saying, but the way he speaks reminds Koba of Mary.

Koba like sign, he replies.

Good, Amol tells him. *We'll do lots of sign.*

"This had better pay off, Amol," Jacobs says, and he walks away.

They bring one the beds they tie him to, and a man

pulls out one of the ugly things that hit him and make him sleep.

He looks up at the man who knows sign.

Koba not big caterpillar, he signs, desperately. *Koba good. No hurt.*

I know, the man says. *Koba smart chimp. Knows sign. We go do sign together.*

Not hurt Koba again?

We sign, the human said.

He turns to the other man.

"You don't need the tranq gun," he says. "Koba will be good."

"It's your funeral, Doc," the fellow says. He steps back, but he keeps the thing—the "gun"?—out.

Reluctantly, Koba climbs onto the table, and they strap him down. He wants to keep signing. He wants to talk. Instead they give him a shot, and he falls asleep.

When he wakes, he can't move. Something hurts at the bottom of the back of his head, and it feels like his back is burning all the way down. The pain is so terrible he can't think.

Koba did good, Amol tells him.

A few days later, it still hurts, but not as much. He can move again, but something is attached to his head and to his back. Black cables come from behind him and plug into machines with lights and pictures of nothing.

Amol comes back.

Now we sign, Amol says. He holds up a blue card.

What color is this? he asks.

Blue, Koba says.

And this?

Yellow.

It goes on like that. Amol just keeps asking questions, and Koba tries to answer them. The screens make pretty colors and weird pictures. Sometimes he sees letters, too, and numbers.

After a while, Mr. Jacobs comes.

"How is this going?" Mr. Jacobs asks. Koba does not like the way Mr. Jacobs looks at him.

"Very well, Mr. Jacobs," Amol says. "I think he's an ideal candidate."

"Good. Continue, then. I would like to see your results at week's end."

"Yes, sir."

Amol asks a few more questions, then he gets a shot needle and goes around behind Koba.

"This will sting just a little," he says.

Whatever was in the back of his skull suddenly seems to come alive with pain. Koba shrieks.

What? What? Koba asks.

The man leans forward.

Study Koba in here, he says, tapping Koba's head. *Maybe help people one day.*

Help Koba, he signs. *Help Koba.*

It's going to be okay, the man says. *Be like a game.*

Amol brings him a button board. It's not exactly like the one Mary gave him, but he likes it. He likes it so much that he hardly notices the injections, and the stuff on his back that keeps him from moving right. He wants to show Amol all of his tricks, because Amol seems to be becoming more and more disturbed. He pays less attention to Koba and more to the funny colors and patterns that appear on his rectangles.

He is agitated.

* * *

It is another day, and the men come to take Koba from his cage. They do not shoot him. He goes willingly on the little bed.

But they do not take him to where his button board is, to the room where he signs. Instead they take him to the place where pain lives.

Amol is there, though, so he isn't as scared.

"We're all done, Koba," he says. "We can take all of this stuff off of you now."

Koba good, he signs. *Koba sign with Amol.*

Amol watches him as he gets the shot. Koba goes to sleep.

Koba wakes in his cage, on the cold floor. He feels sick, as he always does when they make him sleep.

The weight is off of his back, but it hurts again—he can feel the now-familiar tightness of the strings they push through his skin to hold him together after they cut him up. The pain is worth it, though, to have the weight off. He looks forward to Amol's next visit, so they can talk without the weight and the injections. He looks forward to using his button board again.

The lights cycle on and off once, but Amol does not come. Another cycle passes, and still no Amol. Koba loses count of the cycles. He signs to the people who feed him, telling them he wants Amol, but they ignore him as before.

Jacobs comes one day. He squats down and looks hard at Koba.

Koba want to sign Amol, Koba tells him. *Hurt Koba so Koba can talk,* he pleads. *Hurt Koba so Koba can talk. Hurt Koba so Koba can talk...*

Jacobs does not sign. He looks angry.

"You stupid, ugly monkey," he says. "If you had any idea what you and that idiot Amol have cost me... By God,

I wish I could put you down myself. If I were still in charge, I would."

He hits the cage with his hand, so hard that Koba jumps back. Jacobs keeps looking at him.

Then Koba notices something. Jacobs has something hanging around his neck. It has a rectangle on it. On the rectangle there are some letters. He remembers letters from the place with his mother. He thinks it means something, but he can't think what.

Jacobs makes a noise in the back of his throat. Then he leaves.

More light, more dark, light-dark, light-dark blurring together, faster and faster and yet so slow.

Koba stops looking for Amol. He knows Jacobs made Amol go away. He knows Amol will not come back.

Koba begins to pull his hair out again. He begins to sign his fingers against the floor until they bleed. And over and over he sees the face of Jacobs in the blood on the concrete. And the rectangle, with the letters on it.

20

"All of them," Clancy said.

He had heard her crying most of the night. Now she was in the aftershock, he knew—the terrible still place when the initial animal grief finally drains and leaves a numbness that borders on insensibility.

"Mom, Dad, Renee, Jack—how could it happen so fast? I saw them three weeks ago. They were fine." She looked off into the distance. "Like San Francisco was… fine."

"I am truly very sorry for your loss," he said.

She looked at him, and he saw a spark of anger there.

"Do you really feel anything?" she asked.

He shrugged. "To be honest," he said, "I don't know. After a certain point, it's better not to, you know?"

"God," she said. "Why does it have to be you? Why do you have to be the only one I can talk to in this stinking place?"

The remark took him off-guard—not because it was surprising, but because he was thinking the same thing.

"What about this fellow you 'hang out' with? You have your phone now."

"He's an asshole," she said. "I asked him to quietly check something out, and two days later it's on the front page. He never even tried to warn me—I checked. Anyway, it's hard to call anyone, given the shape the network is in. It was a miracle I got through to Uncle Hamm." She closed her eyes. "Ten missed calls from him. I knew it wasn't going to be good, but damn. I was going to see them at Christmas. What the hell am I going to do at Christmas?"

"They don't live here?"

She shook her head. "They're on the other coast, in the DC area. My dad is an engineer and Mom is..." She stopped, started again. "Dad *was* an engineer. Mom *was* an art teacher. Renee was going to graduate high school. Jack was only eight." Tears were rolling down her cheeks again, and her countenance was that of utter devastation. He had seen it so many times he had once joked that it just bored him now.

Do you feel anything?

He really didn't know.

"You have other family?" he asked, more to be polite now.

"I have cousins I'm not very close to," she said. "My grandfather on my mom's side, maybe. Uncle Hamm didn't know if he was okay or not. And Uncle Hamm."

"Well, that's something."

She shook her head. "What if they die, too?"

She glanced over at him.

"What about you? Do you have anyone? A wife?"

"No," he said. "I haven't even tried. There really isn't anyone."

He put his palms on his thighs and pushed himself to standing.

"I think," he said, "I shall take a walk."

She nodded and looked down. Then she started weeping again.

He sighed. "Would you like to come with me?" he asked.

"Yes," she said. "I was alone with this all night. I don't think I can take being alone any longer."

"There's always 'C' hut," he pointed out.

"Right. Get all buddy-buddy with the guys who were maybe going to put bullets in our brains. No thanks."

The fog had retreated for the afternoon, and the sky above was a clear, bright blue. Clancy's words hung with him, and he imagined Corbin placing the barrel of a gun to her head.

He remembered another man, a mercenary.

"What are you thinking about?" Clancy asked.

"I am certain you don't want to know," he said. He glanced up at the trees. "You were right, by the way. They are quite beautiful."

"Yeah," she agreed. "It's kind of weird that the park is so empty. Usually when I came here, there were people everywhere. Now..." She frowned. "What if everyone dies, Malakai?" she asked. "What if nothing stops this disease?"

"I don't know," he said. "It is strange. I haven't thought about it."

"You don't think much about the future, do you?"

"Not so much," he admitted. "Thinking about things that aren't yet real can distract you from the man who is about to kill you."

"I guess when you join the army at twelve, you can start thinking like that." She turned to him. "I mean, have you *always* been fighting?"

"Oh, no," he said. "When I joined Simba, they were almost done already. We killed so many people, more than the other side, perhaps. Just people, going about their lives, with no interest in political matters. There was no sympathy for us in the countryside…"

He stopped and looked at her.

"Why is this of interest to you?" he asked. "My life? The things I've done?"

"I don't know," she said. "I guess because you're the first person I hate and like at the same time. I don't understand it. I don't understand you and I don't understand myself any better, I guess. And I don't want to think about me right now. I guess I keep hoping you'll say something to tip me one way or the other, so I don't have these mixed feelings."

He took a few more steps. Then he shrugged.

"The other guys were also stronger," he said. "The Belgians eventually came in, and the US, as well. Once again my uncle spirited me away. We couldn't go home—it was too dangerous, and there was nothing to go home to. So we went to Burundi. We started poaching chimpanzees."

"I thought chimps were too close to people to eat," she said.

"So my mother believed," he said. "Others did not think so. But we were trying to catch them alive, to sell to westerners. It was there in Burundi I met my wife."

"I thought you said—"

"Well, I don't, now," he told her.

"Oh."

He met Solange when he was seventeen. She was of the Tutsi tribe, and her family had a small cattle ranch in the hills. He and his uncle did day labor for her father. He and Solange began meeting in a place with a waterfall and a small pool. She was fifteen to his seventeen, small, dark-skinned for a Tutsi. Beautiful to his eyes. Some other young men said her face was too round and her mouth too wide, but those were the things that made her appealing to him.

They talked a great deal, and over time there was some fondling and kissing, but she was very Christian, and although he knew he might press her to have sex, he also knew she would regret it, and he wanted her to have no regrets. He felt as if she was a wind coming through him that would blow away the past and bring him a new future.

Her parents didn't dislike him, but he knew that they would never let him marry her if he could not come up with a bride price—which he would never make watching cows and mending fences.

"We'll hunt chimps," his uncle said. "I know a man who knows a man—we can get a good price."

And like that, they went back into the poaching business.

The first morning of the hunt found them in the deep hills, waking around the remains of a fire. Besides his uncle and himself there were two other men, Patrick and Emery, both of whom had hunted chimps before. Malakai wasn't particularly happy with that—he didn't know the men that well. Still, the cage they had with them was heavy enough empty. It would be good to have more men to carry it when it was full of apes.

They ate a cold breakfast of boiled cornmeal and then started out to where Patrick insisted that chimps could be found. Chimpanzees, it turned out, were far easier to find than gorillas. They often used human trails, and their sign was everywhere. And they were noisy.

They caught up to a troop in an upland basin. Patrick was the first to spot one, but by the time he did, the chimps already knew they were there, and were making quite a bit of noise.

"Walk forward slowly," Patrick said. "Try not to seem

threatening. We're looking for a little one, a baby. Those are easiest to carry and to sell. No one wants an old buck."

Malaki kept his weapon down as they moved into the trees. The chimps were scampering all around them, now, and some of the bigger ones were starting to make him nervous—coming too close, making aggressive movements. He tried to count them, but it was hard because they kept moving. He figured there were about twenty.

"There we go," his uncle murmured. He pointed ahead, to where a baby clung to its mother. When the mother saw them, she clambered into the low branches of a tree. One of the big males started screeching even louder as they approached.

His uncle had the net ready, and moved slowly toward the chimp and her baby. When he was close enough, he tossed the net.

The little chimp nimbly dodged it, hopping onto the mother's back. Simultaneously one of the big apes leapt right up into Uncle's face.

Patrick's rifle roared, and the chimp pitched back. The other chimps screamed and retreated, but as soon as the men started toward the juvenile again, they came back with a vengeance. The mother, on the other hand, backed off, letting the rest of the troop defend her.

A big one dropped down right in front of Malakai, and for a moment he was arrested by its gaze—not so much angry as panicked, a look he had seen on plenty of human faces. It snapped at him with its teeth, and without putting a thought into it Malakai shot the beast. It screeched and bounded back, pawing at the wound.

Then Patrick shot the mother.

She tumbled off of her perch and thudded to the ground. The baby managed to jump free, but it immediately leapt down and crouched behind her. She wasn't dead, yet; she reached back and took the baby in her arms, still trying to defend it as she scooted away on the jungle floor.

They were forced to kill fifteen chimps before the troop finally backed off enough for them to retrieve the baby. It was still clinging to the mother. Malakai remembered the mother looking up at him, with the dimming light in her eyes.

He aimed his gun and sent her permanently out of the bright world. They put the baby in the cage and cut some saplings to help them carry it. Then they started back down from the hills.

Three days later he had his bride price, and the next week he and Solange were married. He spent the next couple of years poaching chimpanzees to support them, and the little boy they soon had.

His beautiful boy.

He and Clancy were walking back toward the camp by the time he finished the story.

"What did you name him," she asked, "the boy?"

"Joseph," he said. "After his mother's father. He looked like her."

They were interrupted by the sound of trucks moving up the road. A moment later the first of them arrived, and began disgorging National Guard troops.

"I wonder what that's about," Clancy said.

"I would be surprised if it was anything good," Malakai replied. Then he swore under his breath. For a Humvee pulled up next to the first truck, and out stepped Trumann Phillips.

Phillips saw the two of them and waved them over. Malakai and Clancy met him in the center of the compound.

"Can you find them again?" he asked. "The apes?"

Malakai stared at him for a moment. Something had happened. Phillips was back in charge.

"Yes," he said. "I suppose so. I have some better ideas about how to do it now."

"The mayor wants them captured?" Clancy said, then added, "He said we were free to go."

"He wants us to proceed as planned," Phillips said. "And you are free to go if you wish, but I need you. I wasn't at liberty to tell you this before, but now it's all out in the open, and you might as well know. Gen Sys is responsible for the virus, and the apes have it. We need captive apes to try and find a cure. That's what this has been about, all along. What it's still about."

Malakai considered that. What he really wanted was to be quit of the whole matter. It still stank like a rotting elephant carcass.

"I'll help," Clancy said. Her voice was a little funny, and she had a distant look in her eyes.

"That's excellent," Phillips said. "And you, Mr. Youmans?"

"Sure," he said, trying to hide his reluctance. "I'll help finish this."

21

David watched the television, trying to keep his eyes open. He reached for the glass of water by the bed, but accidentally knocked it to the floor.

After sending the article he'd fallen asleep, and now he came in and out of consciousness. He felt hot one moment, and freezing the next. He wasn't always sure what was happening, and had turned the television on to give himself something on which to focus.

But it wasn't helping. If anything, what he saw there made it worse.

He fumbled with the phone again, to try and call Sage, but the line was still dead.

The images on the screen blurred into each other—scenes of fire and chaos, soldiers, mobs of people trampling over one another. It took him a little while to realize that was he was seeing wasn't local, but scenes of rioting and looting in Paris, London, Rome, Shanghai. A nuclear plant melting down in Byelorussia because it was understaffed. It seemed to go on for a long time. He closed his eyes again, feeling the heartbeat in his side, the liquid fire in his veins.

He most have dozed, because when he woke next, it was to an epidemiologist talking about the characteristics of the virus, how valuable it had been to discover that it had begun as a form of gene therapy, because now they knew it had been engineered specifically to overcome the human immune system.

David felt a flutter of elation. He had finally written something worth writing. Something important. He really owed Clancy big time.

Clancy, he thought. *What's happened to her?* The email she'd sent, supposedly in secret, hadn't been private at all. He knew that now. Someone had found out about it—and tried to kill him, very nearly doing so.

They still may succeed, he mused. But if they had tried to kill him, had they killed Clancy, as well? Had *he* killed her, by publishing the article?

He continued watching. The scene switched instead to a fire, raging out of control. It was a quarantine center, and another case of arson by the organization identified on the screen as 'Alpha/Omega.'

As he stared at the flames, he felt the cloud coming back over his brain. He reached for the water again, and remembered that he had knocked it over.

The images on the television hazed together, and then dimmed into darkness.

Malakai studied the map.

"This isn't going to work," he told Phillips. "Not as it stands."

"Why not?" Philips demanded.

"You're encircling the entire area, then contracting, hoping to force them all to a common point, where you can launch a concentrated strike."

"Exactly," Philips replied.

"It looks fine on a flat piece of paper, but there's a vertical dimension to this. They can go *over* your line."

"If they try, then we'll make it rain monkeys," Phillips said. "Shoot them out of the trees. Some may not survive the fall, but we can't afford to be too precious."

"Beautiful," Malakai said. "But you'll need three times the ground forces you have to make that work—because you have no way to know *where* they will try to punch through your line. They'll find your weakest point, and exploit it."

"There are only so many National Guard to go around," Phillips noted. "We're lucky the governor gave us *anything*, considering the shit that's going on down in Los Angeles."

"Then my point remains."

"Okay, then," Phillips snapped, "What do you suggest?"

"How many helicopters do you have?"

Later, trying to get some sleep, Malakai thought about Hans, the mercenary he had met in Uganda. He was in his thirties at that time, and the mercenary was older by two decades. They were in a camp near the Rwandan border, drinking Scotch, just as he and Clancy had done not so long ago.

And just as it had the other night, whisky loosened tongues.

Hans became a little maudlin, started talking about how horrifying the business could be. Malakai had agreed with him, but in fact nothing Hans had said made any impact on him. As far as Malakai was concerned, the man was just making whinging sounds. Being a mercenary was just a job. You did what you were supposed to do, you got paid, and you moved on.

Don't you feel anything? Clancy had asked.

"There was this one village," Hans said, his voice getting sloppy. "East of Butembo. Tiny place. It was during that whole Simba mess back in the sixties. My first job, actually. Had this real hard-ass Afrikaner boss. He told us to kill everybody. He said if we left anybody alive we would be fired, without pay.

"I doubt any of the villagers even knew what Simba was, or what communism was, or anything like that. And there we were, just shooting them. I remember this one little girl, she didn't have a clue. But I couldn't shoot, you know? I couldn't. And then this kid, this skinny kid, runs up from behind me and jumps on my back. And I just—I just freaked out, you know? The next thing I knew I was hitting him in the face with the butt of my rifle, hitting him and hitting him."

Hans rubbed his red face, then took another drink.

"Jean-Francis," Malakai murmured.

"What?" Hans said.

"Jean-Francis," Malakai repeated. "You know those Congolese—they're all named Jean-Francis."

"Right," Hans said, tossing him a strange look. "Yeah. It's just..." He stared at his drink.

"I guess shit happens, especially in this business," he said.

"I guess it does," Malakai said. He looked at Hans, and wondered if he should kill him. But when he wasn't drinking, Hans was one of their best fighters. They were going to need him. And besides, it would be hard to do it without someone noticing, and then he would likely be executed himself. What would be the point of that?

Hans, as it happened, was killed two weeks later by a land mine. Malakai didn't feel anything then, either.

* * *

He heard a soft knock on his door, and wasn't too surprised to discover it was Clancy. She had what remained of the Scotch with her.

"What do you think?" she asked. "Should we finish it?"

"Sure," he said. *I'll play Hans again, tell you all of my sad stories.*

But she didn't ask him to tell stories. She talked about her own life, about growing up, about her family, as if she was trying to get it all straight in her head. Eventually, though, she got quiet, and he thought she was going to leave. Instead she smiled wistfully.

"The first ape I ever saw was an orangutan," she said. "My dad was working in Malaysia, and Mom and I went for a visit. I guess I was about seven, because Renee wasn't born yet. We went to this place where they take orangs that have been captive or injured, and rehabilitate them back into the wild. Sort of a halfway house.

"We were on this sort of boardwalk, raised above the jungle floor. There was a feeding platform built up around a tree, and when feeding time came, the orangs came in from everywhere. And this one just dropped down next to us, and he looked right at me. We were no further apart than you and I are now. And I saw... Well, there was somebody in there, behind those eyes. A mind, and a heart, and a soul. A person. Not 'almost human,' but *completely* orangutan. Perfect the way he was. Except then I noticed he was missing an arm. I was told later that he'd touched an electric fence, and it basically set him on fire."

An odd, distant look crept into her eyes.

"The thing is, whatever we do with apes—experiment on them, train them to perform, even teach them language—everything we do just keeps them from being what they are. What they're supposed to be. We got kicked out of a paradise, not them. Yet we feel like we have to drag them out with us. I guess misery loves company."

She took another drink of the whisky and passed the bottle to him.

"I love orangutans," she said, and she smiled. "They're my favorites. They're so deliberate..." She frowned. "I've told you this before, haven't I?"

"Yes," he said. "The zookeeper joke."

"Am I boring you?" she asked.

"I didn't say that."

"I think I am," she said. "I'm naïve, and I'm boring, and what else?"

"I think you've maybe had too much to drink," he said.

"No," she said. "Not too much." She suddenly stood, walked over to him, and began to work the top button of his shirt.

"What on earth are you doing?" he asked.

"How long has it been, that you have to ask that?" she said, undoing the second button.

"I'm twice your age," he protested.

"No, you're more than twice my age," she said. "Are you saying that's the line you won't cross? That's the *one thing* you find objectionable?"

"No," he said. "I just didn't think—"

"Just shut up," she said, "I want this, and you're what I've got." She was trying to sound flip, he realized, but then he saw it in her eyes, heard it in the quiver of her voice. She was terrified, and trying to be brave. Again, his respect for her intelligence rose a notch.

He had that one little glance before she bent and began kissing his neck.

She was right about one thing. It had been a while—a long while. But he hadn't forgotten, and his body certainly hadn't. Her skin was soft, and as smooth as glass. No scars, anywhere. She gripped him as if they had been together all of their lives, and at times he actually found himself embarrassed at both her willingness and her dominance. It left him panting, wishing he *was* younger, wishing he was someone else.

When it was done, he wasn't certain what to do, but she snuggled into his arms. He just lay there, feeling his arm go to sleep.

"Thanks," she after a bit. "I know you weren't that into it, so thanks."

"No," Malakai said. "It was... I am very satisfied, believe me. It was such a surprise, you know?"

"Yeah," she said, and she chuckled. "The look on your face was priceless."

"Are we 'hanging out' now?"

"No," she said. "I think this was just a one-time deal. But I enjoyed it. And I made you feel something."

"I suppose so," he said.

"Score one for me."

He thought she was falling asleep, but then she murmured something.

"What was that?" he asked.

"Did you love her?" she said again. "Solange?"

He took a deep breath and let it out, again wishing he had a cigarette.

"Yes," he said. "Very much."

"And your son."

He felt his throat constrict. He nodded.

"I was in the bush," he said. "Hunting chimps. My uncle wasn't with me, that time. He had an infected leg, and so stayed home with Solange and my boy. There was a rebellion, of sorts. Bands of Hutu men, killing every Tutsi they could get their hands on. This was long before the genocide in Rwanda. It was a sort of warm-up to it." He stopped, then continued. "So they killed my parents-in-law, and my uncle who was, of course, not Tutsi, and Solange. And the boy. They had been dead a day when I got back."

"I'm so sorry."

"It taught me something," he said. "It taught me you can't lose something unless you have it."

"That's a terrible lesson," she said. "All the more because it makes sense to me. Last week it wouldn't have. Now it does."

She kissed him on the cheek and sat up. She reached for her shirt.

"I talk too much after sex," she said. "I know this. It's one reason..." She trailed off. "Never mind. Look, I'll let you get some sleep."

He caught her hand.

"Unless you very much object, I would like you to stay for a while," he said.

"Well," she said after a few breaths. "Maybe for a little while."

She lay back down and spooned against him, and in what seemed a short time, she was asleep.

22

Dreyfus rubbed his eyes and closed his laptop. Then he reached for the television remote.

There was little there to give him hope. All of the rough patches of the world were heating up. Serbs and Croats, Hutus and Tutsis, Shi'ites and Sunnis and any of another fifty ethnic and religious groups blamed one another for the plague that was killing them all. Minority groups in eastern China were rising against Beijing and being brutally punished for it.

Indonesia, which had the fewest reported cases of the Simian Flu, had closed its borders and was violently enforcing the isolation. Christians were being burned alive in Egypt and Muslims were being beaten to death in Tennessee. The Ganges was aflame from a chemical spill near the city of Varanasi. Some people were taking it as a religious sign of some sort and were immolating themselves in the burning river.

He absorbed all of that for a few minutes and then switched to a local channel.

He found himself regarding Claire Sang, the Channel Five anchor. The newsroom set was poorly lit, and everything about it looked messy. Sang looked as if she hadn't slept in days, and no amount of makeup could hide the dark circles under her eyes.

"We have breaking news," she said. "Word has come in that detainees in the Haight Ashbury quarantine zone have broken through police lines. Many have armed themselves with police firearms, and have begun moving through town, setting fire to buildings as they go. The police and the National Guard have been able to provide little resistance to this armed and highly dangerous mob."

The screen cut to shaky, hand-held images as she talked, showing hundreds of dirty, desperate looking men and women walking, running, and, in some cases, crawling through the streets. Fires leant an unearthly glow to the scene, and the patter of gunfire rang somewhere off-camera.

Dreyfus felt as if the floor was dropping out from under him.

"No, no, no," he said. "I've got to get down there."

"No you don't," Patel told him.

"We have to stop this!"

"No sir, with all due respect, you've put yourself in the path of too many of these things already." Patel didn't move, and he looked as if he was ready to stop Dreyfus, as well—physically, if necessary. "You aren't running for anything anymore. You're mayor now. The city is your responsibility. That –" he gestured at the screen "– is not the only thing that demands your attention.

"We're up to two hundred thousand dead. Two more hospitals have been torched by these Alpha/Omega assholes. That joker in South San Francisco says they've officially seceded from California or the Union—which one isn't clear—and claims they'll shoot to kill anyone who crosses into their 'sovereign territory.' Meanwhile, city services are down everywhere."

"I know that," Dreyfus muttered, massaging his forehead. "Don't you think I know all that?"

He leaned back in his chair.

"Ah, God," he murmured. "What am I going to do?"

Malakai woke before the dawn. He was alone, so he dressed and went outside, filling his lungs with the cool mist that was in the air, knowing that at last something was happening. Something was moving. A wind was coming.

After Solange and the boy died, Malakai became very still inside. He left Burundi and found work as a mercenary, and he did that work for decades. The faces of the dead became more familiar to him than the faces of the living.

And at last, one day, he found himself back in the Virunga Mountains, along with some of the men with whom he worked. Zaire had become the Democratic Republic of Congo again, and rebel groups had been forced into the mountains. It was different, though—the mountains with their gorillas had become a national park. It was illegal to kill the beasts, and there were rangers to enforce such laws, at least in theory.

Some, he knew, poached the beasts themselves.

But rangers were in short supply, as various forces from the Congo war hid and fought each other in the mountains. Malakai and his mercenaries were one such force. Retreating from a defeat in the lowlands, they were trying to cross into Rwanda, where hopefully the rest of their company would be waiting for them.

However, they were surrounded on all sides, mostly by Hutu militias. The good news was that most of the Hutus didn't know they were there. The bad news was, that wasn't going to make it any easier to move through them. So instead, they went higher into the mountains.

He found evidence of the gorillas on the fifth morning, and took his ragged, half-starved band toward them, thinking that at least they would eat well tonight. But before they arrived, gunfire began ahead. Crouching low in the brush, they hurried to see what was going on.

They found about fifteen Hutu militiamen, firing at a family of gorillas. They shot one in the leg, and laughed as it fell and began to turn in the grass. A big male charged, and they opened up on him, shredding his chest and face. When he went down they starting picking off the little ones, shooting to wound, not to kill. They were plainly enjoying themselves.

Malakai took careful aim at the Hutu leader. The man never even heard the sound of his rifle. Then the rest of his men followed suit, and started firing.

It was over in moments. He went among them, finishing the Hutus with his knife.

The gorillas were watching them. The big one was dead. The one with the wounded leg was dragging itself toward the trees. Malakai put a round in its head.

One of his men, Daniel, raised his weapon to shoot another.

"No," Malakai said. "Leave them be. This is more meat than we can eat or carry. Who knows, we may need them later. And bullets..." He remembered his uncle. "Bullets are expensive."

"But if we leave them, the Hutu will have them to eat."

Malakai watched the females trying to calm one of the little ones that had been shot. She was looking right at Malakai, mixed terror and confusion in her gaze. He remembered the story of the brothers—Whiteman, Blackman, and Gorilla. But it seemed to him that there were really only two brothers—man and gorilla. Men, white and black, killed each other, and for thousands of different reasons. Men killed gorillas, too. But the only time a gorilla ever killed a man was in defense of its own, and even then very rarely.

So there were men, and there were gorillas.

And he was not a gorilla.

"That's a good point," he said. "Kill them all."

He walked away as they started shooting, and began to smoke a cigarette. He thought to go only a short distance.

Instead he kept walking until he was in Uganda. There he withdrew the money he had been saving for almost thirty years, two thirds of every cent he had ever made as a mercenary. The next day he boarded a plane for the United States.

"I guess we're ready," Clancy said, from behind him.

He turned and gave her a little smile. She looked impossibly young in the morning light.

"Last night—" she began, a little awkwardly.

"Was last night," he said. "And today is today."

She nodded.

"Do I still scare you?" he asked.

"Malakai," she said, "you scare the shit out of me. But I like you, too. I can't fix it. I'm not going to try."

It had been too quiet, Caesar knew. No helicopters, no human patrols, nothing. It worried him. So when Koba came hurtling into the camp with news that humans were once again in the woods, it was almost a relief.

Scouts arrived from every direction shortly after. Based on their reports, he knew that the humans were all around them. Maurice held up his hands, forming a circle. Caesar nodded, then called his scouts over.

Find where the circle is weakest, the least humans. Come back and tell.

They went out, moving fast. Nearby, Rocket looked doleful. He was recovering quickly, but was still too slow and stiff to run with the scouts.

Below, the rest of those who were fit enough were gathering together spears. The troop had been making them for days, lengths of wood ground against stone to sharpen them. Even now, Caesar hoped to avoid fighting again—spears against guns would not end well. But they might help intimidate their attackers.

He had been thinking more and more about what would happen if the humans attacked this way. He thought he knew what to do, and had been planning with Maurice and Rocket how to do it. His main worry was that, after their victory in chasing off the enemy, many of the apes seemed overconfident. He was still convinced that the humans had—for whatever reason—simply changed their minds. It had not been a victory.

Now they seemed to have changed their minds again. He thought back to the fight at the grocery store and the conversation near the sea. Were they growing more determined, or was this their last, desperate attempt? Maybe, if his troop could get through this, it would finally be over.

Whether or not that was true, he reflected, they still had to get through it.

He noticed Rocket pointing, and saw the first helicopter, flying from the direction of the sea. It was distant yet, looking no bigger than an insect.

Rocket hooted again, and now Caesar saw another of the flying machines, this one coming from the direction of the sunrise. He scanned the sky for more. In all there were eight, ranged in a vast circle around them, tightening in on them just as the men on the ground were. That would make things more difficult. It meant that only in the mid-canopy would they be relatively safe.

He sent Rocket down to spread the word, and continued waiting impatiently for the news of where the weakest point was in the tightening noose. He could guess a few places where it might be…

But why guess? If they went down into the canyon, the humans would have to come downhill in at least three directions. If apes couldn't climb, it would be bad to be at the bottom of a hole.

But apes *could* climb.

He realized another thing, too. The helicopters were moving very slowly, probably no faster than the men underneath them. They wanted to be able to see the tops and the bottoms of the trees at the same time.

Which meant he already knew where the outside of the ring around them was located—it was where the helicopters were.

He called Koba to his side, and went down to Maurice.

Take them, fast, to the top of the valley, Wait there.

He could see it in his head, almost like a drawing. Wild apes—apes that didn't know human ways—would run from the nearest edge of the circle toward the farthest. That would give the circle time to tighten around them, like a choke collar on a neck. By doing the opposite, by moving *closer* to the nearest edge of the circle, they put the rest of the circle farther away, where most of the humans couldn't hurt the apes.

The humans would bunch there to try and stop them from breaking through, and the rest of the circle would grow thin, especially if they were forced to deal with uneven ground.

Koba, he said. *Find gorillas, brave ones. And some chimps. I need them for a special job.*

Yes, Caesar.

And Koba—tell them they might be captured or killed. Only apes willing to die.

Understand, Koba signed. Then he was away.

There was a rush in the trees as the whole troop began to move. Caesar felt a swell of pride at the sight of them. The orangutans were the best in the trees—it was true beauty, the way their long arms reached and reached, pulling them along. They never failed to find their hold. As unhurried as they normally were, in the trees they could move with impressive speed. Many of them had young chimps or gorillas clinging to them, and the largest carried injured chimps and orangs.

The chimps weren't as masterful in the trees as their orangutan brethren, but they were able to move readily from earth to tree in a way that the orangs, who were clumsy on the ground, could not.

The gorillas moved slowly and clumsily in the trees, and for that reason Caesar hadn't sent any of them out on patrols—they would have left tracks. But gorillas had their own virtues.

Caesar watched them go, then dropped down to where Koba was gathering the volunteers. He surveyed them: six gorillas and five chimps. All of the gorillas were zoo apes, but two of them knew a little sign. None of them had breathed Will's mist, but they could follow simple commands, as they had demonstrated on the bridge.

Two of the chimps were from the shelter. The others were from Gen Sys. He didn't know any of them well enough to know who would make the best leader.

Koba watched him for a moment.

Koba also go, the bonobo signed.

Caesar turned to Koba.

I asked you to find these. You go with me.

Koba straightened a little and put his chin out.

Need leader, he said. *Koba lead. Koba willing to die.*

Caesar regarded the one-eyed ape.

Can Koba think of plan first, Koba second?

Plan first, Koba signed. *Apes first. Koba next.*

Okay, Caesar agreed. *Go that direction. Break through their line, keep them there as long as you can. Draw them to you.*

He looked at the other apes.

"Koba," he said out loud. "Leader."

The apes acknowledged.

Caesar grasped Koba by the shoulder.

Bring them back if you can, he said. *Bring yourself back.*

Koba nodded, then screeched to the others, and they lit out for the trees.

Caesar felt the weight bearing down on him again. They were all counting on him to keep them alive. But not everyone was going to survive today. And what about the day after that? That was for later. There was plenty to do today.

One day Koba is taken from his cage and put in anther cage in a truck, along with some of the big caterpillars. He doesn't pay them any attention, and they, of course, have nothing to say to him. Or so he thinks.

But then one comes over and begins to pick at his fur. He screams, the loudest noise he has made in a long time, and throws himself against the side of the cage. The caterpillar makes funny sounds and tries to touch him again, so he shows her his teeth. Finally, she leaves him alone. He keeps his face pressed against the wires of the cage, trying to pretend the caterpillar isn't there. But deep in the bottom of him he remembers someone doing that to him—picking things from his fur, stroking him.

He remembers that it was good—better than good. But this strange thing that can't talk—having it touching him doesn't feel exactly right. And even if it is okay, he doesn't know what to do, how to respond. Doesn't *want* to know what to do. All he wants is to be alone, to not be hurt.

And he knows that this is too much to ask.

Koba is at the new place, and it is more… white.

The truck takes them to another building, where he is led to another cage, and there it starts all over again. They do things to his eyes. They cut him open and sew him back together again. They stick long needles into the middle of his stomach without putting him to sleep first. But Koba—Koba is going away. He doesn't feel anything anymore. His body isn't his own, and he doesn't care. He is hardly even present.

He *is* his cage. He *is* his pain.

Koba hardly notices when he is moved yet again. He has a new cage, but it is hardly different from the old one.

It is a little later when someone kicks at the door of his cage. Koba looks up and sees a face he remembers. It is Jacobs.

"Well, by God," Jacobs says. "If it isn't the ugliest ape in the world. My fortunes have changed, but I would say yours haven't noticeably improved. Rest assured, there will be no hand-talking nonsense here. You're not human, you know, even if you think you are. You are a chimp, an animal, and you'll act like one."

Jacobs smiles, and it is terrifying.

But Koba isn't terrified for more than a moment. He sits in his cage, and he thinks about Jacobs. And deep inside of him something starts to burn, something that wants out, wants to come out through his hands, through his feet, through his teeth.

There is a reason why all of the things that have happened to him have happened. Roger and Mary took his mother from him. Tommy hit him with the stick and burned out his eye. Countless others have tortured him in more ways than he knows numbers. But behind each of those is a reason, is *the* reason.

And Jacobs has said it.

You're not human, you know, even if you think you are. You're a chimp, an animal, and you'll act like one.

Koba doesn't know all of these words, but he knows what they mean. Mother thought she was human, like Mary, and they both taught Koba he was human, too. They lied, and Jacobs has told him the truth. The reason for everything that has been done to Koba is simple. It is obvious.

The reason is that they are human. They are human, and he is an animal. And everything that humans are, that is Jacobs. It is all him. He is them and they are him. He is their truest voice, and he is here. Koba cannot reach all humans. But maybe he can reach Jacobs.

This way Koba can focus. This way he can be angry.

This way he can fight back.

Now Koba was fighting back, rushing through the woods with other apes, and he belonged to something, something more than anger and hatred. He had other things to keep him going, and that was all thanks to Caesar.

Although, as the flying cages beat ahead and his apes approached the human line, he still had plenty of hate in him.

He saw fog rolling in ahead. That was good—in the fog the humans wouldn't see their real numbers, wouldn't know that there were only a few of them. That the real troop was going to break through in another place. The fog had been their friend from the beginning. He wondered if maybe the trees themselves called it to protect the apes, if the trees had been waiting for them, hoping they would come.

As they entered the fog, his eyes suddenly stung, and his nose began to burn. Confused, he scrambled back, and saw others were doing the same, shaking their heads, trying to clear out the pain. This fog was *not* their friend, and it kept coming.

Koba scrambled up a tree, trying to get above the burning mist, and there he saw something it took him a moment to understand. One of the flying cages was weaving back and forth above them, and the fog was pouring from the machine.

The circle closing in on the troop was not just men and machines—it was also this stinging cloud. The humans were counting on it forcing them back, until all apes stood in one place, surrounded by humans and their machines.

He jumped down and skittered over to Roy, a chimp who knew some sign.

Find Caesar. Warn him of the fog that stings.

Roy hooted and set off back the way that had come.

And now he had one fewer.

The remaining apes in his band were slowly retreating, backing away from the mist.

He remembered once, in the white place, they had pulled back his eyelids and pinned them open. Then they had sprayed something in them. It hurt like this, but worse. Even his dead eye hurt, and he couldn't blink to try and relieve the pain.

It had hurt, but it had not killed him.

He stood up straight and gestured into the fog. He wiped his palm over his eyes and closed them. Then he opened them and stabbed his fingers back at the fog. He went into it, walking upright, like Caesar.

"Ohgk!" he barked. He had been trying to say "go," as Caesar did, but it didn't come out right. But they understood, and when he plunged into the mist, they came with him, eyes closed.

Once again Koba's eyes burned, but now he *chose* to keep them open, to guide the gorillas with the sound of his voice, with the prod of his hands. Suddenly, through the mist, Koba saw a silhouette that stopped him for an instant. It stood like a human, but the face was oddly shaped, more like a chimp...

Then gunfire erupted, and Koba saw that it was a human after all, but wearing something on its face. And he wasn't shooting darts. It was far too loud for that. They were not trying to capture him. Which was just as well.

Koba scrambled behind a tree, then up it, and flung himself over the human. The man followed him with the gun, and Koba heard the hiss of bullets passing near. Then he was down. The man let out a muffled scream as the hulking forms of the gorillas appeared. He backpedaled and hit a tree, dropping his weapon.

Koba screeched and ran forward, propelling himself now on all fours. He wished Caesar would let him hit the humans, knock them down, but that was specifically forbidden, and a part of Koba knew that if he started attacking them, he might lose control and be unable to lead. And he wanted to lead.

He felt that now.

More shots rang out, now from the sides. That meant humans were leaving their positions in the circle, coming to him. One of the gorillas moaned as bullets struck him. Koba screamed, pushing him, inducing him to go on.

He pushed them all forward, half-blind, his throat closing—but now the burning mist was starting to thin. He looked up and saw the flying cage turning to come back. Shouts from his left and right told him that even more humans were running toward them. That was what Caesar wanted. He had to pull them here, make his few seem like many. So instead of just breaching their line and continuing on, Koba led them back into the burning mist.

A chimp screamed as bullets ripped through his body. Koba hoped his troop would live long enough to make a difference.

23

"They're trying to breech the western perimeter," Corbin reported. "Is everyone ready?"

"Sure," Clancy said, slinging her backpack over her shoulder.

"Quite," Malakai said. And he meant it. For the first time since this whole mess had begun he felt complete, with a tranq rifle on his shoulder and a Glock at his side. He no longer felt naked in the land of the clothed or, perhaps more aptly, like a balloon surrounded by needles.

"Everyone knows the drill, right?" Corbin said. "We find the apes, start bagging them while everyone else shows up. This time we *will* have air support."

"Got it," Malakai said. He saw Clancy nod.

They piled into the Humvee.

"Western perimeter, here we come," Corbin said as he started the engine.

"Nonsense," Malakai said. "That's a diversion."

"Not the way the guys on the line are talking. It's the full-on thing."

"So they're pulling men from the encirclement north and south?"

"Yeah."

"As I said, it's a diversion," Malakai told him. "Do or do you not want to succeed this time?"

Corbin stared angrily at him for a moment.

"I want to get this over with," he said.

"Then go where I tell you to," Malakai replied.

Caesar could already hear the helicopter ahead when Koba's messenger reached him. He brought the troop to a halt, and the scout told him about the fog that stings. He quickly passed the news to Maurice and Rocket.

We go, and we go fast, he said. *If we hesitate, mill about, they'll see us. As it is, with the smoke they're making themselves, we might succeed. Prepare the apes. Strengthen them. Apes together strong.*

He waited a moment for it to be passed around. Then he walked out in front, dropped to all fours, and began to run.

When the power went out, Dreyfus was on his way back to his office from a meeting of what was left of the Board of Supervisors.

"That's great," he said. "That's all we need."

He waited for the generators to come on, but after a few moments they still hadn't, and all he had was the light filtering through the window in his reception area. He continued on, and thought he heard a distant popping sound.

Just as he reached his office, the windows shattered inward, and this time he heard the distinct chatter of firearms. Longtime instinct took over, and he threw himself flat, then crawled over to his desk, where his old service revolver was waiting in a drawer.

There was a lot of gunfire now, but none of it seemed to be coming through his window. He got to the wall, stood against it, and peeked out.

Hundreds, maybe thousands of people were gathered below. It was not a peaceful gathering—that was demonstrated by the now constant gunfire. He couldn't tell who was shooting whom, either.

He heard a noise behind him and whirled.

"It's me," Patel said. He had several policemen with him.

"What the hell is going on?"

"Sorry, sir. We've been out of communication with the chief, and almost all the news outlets are failing. We should have been following Twitter. There are riots all over the city, but that armed mob from the quarantine—a lot of them still have phones, apparently. They've been tweeting about a cure—claiming it's here. Now that's drawing mobs from all over the city, including Alpha/Omega, who are here to 'exterminate the infected.'"

Dreyfus rubbed his forehead.

"I need to talk to them," he said. "I can talk them down. They trust me."

"Not this time, Mr. Mayor," Patel said. "You go down there, and someone is going to shoot you, sir."

"Just come with us, sir," one of the officers said. "They've already broken through the west entrance."

"Well, how are we getting out?" he asked. We can't walk through that."

"There's a helicopter on its way," Patel replied.

"There's no helipad up there," Dreyfus said.

"The FAA can fine us later," Patel replied. "Now we have to go."

As they entered the hall, Dreyfus could hear gunfire below, bullets ricocheting off of the limestone walls. There was the clatter of footsteps, and as they ran for the service stairwell, gunfire burst from behind him. He saw that it was one of the cops, firing at part of the mob that was running up the grand staircase and charging toward them.

Bullets spattered around them as the mob returned fire.

The officers led them into a stairwell Dreyfus had never been in before. It looked old, with chipped paint, and it was narrow. They had gone up about two floors when deafening gunfire erupted inside of the stairwell itself. He heard someone scream, but that was cut short by another round hammering out.

A few moments later they burst onto the rooftop. There were only two policemen left, and they planted themselves on either side of the door. Dreyfus could see the lights of the chopper coming in the distance. He didn't think it was coming fast enough.

The door burst open, and the first man through died, as did the second and third. Then one of the officers dropped.

Dreyfus had had enough. He lifted his thirty-eight and walked toward the door, taking careful aim and squeezing the trigger. A man dashed out with an assault weapon. Dreyfus shot him in the middle of the chest. He kept blasting away at the stairwell until the revolver was empty.

For a moment there was quiet.

The remaining cop picked up the dropped rifle.

Then more gunfire flared from the stairwell.

"Sir!" Patel was frantically tugging on his sleeve.

He realized that the helicopter had landed. It was a military chopper, with built-in firepower. He turned to the cop, who was blazing away at the stairwell with the rifle.

"Come on," he shouted.

"When I'm done, sir," the officer shouted.

Dreyfus numbly let Patel drag him to the helicopter. He was just boarding it when the cop ran out of ammunition.

"Come on!" he yelled, trying to send his voice through the sound of the propellers.

But the cop pulled out his pistol again. He fired once, then staggered and fell.

"Get us out of here!" Patel shouted.

The chopper began to lift as armed men poured out of the stairwell and began firing at them. The bullets *spang*ed on metal, then the helicopter gunner began shooting. Dreyfus watched the attackers collapse or run for cover.

"Damn," he said. "Goddamn. Patel, where are we going?"

But Patel didn't answer. The bullet hole in his cheekbone explained why.

Humans were everywhere now, the hammering of their guns the only sound Koba could hear anymore. Almost every one of his band was dead or dying. Screeching, he led those who remained back into the mist.

He knew it was nearly over.

Two men—two humans—approach Koba's cage. He holds out his hand for a cookie. One of the men looks at the outside of his cage. Then he looks straight into Koba's face and nods.

"Koba," he says. "Hi, I'm Will."

He talks to Koba like he knows Koba understands.

Koba doesn't care about that. He knows Will is like all of the others. Like Jacobs. He takes the cookie they give him, then thrusts his arm out for another.

He is doing a trick now. The trick is to seem cooperative. The kind of chimp they can trust to do his part, take the pain, take the treat, lie quietly in his cage. Because in the cage he can do nothing. Jacobs is not in the cage.

Will looks at him.

"This one," he says.

Koba eats the cookie.

Later they come for him. He goes easily. He knows his job. He lies on the rolling bed, and they put straps on him. He wonders how they will hurt him this time.

"He's very calm," Will says.

"I know. Yeah, this guy's seen the inside of a whole lot of labs. He knows the drill."

They stop in a room. Koba hears a knock on glass. He rolls his head and sees Jacobs standing outside, grinning, ready to watch Will and the other man hurt Koba.

"I thought I'd join you," Jacobs says, his voice muffled by the glass. "Watch our progress."

"Get him prepped," Will says.

Jacobs comes into the room. He is wearing the blue clothes the other humans are wearing, and like them he puts something over the bottom part of his face. But Koba can see his eyes. His is so close.

They put a thing over Koba's mouth and nose, too. This has happened before, more than once. Once it made him go to sleep. Another time it had made him cough. He coughed for two cycles.

They turn it on, and a kind of wind starts in his mouth, but all Koba can think about is Jacobs, how close he is. And how the straps that hold him down are looser than usual. And he feels the heat that wants out of him, through his hands, through his feet, through his teeth.

He screams and heaves towards Jacobs, and one of the straps snaps off of him. He sees Jacob's scramble back, arms raised in fear, his eyes full of panic, and he likes it. Koba strains to get off the table, but then they slam him back onto it, and before he can struggle back up, they strap him back down.

Tightly, this time.

They put the thing back on his face, and he has no choice but to breathe whatever it is.

Koba is back in his cage. He is tired and disappointed. He wants to sleep. But when he closes his eyes, he sees things—bright flashes of light, flickering patterns. He remembers his mother's face, the smell of Tommy's smoke-stick.

He remembers outside. He feels as if somehow he is in the sky, getting bigger and bigger. Like the sky is inside of him, or some great space. It was empty, but now it's starting to fill up.

He remembers the things Will and the other man said. They chose him because they think he is docile, just as he planned. It was easy for him, because for so long he has been docile. The man with Will had seen that in him.

But now they know he isn't docile, and he understands that his chance to punish Jacobs—for all he has done—might now never come. He should have waited until a better time.

He sleeps, and he dreams strange, colorful dreams, and he wakes with something bothering him. He remembers Will looking at something and then saying his name. How did Will know Koba's name?

It is a little later when they come for him. As they take him from the cage, he looks back. He sees letters there, and now he remembers how Mary taught him to spell his name. K-O-B-A.

Will can read the letters. The cage tells Will his name.

And now he understands why that bothers him. Because he has dreamt of letters—not the letters of his own name, but those that Jacobs had on the rectangle around his neck. The letters told people who Jacobs was. And those letters are clenched in Koba's mind as in a fist, along with the face and the sound of his name.

They take him to another room, and this one has toys like he remembers from the place where his mother was. There are two button boards on the wall. He stares at them, remembering. Then he begins to play with one. Outside of the glass, the humans are watching something.

"You've done this before," Will says.

Koba signs, *Yes*.

"And you sign," he says. "I knew you were a good choice."

"Aside from the fact that he attacked us," Franklin says.

"Enjoy yourself, Koba," Will says. "I'll be back later."

The humans leave him to play.

He tires of the button board, because no one is asking him questions. He finds another game he remembers. It involves circles with holes in them that fit onto sticks. When he gets bored of that he sees something else that looks familiar, a flat dark rectangle. He touches it, and a spot appears. Intrigued, he begins drawing patterns. He draws some angry bananas.

He hears a sound, and from the corner of his eye he sees Jacobs enter the room beyond the glass. He isn't wearing a rectangle with letters on it, but Koba remembers. Carefully, he writes them on the screen: J-A-C-O-B-S.

Then he glares at Jacobs. He wants Jacobs to know he is thinking about him.

But Jacobs smiles.

After that, they make him play many games. They all seem pleased.

* * *

Koba is back in his cage when the noises begin. At first he thinks it's just the caterpillars getting upset, but then he hears humans screaming and glass breaking. He looks out and sees that some of the caterpillars have escaped, and are freeing the rest, smashing the buttons that control the cages. He hears the latch on his cage click, and he gives it a push.

It swings slowly open.

Carefully he creeps out of his cage, uncertain what is going on. He peers around the corner and sees one of them, standing like a human. Giving orders. Commanding. And he realizes that these are not dumb caterpillars. These are not humans. These are apes, like him. And their leader...

He feels a strange pull inside, like the invisible thing that brings him back to the ground when he leaps. This is an ape fighting the humans. Fighting Jacobs. Tearing apart the things Jacobs has made.

And now *he* is torn. He wants to be part of whatever this ape is doing. He wants to help him. But he wants Jacobs more, and so he turns away to search for him.

In the chaos, he cannot find Jacobs. The caterpillars are running everywhere, breaking everything. But a strange thing happens—the chaos begins to become more still, and Koba realizes that the apes who freed everyone are gradually taking leadership of the caterpillars. And they are leading them outside.

The pull strengthens. The leader has a plan. He is going somewhere. Somewhere outside. In that moment Koba understands that he wants more than revenge. He wants...

He doesn't know the thought or word or sign for what he wants. But he knows that this leader, this ape who freed him, is the key. So he turns from seeking Jacobs, and instead follows him—follows Caesar.

He does not regret his choice.

* * *

Koba swung up into the nearest tree and glared at the approaching humans. They saw him now. The gunfire trailed off.

"That's the leader!" one of them shouted.

Koba knew that wasn't the truth, but he liked to hear it. And it meant the humans were still falling for the trick. So there was only one thing left to do.

The survivors clustered around him, their presence giving him strength. He knew they were with him.

With a defiant shriek, he leapt toward the humans. Their guns made thunder.

24

Corbin pulled the Humvee to a stop and Malakai got out.

"Everyone quiet," he said, holding up his hand.

The forest stretched out into the valley below them. A helicopter was making its way along what must be the perimeter not far away, spraying tear gas. But as they watched, it suddenly veered and began moving down the valley.

"See?" Corbin said. "They're calling it in. That's because they're on the western perimeter."

"They're wasting their airpower, then," Malakai said. "Listen."

Corbin shut up, and a little frown appeared on his face. "What?"

"Follow me," Malakai said. "And whatever you do, don't start shooting unless I tell you to. If they know we're here too soon, this won't work."

He led them to a line of rocks just next to and overlooking the upper end of the valley.

"I hear them," Clancy whispered.

"Shh," Malakai admonished. He could already see movement in the trees, not in one spot, but everywhere. A *thutter*ing, thumping sound came from woods, almost like a cattle stampede. The limbs of the trees began thrashing.

And then they burst into the clearing—first a chimp, running furiously, one hand gripping what looked like a spear. Just behind him were the gorillas, their knuckles tamping out the beat of the charge. Flores raised his rifle, but Malakai pushed it back down.

Now chimps and orangutans were sailing by overhead, carrying wounded and infants, and without doubt some of them were armed with spears. He remembered being thirteen, and holding a spear, surrounded by children holding spears and clubs. He remembered the flame spitting from the machine-guns of the mercenaries as they charged with those crude weapons, confident that the bullets could not hurt them.

But the shamans had lied, of course, and they fell by dozens. He didn't remember how it ended—only later, being carried by his uncle once more into the shelter of the forest.

Only when he judged that most of the apes had gone by did he raise his rifle and take aim at a young, straggling orangutan.

His shot went true, the tranquilizer dart striking it in the neck. He worked the bolt action and put in another dart as Corbin and Flores began to shoot, as well. Malakai aimed and knocked another one down, this time a limping gorilla. A chimp traveling beside him noticed, and her gaze flashed to him.

Flores shot at the chimp, but she skipped behind a tree and darted off through the branches. The gorilla, looking confused, went a few more steps before slumping against a rock, panting.

Then the last of them were past.

"That's six," Corbin said. "That's good enough. I'm calling in the strike."

* * *

Higher up the slope, the forest began to break up, and Caesar brought them to a halt. They were clear of the stinging gas, and the helicopter was gone. They had succeeded, for now, and his troop needed rest. Then they would go over the mountain and keep going. His dream—of living in his beloved woods, where Will used to bring him—was over.

He wondered if Koba had survived. He hoped so.

He heard excited *Waaa!*-calls from downslope, the kind that signified danger. He dropped from his branch and went to see what the matter was.

It was Cornelia.

Humans, she signed, pointing downslope. *Hiding. Shot Herman with sleepy gun, shot others, too.*

Caesar felt his belly tighten. Then he began singling out apes.

Maurice came down.

You need orangs, to carry. Herman heavy.

Caesar nodded, and with six orangs, three gorillas, and five chimps, he started back downslope.

He noticed that Cornelia was with them, and motioned her back.

I know where, she signed, defiantly.

He realized she was right, and he couldn't waste time arguing with her or putting her in her place. So he gave her a curt nod as they continued on.

Corbin took the walkie-talkie from his belt.

"Stop," Clancy said.

Malakai turned, but he already knew what was happening. He had known last night, for that matter.

Corbin didn't turn until he heard the gun cock.

Clancy was pointing a pistol at him.

"They deserve their chance," she said. "We had ours. They deserve theirs. Don't you see? They're not just apes anymore. They aren't human either. They're something… different."

"I'm just calling the capture team."

"No," she said. "You're not. We've live-captured all the apes Gen Sys needs. There's no need to capture all of them for what they want. You said 'strike.' You're going to bomb the shit out of them, aren't you? That was always the plan."

"Smart girl," Corbin said. "But you're being real stupid right now. Drop that thing, and I'll forget about it."

"They haven't done anything," she said. "They could have killed us. But they didn't."

"They started the plague," Flores said.

"No," she said. "Gen Sys did. They're just cleaning up their mess. Call the strike somewhere else—anywhere. In a week no one will know or care about these apes. Then they can survive or not, on their own terms."

"Put the gun down, Clancy," Corbin said.

At the moment, several apes broke into the clearing. Clancy's hands were already shaking, and now her eyes shifted. Corbin drew his pistol and shot her. She looked vastly surprised and backed into a tree.

Corbin lifted the walkie-talkie with the other hand.

"HQ, we have the flock, repeat, we have the flock. Outside strike radius from these coordinates, running north. Will advise when clear."

Malakai had never felt so calm, so at peace in all of his life as when he drew his pistol and shot Corbin between the eyes. Flores still hadn't figured out what was going on when the next bullet took him out of the bright world. The next was for Kyung, who almost got his rifle up in time.

Then Stillman shot, and a white heat exploded in Malakai's gut. He turned a little and shot Stillman. He fired at Ackers as he felt two more bullets strike him. Ackers fell—that left only Byrd.

But now he couldn't raise his gun arm, and Byrd had a bead on his head.

Ah, well, he thought.

But then a gun fired, and it didn't belong to Byrd. He saw Clancy, sitting with her back against a tree, her pistol raised, breathing in great heaving gasps. Byrd dropped without a word.

"Thank you," Clancy told him. "It was... the right thing."

"Yes," Malakai gasped, looking with mild disbelief at the damage done to his body. It wasn't only gorillas who looked confused when they were shot. He had seen plenty of people who didn't know they were dead.

Then Malakai saw the apes approaching.

"You have to stop the strike," Clancy said weakly. "You..."

Her arm dropped and her chin fell to rest on her chest. She took one more breath.

Malakai looked up into the eyes of the chimpanzee, its strange, green-flecked gaze, so full of life and intelligence.

"If you can understand me," he said, "You need to get your troop out of here, and go fast. There's going to be fire, do you understand? A lot of fire. I can give you a little more time. Hurry."

The chimp held his gaze for a moment, and he was suddenly back on Mount Virunga, staring into the eyes of his first gorilla. Into the eyes of every ape, every man he had ever watched die.

"I'm sorry," he whispered.

The ape knelt by him.

"Thank you," it croaked.

For a moment he was so stunned that he couldn't say anything.

"For God's sake," he finally gasped. "Run!"

And with no more hesitation, the chimpanzee ran. The other apes followed, carrying their drugged comrades.

25

From the cover of the trees, Caesar glanced back at the dead and dying humans. He had really begun to despair, to believe that maybe Will, Charles, and Caroline were the only ones in the world who weren't monsters. But now…

He didn't know what exactly had happened back there, yet one thing was clear. Two humans—humans he had never met, and did not know—had just given their own lives so that he and his troop might survive. Why they had done so he would probably never know.

But he did not intend to squander the opportunity they had provided.

Maurice, with his long, carrying call, had roused the troop to readiness before he arrived. They only awaited him to tell them which direction, and soon they again were in full motion, as they had been not so long ago. He knew they were tired, that many had little left to give, but he pressed them to follow him, and when that wasn't enough, he left Maurice at the front and went to the back, where Cornelia and others toiled to keep the wounded and drugged in motion.

He heard the sound long before he saw it—a long hushed tone, growing in pitch. Urging Cornelia to keep everyone moving, he hurried to the upper branches. There he saw something coming. It did not look like a helicopter—it was sleek, like a fish. It was distant, but it was turning toward him, coming from the direction they had come.

Panting, Malaki took out his walkie-talkie.

"HQ," he said. "Be advised. We are not clear yet. Experiencing difficulty."

"What sort of difficulty?" the device crackled back.

"Flat tire."

"Well, high-tail it on foot," the voice demanded. "Where's Corbin?"

"Will advise when we're clear," Malakai said.

"The drones are on their way. Get clear, now. Corbin, answer!"

It was getting harder to breath, and his head felt very light.

"Will advise when we're clear," Malakai said again.

He propped himself against a tree and stared out at the wide, beautiful valley, at the sky and hills. He felt the wind start to blow through him.

"Clear," he murmured. The walkie-talkie dropped from his hand.

Clear. And he was.

Caesar bit back a shriek as the first plume of flame erupted, engulfing the tops of the redwoods, spewing into the air and falling in long globs and streamers back into the forest. The trees instantly became cyclopean torches. It happened just about where they had stopped; without the warning of the human, his troop would now be burning.

The fish-thing flew on, not directly toward them but a bit to the side.

Another monstrous explosion sent shock waves rippling through the leaves and branches in every direction, and Caesar saw what was happening. The flying thing was making it impossible for them to turn this way or that; it was making an arc of burning trees which would eventually be a circle. They would have to outrun it, be ahead of where the circle closed.

Caesar didn't wait to see more. The thing was coming fast, leaving death behind it.

The forest shuddered under the force of another explosion as he caught up to the troop. His gaze flickered frantically about, trying to remember if they had been in this place before. He couldn't allow himself to become disoriented.

A glance back showed flames visible through the trees now.

Then he saw what he was looking for, the flicker of light on water, and he remembered where he was. Bounding ahead, he turned the troop. They were starting to panic as the explosions grew louder, but at the sound of his voice most of the others seemed to steady. They scrambled downhill and into the river below. It wasn't as deep as he had hoped, not nearly deep enough to save them if they were hit straight on. But it was better than nothing.

Stay in the water, he told Maurice, and then once more he sprinted to the back. Where Cornelia was.

By the time Caesar reached Cornelia again, he could feel the heat from the nearest flames. Squirrels, deer, and animals he didn't recognize were running past, fleeing for their lives.

He waved on the stragglers, ashamed of the deep part of him that wanted to leave them, to grab Cornelia and make her flee. But they were all his troop, and all his responsibility, and he knew he wouldn't—couldn't—abandon any of them.

The rearmost stragglers reached the water's edge. He grabbed Herman's arm and started dragging him deeper into the stream. The gorilla wasn't asleep, but he was having trouble using his arms and legs, a feeling Caesar remembered all too well from having been tranquilized, himself.

Suddenly everything was yellow, and for a single, suspended moment there was an impossible stillness as if he, Herman, Cornelia—all of them—were embedded in amber, like the bug Will had once shown him.

And then the wind came, like the sun breathing on them, searing them and slapping them down in the same instant. He smelled his own fur as it singed.

He shoved Herman underwater, though there was only just barely enough to cover him. The others were all staring at the billowing orange maelstrom above them, so he continued, pushing them down, one by one. Cornelia saw what he was doing, and she began helping him.

Then the fire began raining down on them, and there was no time. Caesar pushed Cornelia into the water, covering her with his body.

Dreyfus stared at the blinking phone, wondering why Patel hadn't answered it. Then he remembered that Patel was dead, that what remained of the city government was holed up here, in the National Guard Armory. That the city was tearing itself to pieces outside.

He picked up the phone.

"Dreyfus," he said.

"It took them long enough to find you," the voice at the other end said.

"Who is this?"

"It's Phillips."

"Right," Dreyfus said, wearily. "What do you want?"

"It's done," Phillips said.

"I thought I told you to go away."

"I'm going," Phillips said. "I just thought you would like to know."

"Come in," Dreyfus said, after a pause. "We can use you on something else."

"Dreyfus," Phillips said. "We were here to do a job. It's done. There's no way I'm dragging my people into that plague-infested hell-hole."

"It's an order," Dreyfus said.

"I don't work for you," Phillips replied. Then the line went dead. Dreyfus stared at it for a moment, then turned it off.

He looked at his monitor, at the reports flooding in. He had predicted panic. He hadn't predicted *this*.

He reached for the phone and tried his home number. It was busy, just as it had been the last seven times he had tried it. So was Maddy's cell.

"Sir?"

"Yes, Mr., ah—"

"Pinheiro, sir."

"Yes, what is it?"

"You said you wanted to talk to the prisoner."

Dreyfus nodded wearily. "Let's go."

The prisoner was young, clean-shaven. He had good teeth. Aside from the Greek letters tattooed on his forehead and the dirty urban camouflage he was wearing, he looked no different from any suburban kid. He sat in a small white room, staring, unperturbed, through the glass.

"What's your name, son?" Dreyfus asked.

"I am the Alpha and the Omega," the boy said. "The first and the last. The beginning and the end."

"Ah," Dreyfus said. "You're Jesus, then. How comforting."

The boy just smiled.

"You were involved in firebombing the quarantines," Dreyfus went on. "Men, women, children, burned alive. What possible justification could you have for that?"

The boy looked at him as if he was speaking gibberish.

"They were dead already," he said. "You know that. Dead, and damned, as well. Don't you get it, man? The disease, this virus—it's not a curse. It's a gift. It is cleansing the world of the impure. It is burning away the chaff. The miscreants, the misbegotten, the miscegenate, the weak, all will be swept away. All who struggle against the purification will die and become as dust."

"So you're just helping out," Dreyfus said.

"Look around you, man." He swept one hand in a wide arc. "Look at these people. Two weeks ago, they thought they were civilized. They went to church, went to their book clubs, bought all the shit they were supposed to buy from the places they were supposed to buy it from. They thought they were good people, great people. Now look at 'em. Look what they're capable of, how wasted they are on the inside. There was nothing in there, man."

"So why not burn a few," Dreyfus said.

"It's our duty."

"Right," Dreyfus said, thumbing through a file folder. "Here's somebody—Louisa Vega. She joined the army and became a field medic. Later she worked for aid organizations all over the world. In Africa, she nursed in a village that was essentially wiped out by Ebola. And she was in the Alameda Point quarantine when you assholes shot it all to hell and torched it. She wasn't weak, and she wasn't chaff, and she wasn't 'empty' on the inside, whatever the hell that's supposed to mean."

He stared directly at the prisoner.

"She was someone who dedicated her life to helping the sick. And she wasn't the only person like that who you killed. Real people, who see their duty not as hiding behind masks and chucking firebombs, but working to hold something together, build something."

The boy laughed.

"You think you're going to hold this together?" he said.

"I know I'm going to try," he said.

"Well, good for you," the boy said. "When this is all over, and the select inherit our kingdom, I'll think of you."

"Oh, son—didn't anyone tell you? You won't be inheriting anything. Nobody comes in here without a screening. Why do you think you're behind glass?"

For the first time, the boy looked uncertain.

"See, turns out you're part of the chaff," Dreyfus said.

"No," the boy said. Then louder. "No!"

"Put him in quarantine," Dreyfus said. As he left, the boy starting shrieking in earnest.

Back in his office, Dreyfus dialed home again, hoping against hope he would get through this time.

To his relief, the phone rang, and to his greater relief, Maddy answered.

"Maddy," he said. "Thank God. Listen, I've sent a car for you and the kids. They should be there in half an hour."

He was answered by a long pause.

"Edward has it," she said, her voice trembling.

"Has it?" he said. "Has what?"

"The plague. The Simian Flu."

A deep cold buried itself in Dreyfus's chest.

"Maddy," he said, "You don't know that. You're not a doctor—"

"He's sneezing up blood," she said. "Everyone knows the symptoms."

His head was pulsing.

"You don't know," he said.

"I'm so scared," Maddy said.

Dreyfus looked past his door at the confusion outside, at the boards showing riots and fires and armed conflicts. He felt like he couldn't breathe. He felt imbalanced, like a man on a high wire that was starting to shake.

"Maddy," he said, "I'll be home as soon as I can. I'm on my way now."

"You can't," she said. "You'll be exposed, too."

"I'll be there soon," he said, and put the phone down. He picked up his jacket from the chair he had slung it over and put it on. He found Pinheiro.

"Have my car brought around," he told the young man.

"Sir, it's dangerous out there," Pinheiro replied. "I don't think—"

"Just do it, son," Dreyfus said.

"Yes, Mayor Dreyfus, sir," Pinheiro said.

"It's just Dreyfus now," he replied, softly, and left the office.

When Caesar lifted his face up for air, at first all he saw was fire. It danced in the branches above, it raged on the ground, some even hissed and sputtered in the river. But, looking around, he could also see the end of it. If they could make it a little farther, they would be with the rest of the troop.

Safe.

He pulled Cornelia up. Most of the others had already

come up for air and were looking around, even Herman. The air, however, was not very good. It was thick with smoke, and at the same time seemed somehow thin.

"Come!" he roared, pulling Herman's arm. "Come!"

They gathered themselves, then began shakily wading downstream. Burning branches began to fall all around them. The smoke grew thicker. Caesar saw another gorilla slump down, and understood that the smoke was making them all weak, taking their strength. That they weren't going to make it. He exchanged a glance with Cornelia.

Sorry, he signed.

She shook her head.

No sorry, she said. *Cornelia not sorry.*

Then she stumbled and fell into the river.

Caesar dropped to a crouch, unable to support Herman anymore.

His eyes filled with tears from the stinging smoke.

Most of them will survive, he realized. Maybe the humans would think they were dead, burned up with the forest, and leave the others alone. Maybe if the humans found his body, it would be enough.

He thought he was hearing things as first, sounds in his head as the smoke put him to sleep. But then he heard a hoot, and another, and splashing in the river. Through blurred vision he saw shadowy figures helping Cornelia to her feet, dragging Herman downstream, and as the last of his consciousness faded, he felt a shoulder come up under his.

Caesar is the smartest, he remembered Cornelia saying. *Still, should listen to others, take help from others. Caesar alone strong. Caesar with apes, stronger. Apes together, strong.*

Then he passed into darkness.

* * *

The lights went out again, just as Talia finished closing up a ten-year-old boy. She worked by candlelight—a precaution they had taken a few hours before. She knew this would be her last session. She was working with an IV in her own arm, just to keep her on her feet a little longer.

She heard someone scream, and then an abrupt burst of rifle fire.

"Get down," McWilliams hollered, drawing a pistol from beneath his surgical gown.

Talia saw the men as they came in through the door. They had on masks and were carrying rifles. As she threw her body across her patient, she heard McWilliams' pistol roar, and then the stutter of rapid rifle fire. She felt three hard thumps in her back and side. She wished she could see her father one more time, have one more dinner with him. Tell him it was all right.

Across town, David woke abruptly from fevered dreams. His heart wasn't beating right, and he didn't know where he was. He could barely even move, but he managed to tilt his head a little, and in the darkness he saw the glowing numbers of a digital clock.

It was four, he realized. He would have laughed, but he didn't have time.

Caesar awoke, feeling clean, cool air in his abused lungs. Someone dribbled water on his face.

He lay there a moment, letting the last of the dizziness pass. He did not smell smoke anymore. He opened his eyes and found an ape squatting by him, concern writ large on his ravaged face, in his single good eye.

"Koba," Caesar croaked.

Koba nodded. His fur was singed in places. He was bleeding. But he was alive.

Caesar stood up, feeling shaky.

Koba brought himself back, Koba said. *Brought two others, only. Koba is sorry if he failed.*

Caesar regarded the other ape for a moment, then stepped forward and embraced him. For a moment, the bonobo was rigid, unyielding.

"Koba did good," Caesar said. "Good."

At that, Koba finally relaxed, and hesitantly returned the embrace.

Caesar pulled away from him.

You are my brother, he told Koba. *We are all of us family.*

EPILOGUE

That night, Caesar climbed to the top of the tallest tree he could find. He looked out over the woods, at the conflagration that was still sending clouds of sparks whirling into the sky. While he was unconscious, Maurice, Koba, and Rocket had taken the troop against the wind until they thought they were far enough away to be safe.

Although it was still a terrible sight to behold, the fire looked as if it was beginning to diminish. As if the trees were winning.

And his scouts told him the humans were all gone, or leaving the woods. It felt like the apes had won, or at least gained a reprieve.

Beyond the burning woods, Caesar could see the city, the place that had once been his home. There were fewer steady lights than ever, but there was a new light—an orange, flickering glow, cousin to the flames that had nearly killed him.

Like the woods, the city was on fire.

He wondered what that could mean.

And, as he wondered, Cornelia quietly climbed up beside him and began to comb through his fur.

ACKNOWLEDGMENTS

It's been a great honor and great fun to play in this playground, so thanks to 20th Century Fox for the invitation and all of the support, advice, and feedback I received while doing so. Thanks especially to Josh Izzo and Lauran Winarski for finding answers so quickly and efficiently when I had questions—and I had questions often.

On the Titan side of things I would like to thank Steve Saffel for quick and skillful editing. I would also like to acknowledge the hard work and contributions of Nick Landau, Vivian Chrung, Katy Wild, Cath Trechman, Alice Nightingale, Tim Whale, Jenny Boyce, Katharine Carroll, and Ella Bowman.

Thanks also to Dafna Pleban and BOOM comics for helping coordinate this enterprise. Finally, many thanks to Warren Roberts and Terri Hunnicutt for letting me tap their years of experience with great apes. Any mistakes herein are mine, not theirs.

ABOUT THE AUTHOR

John Gregory Keyes was born in 1963, in Meridian Mississippi to Nancy Joyce Ridout and John Howard Keyes. His mother was an artist, and his father worked in college administration. When he was seven, his family spent a year living in Many Farms, Arizona, on the Navajo Reservation, where many of the ideas and interests which led Greg to become a writer and informed his work were formed.

Greg received a BA in Anthropology from Mississippi State University, and worked briefly as a contract archaeologist. In 1987 he married Dorothy Lanelle Webb (Nell) and the two moved to Athens, Georgia, where Nell pursued a degree in art while Greg ironed newspapers for a living. During this time, Greg produced several unpublished manuscripts before writing *The Waterborn*, his first published novel, followed by a string of original and licensed books over the following decade and a half.

Greg earned a Masters in Anthropology from the University of Georgia and completed the coursework and proposal for a PhD, which thus far remains ABD. He moved to Seattle, where Nell earned her BFA from the University of Washington, following which they moved to Savannah,

Georgia. In 2005 the couple had a son, Archer, and in 2008 a daughter, Nellah. Greg continues to live with his family in Savannah, where he enjoys writing, cooking, fencing, and raising his children.

Dawn of the Planet of the Apes: Firestorm is his twentieth published novel.